I0721433

IN COLD BLOOD

A Wild Fens Murder Mystery

JACK CARTWRIGHT

IN COLD BLOOD

JACK CARTWRIGHT

PROLOGUE

EMMA JACKSON'S BOOT CRUNCHED THROUGH THE CRISPY LAYER of frost, then sank into the few inches of mud beneath. The surrounding fields were obscured by a thick fog that rolled in off the fens. Occasionally, a break in the clouds revealed the sky above, laden with stars so close she could almost reach out and grab them. Though they would simply slip through her fingers like everything else she cherished.

She found him staring out into their field, watching the mist as they had done together on many occasions. She slipped her arms around him to nuzzle into his back.

She said nothing. Not at first anyway. Enough had been said already, and nothing had changed. She was still leaving.

His body tensed at her touch and did not relax when she squeezed. Not the way it used to. Not before the old man had died.

"I'm sorry," she offered, and heard how feeble it sounded. "I've ruined everything."

Somewhere out in the field, beyond the blanket of fine mist, a neighbour's dog barked at something. There was nothing unusual there. Almost every household in Wasps Nest had a dog, and one of them would always find an excuse to bark, even in the early hours.

"Will you call when you get there, at least?" he asked. "Wherever *there* happens to be."

"No," she replied without hesitation. "It's better if I don't."

"How will I know you're safe?"

"You won't. You don't need to anymore," she said, though it pained her to say the words.

"Emma–"

"I've made up my mind, Jason. Don't try to change it. Please."

He turned in her arms before she could stop him, and he held her by her shoulders, searching her eyes for a weakness to exploit. That was his way.

"You don't have to leave," he said. "Who cares what people think?"

"Don't. Please."

"No. I won't let you go. What about our dream? The farm. The bed and breakfast. Kids even–"

"Oh, come on. We both know you never wanted–"

"I do. I do. If that's what it takes, then I do want them."

"It's too late for that."

"Then we'll both go. We'll sell up. It's nearly Christmas for crying out loud."

"I see the way you look at me."

"What?" he said, and pulled away, turning to stare out at their field.

"There's doubt, isn't there?" she said. "In your mind, there's doubt. You're not sure if I did it or not."

"Of course I'm sure," he said, and reached to stroke her hair.

"Really? So look me in the eye and tell me you believe me."

He turned away to gaze into the fog once more.

"Jason? Come on. Look at me and tell me there's not a shred of doubt that I'm innocent."

"You're being stupid, Emma."

"And you're lying. How am I supposed to live with this? How am I supposed to run a bed and breakfast? Who's going to want to stay at a place run by a killer? A loser."

"You're not a killer, or a loser."

"As good as," she said. "In their eyes, I'm as good as."

"You were found not guilty. The jury said so. It's all in your head. You're being stupid and–"

"And what, Jason?" she said, and her temper flashed red, like a pulse of blood behind her eyes. She exhaled, and softened her tone. "And what?"

"Selfish," he said flatly. "You always were selfish. I should have known you'd do something like this."

"No–"

"I should have known you'd bail on me as soon as it got hard. It was never going to be easy, Emma. I told you there'd be times when we had no money. When we'd scrape a living doing whatever we could. That's what you have to endure. That's the price you pay to get what you want. Suffering."

"To get what *you* want, you mean."

"Oh come on, this was your dream as much as mine. Now you're going to leave me to run a bed and breakfast. What am I supposed to do out here on my own? We're in the middle of nowhere, Emma."

"You chose it–"

"I *found* it. We chose it. We chose the place where we could both be together away from everyone. We – just you and me, we don't need anybody else. Now you're bailing on me, and I'm stuck out here."

"A man died in my care, Jason," she snapped. "I'm plagued by death. I've lost the game."

Her words carried across the field, startled some birds, and that dog began barking again. A dark shape flashed then was lost to the mist once again. A trick of the light maybe?

"I have to live with that," she said. "Regardless if people think I did it or not. Regardless if even you think I did it–"

"Which I don't–"

"I have to live with it. I have to live knowing that, had I done something differently, he might be alive. Had I not left him alone for a few minutes, he might still be alive. I have to live knowing that had we chosen someplace else, we might have had more money behind us. I wouldn't have had to clean up after old men, and heat up their rancid dinners, or wipe their bloody arses. And you know what? I might even sleep at night. I might even enjoy being with you, being here. But I don't."

"Sleep at night?"

"Neither, Jason. I see it in your eyes. I see the doubt. It's bad enough that I can't step foot in the local shop anymore–"

"Of course you can. People take time, that's all."

"They hate me, Jason. They bloody hate me. A car nearly knocked me down yesterday when I was walking up the lane."

"Oh, come on, it's a narrow lane."

"The driver sped up when he saw me."

"It was a man, was it?"

"No. I don't know. It doesn't matter. You don't bloody get it, do you? I'm scared to leave the house, and when I see the doubt in your eyes, I'm scared to be here with you. I can't go on like this. I need to go."

"Go where? You have nowhere else to go."

"Anywhere. I need to go where nobody knows me," she said softly. "I need to start over."

"Then we'll both go."

"No," she said, as she stepped out of arm's reach. "No, I have to do this alone. I dream there's somebody standing over me when I sleep. It's so real. Like, I can feel a sharp point on my throat."

"It's all in your mind, Emma. You've been through a lot."

"Three months on remand. Three months locked up with

bitter women with nothing to lose. But you know what, I felt safe there. I felt like I belonged. Like I deserved it. I slept, too," she said, hearing the fondness in her voice. "There was no man standing over me while I slept. Nobody tried to run me down on the lane. I'm going, Jason. This is no life for me, and it's no life for you either."

"Shh," he said, and he half-turned, holding his finger to his pursed lips. "Did you hear that?"

"Hear what?" Emma said. "I didn't hear anything."

"Who's there?" he called. He hurdled the fence to run out into the field where the long fingers of mist seemed to envelop him.

"Jason, wait," Emma called, and she unstuck her boot to climb onto the fence, then swung a leg over just as she heard two footsteps in the mud.

But her loving boyfriend did not run out of the mist, and the footsteps ceased.

"Jason? Where are you?" she called, stumbling into the field. She tripped once on the rough terrain, then dropped into a divot their little tractor had created, and fell to her knees. "Jason?"

And then she saw him. Through the fog just twenty feet ahead. A dark and lifeless form lying in the frost. A wave of mist formed, then passed, but the spot where he had been lying was empty.

"Jason?"

And then she smelled it. The chemical scent of oil.

And then she felt it. The rough, gloved hand that clamped over her mouth, and the cold bite of a steel blade against her throat.

CHAPTER ONE

Detective Inspector Freya Bloom opened her eyes and took in the room for perhaps the fiftieth time. Maybe it was more. She couldn't remember. But each time had been the same. Stale, yellowing walls, stippled, Artex-covered ceilings, and heavy, wine-coloured drapes that blocked the winter sun, except for a small slice where the two curtains failed to meet.

There wasn't a flat wall in sight, each one marred with aging plaster, and the gaps around the windows were so large that a breeze set the drapes in motion.

The toilet flushed in the downstairs bathroom, and the cistern being refilled rattled the pipes somewhere in one of the walls.

Freya closed her eyes and pulled the heavy duvet over her head. The duvet was the only useful thing she had taken when she had left her husband in London and ventured to Lincolnshire, claiming their motor home as her new home. Thankfully, a colleague's father had offered the rental of the old farm cottage. It would have been lunacy to sleep in the motor home in what must've been single digit temperatures.

Footsteps sounded from the old, wooden staircase, and Freya rolled over, feigning sleep. The bedroom door squeaked open, reminding her of the incident room at the station. Did every door in Lincolnshire bloody well squeak or creak? Were there no silent doors?

"I'll be off then," her guest said, and she heard him pulling his jacket on.

She raised an arm from the duvet, offered him a farewell wave, then retreated to the warmth.

"Will I see you again?" he asked, his Irish accent stirring memories of the previous night when they had talked, and talked, and...

God, what had she told him?

She sighed audibly, and rolled over awkwardly. Her dress had pulled tight and to get comfortable would take considerable effort.

"I'll take that as a no then, shall I?" he said, and he laughed once, a deep, throaty chuckle. "I'd accuse you of using me for my body, if you hadn't fallen asleep."

"Leave your number," she said, refusing to raise her head above the covers. "I'll call you."

"That old chestnut."

She sat up in bed suddenly, and a few moments later, her brain caught up. She stared down at her dress. It was her blue number, stylishly long with a tantalising slit up one leg. She wasn't wearing a bra, but the material was so fine, she had yet to find a bra that worked with the dress.

"Did we...?" she asked, and he leaned on the door, smiling at her.

He shook his head.

"I'm still dressed."

"I can see why you're a detective."

"How did I—"

"I carried you up."

"Carried me?" she said, piecing the previous night together. Nope, there was no memory of being carried.

"But where did you–"

"The couch," he said. "It's okay."

"Most men would have–"

"I'm not most men," he said.

"I'm forty-five years old," she said, and stared at him, marvelling at his grey eyes and dark hair. Unsure if it was just the hangover working its magic or if he truly did look like a film star, she continued voicing her thoughts, "I've been in relationships with men for nearly thirty years, and never once has one carried me to bed and let me sleep fully dressed."

"You have no idea how special that makes me feel," he said.

"Oh god, that makes me sound terrible. I'm not... I mean, I don't do this often–"

"Can I get you a coffee before I go? You look like you might need one."

"A coffee? Yes. Wait, I'll make some. I can make coffee," Freya said, and tried to climb from the bed, but found her legs entangled in the sheets and the dress.

"It's no bother. I'm forty-two years old. I've been using a kettle for thirty years now. Not once has any of them ever outsmarted me."

Freya hung her head in defeat. Either he was too witty for her, or she was just plain old drunk still.

"Martin?" she said, and raised her tangled legs and covers as high as she could muster. "I need help."

"And you don't do this often?" he asked, as he took a single step across the room, grabbed hold of the duvet, and pulled her free. She watched him help her, and he even averted his eyes so that she didn't flash him her underwear.

She didn't even know if she was wearing any, but a smooth reach down to straighten her dress reassured her that she was. He tossed the duvet so it covered her entirely.

"I'll work my magic with the kettle," he said, and his footsteps trailed off down the loud and creaky stairs.

"Oh god." Freya cringed and rolled over into another mess. It was then that she thought of him downstairs alone. She thought of the dining table with her case files. Springing out of the bed, she pulled on her dressing gown, a satin number with an Asian floral print, and tied it as she descended the stairs.

Expecting to find a scene from a horror movie, Freya was half-surprised and half-embarrassed to find that, not only had Martin tidied the couch and straightened the cushions, but he had also tidied the entire living room, where she was sure they had spent most of the evening. There was no sign of wine, or the takeaway they had shared, and the dining table had been organised with her case files and paperwork neatly stacked at one end.

The kettle was raging in the next room, and she felt rather than saw Martin emerge into the hallway.

"Hope you don't mind," he said. "I figured I'd straighten it out for you. My way of saying thanks."

He said the word thanks like there was no H. *Tanks*, she thought, and smiled. She could get used to that accent.

"You're one of them, are you?" she asked.

"One of them?" he said.

"A neat freak."

"Oh." He laughed again, and Freya enjoyed listening to the rumble of his throat. "I have three sisters and four brothers. If I didn't tidy my stuff away, it would be lost to the chaos. I guess it stuck with me. Old habits, and all. I do fart though. From time to time."

She smiled.

"So, you're human then, are you, Martin?"

He looked slightly bemused at the comment, but brushed it off with one of those broad smiles that had caught Freya's attention when she had first seen his photo.

"Something like that," he said, and he placed a large, warm hand on her back as he leaned to kiss her on the cheek. She was grateful he hadn't gone in for a full kiss before she had a chance to freshen up. "You take care now, Freya Bloom. I've left you my number in your kitchen. I'm not sure I can live up to your wild expectations, but I can give a damn good try if you're game. I'll cook you something."

"You cook, too?" she said, impressed at his growing skill set.

"I try," he said, opening the front door. He nodded and gave her a wink that in any other circumstance would have been corny and off-putting. But she found herself smiling in response. "I'll be seeing you, Freya Bloom. And if I don't, well, enjoy Christmas."

The door closed behind him, and he seemed to linger outside for a moment, the frosted window framing his dark hair and broad shoulders.

Freya considered him to be a conventionally attractive man, with dark and rugged features. His uniqueness was in the way he carried himself, carefree yet confident.

The aroma of Ethiopian coffee wafted in from the kitchen and she followed the scent. The coffee pot was full, not half-filled as Greg used to do. Something that annoyed the hell out of Freya. Not only did she have to make more coffee, but it wasted a filter, too. Martin had prepared a cup, some milk, and a small bowl of sugar, beside which he had left a note written on a piece of paper torn from her little notebook.

Sleeping beauty, I wasn't sure how you like your coffee, but I'm willing to learn. Call me.

He had written his number below the message, and then signed off with a playful yet flamboyant signature that unmistakably read...

Mark.

"Mark?" she said. She could have sworn his name was Martin. "Oh, bloody hell."

She leaned on the kitchen counter with an almost certainty that he had found the mistake funny. But that mean, old hangover added a torturous element of doubt. Maybe he had been toying with her, secretly offended that she had confused him with some-body else.

"What an idiot," she said, pouring herself a black coffee and stirring in two sugars. The sugar was naughty, she agreed with herself on that one, but the lack of milk somehow made it okay.

Three raps on the door startled her, and she leaned out of the little kitchen. Through the frosted window was that familiar shape. Dark hair, broad shoulders.

Cursing herself for not freshening her breath at least, she opened the door, clutching the collars of her gown while forming a friendly, inviting smile.

Ben Savage was standing there.

"What are you grinning at?" he asked. "Aren't you dressed yet?"

"Why would I be dressed?"

"Didn't you get my message?"

"Message?" Freya said, and a sense of dread washed over her.

"A body. Female. Mid-twenties. I'll wait in the car."

CHAPTER TWO

They were just two minutes into the short journey to Nocton when Freya lowered the passenger window. The cold air filled the car almost immediately.

"Heavy one?" Ben asked.

"Wasn't meant to be."

"Was he worth it?"

Freya didn't reply. Instead, she turned away from Ben to stare out of the window.

"He seemed like a nice guy," Ben said. "I mean, it's not often a bloke high-fives you when you walk up a garden path."

Freya turned to him, her face aghast, before she caught the joke.

"Nothing happened, alright. He stayed the night, and before you say anything else, he slept on the couch."

"Where'd you meet him?" Ben asked, trying his best to sound as positively interested as he could.

"Oh, just around. What do we know anyway? Cause of death?"

"I'd say male, early forties, six foot one. Hung like a–"

"The victim, Ben."

"Ah, I see. Female. Mid-twenties. Non-smoker."

"Cause of death?"

"Exsanguination."

"She bled out?"

"Slashed throat."

"Are you going to string a full sentence together? Or is today going to be bullet points in list format?"

"I'm guessing Tinder."

"What?"

"Tinder. I'm guessing you met lover boy on Tinder."

"Oh for god's sake, Ben."

"There's nothing wrong with that. I was on there once. It's the done thing these days."

"I'd prefer it if we could talk about the investigation."

"Sure. Just as soon as you give me all the dirty details."

"How do you know she's a non-smoker, anyway?"

"The FME is already on site. He called me while I was waiting for you to get ready. It's just his assessment. We'll know more when the lab results come back."

"Promise you won't say anything?"

Ben indicated to exit the main road into Nocton and slowed to wait for the oncoming traffic to pass.

"I'd have hoped you had a little more faith in me than that, Freya."

"I'm not used to sharing my personal life, that's all. And yes, I met him on Tinder."

"Oh good for you. First date? Second date?"

"First," she said, as Ben navigated onto Nocton Fen Lane, a narrow lane with fields on either side. "Which is why he slept on the couch."

"Ah, who am I to judge?" Ben said. "You go, girl. If you like him, then don't let what anybody else thinks stop you."

"I shan't," she said, releasing a flavour of her middle-class upbringing. "Sorry. I just... I don't know. I feel like it makes me look desperate or something."

"What, online dating? Get over it. It's the norm now. Kids don't meet in nightclubs anymore. They meet online. My brother does it all the time."

"All the time? So it's not worked well for him then, surely?"

"Or it *has* worked well," Ben said, not even trying to stop the sheepish grin that was spreading across his face. "He'll settle down one day. He's not doing anything any of us didn't do when we were younger. He's just saving time and money by getting all the small talk over and done with online. If you think about it—"

"Don't even try to convince me it's efficient, Ben. It's not as easy as you might think."

"Ah, you'll get the hang of it."

"I don't want to get the hang of it. In fact, hopefully I can remove my profile. It was a frightening experience. I felt like a piece of meat on a digital shelf."

"So it did go well then. When are you seeing him again? Will you be calling him tonight? Or are you one of those that has to leave it a day or so? You know, to make you look calm and collected."

"Trust me, calm and collected is the last thing he thinks I am."

She turned to stare out of the window again.

"Why?" Ben asked, then sighed as he caught sight of the emergency vehicles parked in a property a few hundred yards away. "What happened?"

"You don't want to know."

"Freya, who else have you got to talk to? None of your girlfriends are in Lincolnshire, and honestly, don't mention any of this to Jackie. You might as well call the newspapers when it comes to keeping a secret."

"And don't I know it," Freya said, and Ben caught the reference to a previous secret that Jackie had somehow managed to let loose regarding Freya's mental health.

Ben pulled the car to a stop outside the gates to a small farm.

He checked the address on his notes, and spied the various vans belonging to CSI on the drive.

"You can tell me anything. I won't say a thing to anyone. Mostly because I don't really have any friends, but also because I'm loyal," he said, and offered a smile.

"You tell anybody and I'll make your life hell."

"Cross my heart," he said.

Freya sighed and turned away, mumbling something inaudible.

"What?" Ben said.

"I fell asleep, Ben."

"Eh? When?"

"I don't know. Sometime after dinner. We were talking and–"

"You fell asleep?" Ben exclaimed.

"Alright, alright, keep it down."

"Freya, it's the bloke's job to fall asleep, and to be honest, not until after–"

"Okay, enough. I knew I shouldn't have told you."

"I'm sorry. I shouldn't laugh. But you said he slept on the couch?"

"He carried me upstairs, and put me to bed," she said. "Fully dressed, I might add. That was my next problem."

"What was?"

"He woke me up before he left, and somehow during the night I had managed to get my dress and the sheets all tangled around my legs."

Ben shrugged. "So?"

"So, I had to ask him to help me out. I felt so bloody stupid, Ben. Lucky I..." She paused, clearly stopping herself from saying too much. But Ben stared at her, eyebrows raised. "Lucky I was fully dressed."

"Oh, my word, Freya. How boring is my life?" Ben said. "I woke up, had breakfast, answered a call from DS Gillespie, then left a message on your phone. That's it. That's all I've done. You, on the other hand, have managed to–"

"Ben, Ben," she said, holding her hand up in defeat. "Quietly please. My head."

"Oh dear, Freya. Well, here's me thinking that you were our only chance at bringing some refinement to us country folk."

"That's not the end of it either," Freya said, and this time she smirked at the memory and met his gaze without shame.

"Go on," Ben said, as he unclipped his seat belt and made himself comfy.

"I spent all morning calling him Martin."

"So?" Ben said with a shrug.

Reaching into her pocket, Freya produced the page torn from her notebook. She covered the message with her finger, then displayed his signature.

"Mark? You called him the wrong bloody name?"

There was a moment of silence as Ben digested the tale of woe, then each of them burst into a fit of childish laughter.

"Well, if he comes back, you'll know he likes you, and that's when you'll need to watch out."

"And why is that?" Freya asked, as Ben opened his car door. Every so often, she overpronounced the word *why*, adding emphasis on the H. He wasn't sure why, but it irritated him a little.

He leaned on the roof and waited for her to do the same.

"He sounds like the perfect man for you. Good looking, well-mannered, a gentleman," he said, and cast his eyes downward referring to Freya flashing him her panties.

"But?" she said.

"You fell asleep on him before anything happened. I mean, that must be some kind of record. How boring must he be?" said Ben, as he clicked the key fob to lock the car, and turned to walk toward the gate, leaving her behind pondering his comment. "Don't delete that profile just yet, Freya," he called. "Swipe left and carry on, as my brother would say."

CHAPTER THREE

THE MAIN HOUSE WAS SINGLE-STOREY AND BRICK-BUILT WITH windows that needed replacing fifteen years ago. There was no double-glazing, and there seemed to be at least one cracked pane of glass for every three that were intact. A uniform named Griffiths nodded his greeting at their arrival, and he raised the tape for them to duck beneath.

Set to the side of the main house were what looked to be some old stables that had either been poorly converted into accommodation or were still in the process of being converted. The ground before them was muddy and glistened with the melting frost, but despite all the negatives, the fog that had hugged the ground when Ben peered through his kitchen window that morning was lifting, and revealed a place of beauty.

The surrounding trees provided privacy where privacy was needed. Yet, in those spaces where a man might stand and gaze, the landscape provided a suitable canvas.

"So this is Nocton, is it?" Freya said, as she came to stand beside him.

"Technically, this is Wasps Nest. Nocton is the village we

passed through. There's not much out here except for what you see."

"Peaceful," she said, then brushed it off, as any city girl might. "Come on. Let's find this body."

They walked around the main house and emerged in a small, fenced garden, where Ben could see some effort had been made to make it homely. Beyond the fence was a small field, less than an acre in size. Two people in white suits crouched in the field, one of whom waved when they saw them.

"Looks like Michaela is on the case," Ben said.

"You can tell who it is from here?"

"This isn't London. You get to know the teams over time. Besides, look at her. She's five foot tall with long, blonde hair and bossing the bloke around like she's six foot six."

He glanced down at Freya, noting her smaller stature. She wasn't quite as short as Michaela, but the two women shared certain qualities.

"Let's see what she has to say," Freya said.

"Do you need help with the fence?" Ben asked, as he stepped onto the first rail and swung his leg over. He rubbed his hands together and blew into them to heat them up, the way her father used to.

Freya shook her head in disbelief. "If you recall, Ben, I was faster over the stile in Anderby than you were."

"You were not," he scoffed, remembering the time a girl they wanted to question had done a runner. "You were *as* fast, at best, and you had adrenalin on your side then. Right now, all you have is a coffee and a hangover."

He dropped to the muddy ground below, then turned to watch. She had just raised one leg to the first rail when a familiar face emerged from the main house.

"Now then," the man called, using that age-old Lincolnshire greeting. He smiled as he strode over to them. Dropping her leg back down, Freya straightened her trousers and boots, then turned to see who it was. "I was hoping I might see you here. Never pleasant, but a familiar face brightens the mood."

"Doctor Saint," Ben said, and extended his hand for him to shake. "How have you been?"

"Oh come on, there's no need for formalities. Call me Peter, and yes, I've been okay, thank you," he said, then added under his breath, "aside from the company I keep of course."

As a local forensic medical examiner, Peter Saint was at the top of his game. From previous experiences, Ben knew him to be called to crime scenes all over Lincolnshire, as far north as South Yorkshire, and even venturing further south to Norfolk and East Anglia. Ben was always fascinated by him. They had first met before Freya had moved to Lincolnshire, when Ben was working beneath DI David Foster. That was before David's cancer had taken hold, and subsequently devastated the team. David's death, however, had opened a door for Ben to move up to DI. A move that had been thwarted by the arrival of a newcomer from London. Detective Inspector Freya Bloom had seconded to Lincolnshire following a harrowing investigation. It was a diversion to what was otherwise looking to be a promising career.

Meanwhile, Ben's promotion hung in the air like a spent helium balloon – falling slowly back to the ground with every passing day.

Peter Saint was one of those men who had been born with unnaturally large features. His ears, nose, mouth, and jaw all seemed giant-like but in proportion to each other. And his hands and fingers were so enormous that Ben wondered how he managed to control such implements as small as a scalpel.

"What are we looking at here, Peter?" Freya asked.

"DI Bloom, wasn't it? Apologies if that's wrong."

"No, that's right. You have a good memory."

Beaming down at her, Peter slipped his giant hands into his pockets. He wore a V-neck sweater over a pale blue shirt, and on top of all that, he wore a bright blue mac. The raincoat looked to be two sizes too small for him, but then Ben imagined the man probably struggled to find anything to fit him at all, and he had done well to find the sweater and shirt.

"I gave my report to DS Gillespie," Peter said, and he waved back at the house indicating that Gillespie was inside. "I've got to get to Hull fairly sharpish. However, you're looking at a single wound to the girl's throat."

"She bled out, did she?"

"That's right. It would have been fast." He nodded to the two white suits in the field. "Whoever did this hasn't left us much to go on. Very clean. You never know, we might get lucky. Anyway, I'll be sending a full report through, and as I said, Gillespie has my preliminary findings. He's an interesting guy, you know?"

"Gillespie?" said Ben.

Peter nodded. "He seems like a safe pair of hands. A bit like you really, Ben, only not as tactile. He's the type of guy I'd want on my side in a fight, but not on my team in a quiz night, if you know what I mean. He was first on the scene and had the place locked down so tight I had to show my ID to get in. I can't remember the last time I even got it out of my wallet."

"Gillespie usually works for Detective Inspector Standing. Another team," Ben explained, smiling at Peter's candid feedback. "He's okay on his own, but he can be a handful when he's with his boss."

"Ah, yes. Well, a little team rivalry never did anybody any harm, did it? Seems like a nice chap," said Peter. Then he leaned in close, took a quick glance back at the house to make sure they weren't being overheard, and whispered, "Can't understand a bloody word he says, mind you. But I nodded when needed, and it seems to have done the trick."

He winked, grinned, then pulled the raincoat cuffs down as far as they would go, which wasn't far enough to cover his watch.

"I'll be seeing you," he said, as he turned to leave. As he

reached the side of the house, he called out to Ben once more, "I might pay David a visit. I seem to recall the service being local."

"That's right," Ben said. "Follow the road back to Nocton. You can't miss the church."

He waved his giant hand, then disappeared from sight. Feeling Freya staring up at him, Ben turned to her.

"Sliced throat," she said. "Are you thinking what I'm thinking?"

"That depends what you're thinking. If it's that this doesn't seem to be a random act of violence, then yes."

"Why in the field and not in the house? This was planned, Ben."

"Let's not make too many judgement calls," Ben replied, just as a heavy boot crunched in the mud behind them.

Turning toward the sound, Ben found DS Gillespie standing outside the back door to the house.

"About time you two showed up," he said, his thick Glaswegian accent adding more than a hint of aggression to his choice of words. "I've damn near solved it on my own already."

CHAPTER FOUR

"DID YA BRING US COFFEE?" GILLESPIE SAID, AND LOOKED AT each of them as if he was watching a short tennis match.

"Coffee?" said Freya. "Damn it, I knew we forgot something. How stupid of us to turn up to a crime scene, where the aim is to control substances and fluids to preserve evidence, and forget to bring coffee. Shall I run and get you one? Wait, don't tell me, you're a vanilla latte type of guy. Am I right?"

"Aye well, Steve always brings us coffee," Gillespie said. "But nay bother if you're going to be funny about it."

"How long have you been here, Gillespie?"

"I was first here. About two hours now. Two hours and all I've had for company is the gentle giant and sleeping beauty over there."

"The gentle giant?" Freya asked.

"Aye, the big fella. Ears like satellites and hands like dustbin lids."

"You mean Doctor Saint?" Freya said. "The FME, one of the most respected men in his field?"

"Aye, boss. That's him."

"Where's DC Nillson?" Ben asked, pushing the conversation on. "I thought you were both attending the scene?"

"Aye, we did. She took off with the scrote who found her. Doing her family liaison bit, she said. Rather her than me. I'd sooner sit with the bleeding corpse than make tea."

"Doctor Saint spoke highly of you. You seem to have made your impression on him," Freya told him. "Sadly, I'm yet to be convinced. Perhaps while we wait for CSI to finish up, you can show me just exactly how you single-handedly solved the crime?"

"Aye. It'll be my pleasure," Gillespie said, his confidence swelling. He presented the way with a sweep of his arm, and stepped to one side, adding a charming smile to the gesture.

"Have forensics finished inside?" Ben asked. "Shouldn't we wait?"

"There's another CSI team processing the house." He stopped and turned to face Ben, leaving Freya at the doorway. "But I'm not as daft as I look, Ben. I always carry protection."

On the ground outside the back door was a small box of disposable shoe covers. Freya gave Ben a smile behind Gillespie's back, and began to slip a pair over her shoes. As if to compliment Freya's gesture, Gillespie pulled a pair of latex gloves from his inside pocket and winked at Ben before revealing the truth behind his preparedness.

"If I'm honest with you," he began, "I never used to carry a thing with me. But when I came down here from Glasgow, and started working with Steve, he'd never let me hear the end of it. If you forget something, he'll beast you until it never happens again."

Ben pondered Gillespie's final sentence, struggling to make any sense of it, but put it down to his brash mannerisms. Although he'd never worked with Gillespie, he had heard good things about him from his boss, Steve Standing. And from what DCI Granger had told him, he was a sharp individual who never missed a trick. But what let him down was his bullish approach, and willingness to let the rule book slip when the occasion suited, a trait that the force did not seek when filling leadership roles.

"How've you been, anyway, Ben? You know, since David and that," Gillespie said, as they each balanced on one leg to pull the covers on.

"So so, Jim. You know how it is."

"Aye. Weird, isn't it? We've been working from the same room for the past year, and this is the first case we've been on together."

"Small towns, small crimes," Ben said. "There's no reason for two detective sergeants to fight over who does what."

"I guess, there's that. Anyway, it'll be nice for a change. You know? See how the other team do things?"

"Aren't you just handing it over to us? This is our jurisdiction," Ben asked, and he looked at Freya who by now was already in the rear entrance to the kitchen looking around. She turned, and, with little hesitation, summarised the situation.

"Gillespie will be with us on this one, Ben. So you both might as well get used to each other. If DI Standing objects, then I'm sure I can persuade him otherwise. But seeing as DS Gillespie was first on scene and has a good lay of the land, I think we could use him."

"The boss has spoken, Ben," Gillespie said, then addressed them both. "Now then, shall I walk the pair of you through what happened?"

Ben opened his mouth to correct him, but Freya, ever the diplomat, quietened him with a subtle wave of her hand, as if she were patting a child on the head.

"DI Standing always makes us keep our hands in our pockets," Gillespie started, as he made his way out of the kitchen into the hallway, rattling on as he went. "Says it stops us touching stuff we shouldn't be touching." Stopping at the doorway to a bedroom, Gillespie stepped to one side. "This here's the master, though it's a bit poky for my liking. You'll note the suitcase on the bed. I took a wee look inside. It's the lass's clothing."

"Who else's might it have been?" Freya asked.

"I'm glad you asked. You'll note the open wardrobe door and the items on the floor. Male clothing. Far too big for that wee lass," Gillespie said. He turned away from the bedroom and strode confidently toward the end of the hallway, and stopped outside the final door. "Then we have this place."

"And this is?" Ben said, peering into the gloomy room, which he guessed to be three metres by three metres, and had been furnished with two makeshift desks and an old filing cabinet. The drawers had been pulled open and paperwork had been rifled through, some of which had fallen to the floor, while the rest had been scattered across the work surfaces.

"Office. Looks like they had a good rifle through looking for something," Gillespie said, and he pointed to a bank statement on the floor. "The victim's name is Emma Blanch."

"No, the person whose bank statement that is is Emma Blanch," Freya said. "At this stage, I haven't even seen the body. It could be anyone out there."

"I've seen her." Gillespie adopted an expression far more serious than he had until now. He nodded at the wall where a framed photo hung of a young woman standing at a pair of gates. Behind her was a beaten-up Volkswagen truck, and the unmistakable front door to the property. She looked to be in her twenties, and wore a woolly hat and a big scarf. Her long, blonde hair poked out from beneath the layers, and she had her arm around a man of a similar age. It was a picture of love and family, and, Ben guessed, new beginnings. "That's her."

"We don't know that's Emma Blanch, though," Ben added.

Despite his rough-around-the-edges mannerisms, Gillespie had foreseen Ben's comment. He retrieved his phone from his pocket, fumbled with the pass code in his latex gloves, and eventually held the screen up for both Freya and Ben to see. It showed a Facebook profile belonging to the girl in the image on the wall.

Her profile picture was different, but it was clearly the same person. The name on the profile was Emma Blanch.

"So, it is her," Freya said. "We'll still need a positive ID, but good work, Gillespie. Any news on her male friend?"

"Scarpered," Gillespie said, and he waited for one of them to coax him to embellish the single-word statement.

Neither did, and he relented with a sigh, clearly enjoying the limelight that perhaps DI Standing did not often afford him.

"I ran the number plate through ANPR while I was waiting for you. It's faster than it looks. It was caught going through a speed camera on the B1189 at three-thirty this morning."

"Which direction?"

"South, but it didn't go very far. It turned off a few miles before Billinghay, and hasn't been seen since."

Freya looked back toward the bedroom, and then into the office. Finally, she stared at Gillespie.

"So, your theory is that she argued with her partner—"

"Jason Cross," Gillespie added, and raised his phone again to show another Facebook profile.

"Right. He killed her, and then took off in the truck?"

"It's about as simple as it gets, and simple is often accurate."

"So why did he ransack this place?" Ben asked.

"Maybe he was looking for something. Maybe he slotted her and panicked, and searched this place—"

"For?" Freya asked.

"I dunno. It's just an idea."

"I thought you said you solved it?"

"Aye, well... I mean, I established their identities, at least."

"As far as I can see, Gillespie, you waited in here in the warm, browsing Facebook until we turned up," Freya said. "Do me a favour, will you?"

"Aye?" he said, his confidence on the floor.

"Find me that vehicle. DS Savage and I will take over here."

CHAPTER FIVE

For DC Anna Nillson, the role of family liaison was not limited to the dedicated resources the force provided. The role was the responsibility of any officer close to grief, and was more than simply comforting a person affected by crime or death-related stress. A FLO acted as a link to the investigating team, a spy deep underground, the eyes and ears behind closed doors.

"There you go," she said, as she placed a tray of tea and biscuits on the coffee table between Mr and Mrs Cross. Her phone vibrated once in her pocket, indicating a message. She ignored it, and took the spare armchair, composed herself, and then in the softest voice she could muster, she began.

"So, Mr and Mrs Cross, there's a few formalities I need to go through with you. I understand this is a very difficult time for you both. You can stop me at any time, and if you have questions, then feel free to ask. I'll answer them the best I can. Is that okay?"

Mrs Cross' face was buried in her hands, but Mr Cross nodded once, his face steeled in preparation for what she might say.

"Mr Cross, I just need to go through the sequence of events. Like I said, it's just a formality—"

"Cyrus," he said, in a thick local accent. A red ring had formed around his wrinkled eyes, and although his appearance was what she might call weathered, the experience had clearly shaken him. "Call me Cyrus. Please. And this is Mary. You're in our home. There's no need to stand on ceremony."

"Thank you," she said, touched by their hospitality. In her experience, the FLO was open to abuse. To find the couple accepting of what she was trying to do was warming and encouraging.

"Cyrus," she began, "am I correct in saying that it was you who made the call to the emergency services this morning?"

"S'right," he said. "About five-thirty. Give or take a few minutes."

"May I ask what you were doing up at your son's house at five-thirty in the morning? Just in case I'm asked. Forearmed is fore-warned, as they say."

Her phone vibrated once more, again just once, another message. But to look at her phone while the old couple were dealing with the discovery would be plain rude. As if to tempt her to take a peek, another message came through. The sender would either be DI Standing or her boyfriend, Keiran. And seeing as DI Bloom was running the investigation, she presumed it would be Keiran. He was persistent like that. Unnecessarily needy, her mother would say. Sitting with Mr and Mrs Cross reminded Anna of her mother, and she could almost hear her say in her high-pitched, been there, seen it all, got the t-shirt tone, "There's nothing so unattractive as a needy man."

"Feeding chickens," Cyrus said, as a matter of fact. "I said I'd help them when them came here. I feed the chickens for her, amongst other things—"

"They were for the bed and breakfast, you know," Mrs Cross added. She was far frailer than her husband, though they both appeared to be in their early seventies. "The eggs, dear. The bed and breakfast is due to open in a few weeks. I think there are

even some bookings. Someone will have to deal with all that..."
She broke again, and rested her head on her husband's shoulder.

"So you were tending the chickens and collecting eggs, were you? Is there anything else you did for..." Making a show of searching her notes for the name, Anna waited for Cyrus to finish it for her.

"Emma," he said. "Emma Blanch. That was her name."

Anna wrote the name at the top of her notebook, while Cyrus' eyes bored into her.

"And you're sure that it was Emma?" Anna asked. It was a terrible question, and she knew it the moment the words left her mouth, but without a formal identification, the enquiry would come to a standstill. "You said it was dark and foggy–"

"Course I'm sure," he snapped, then softened. "I'd recognise her with my eyes shut. It's her. I checked."

"And how did you know Emma, Cyrus? She obviously trusted you to look after her chickens."

"I don't just look after the chickens. Oh no. I damn well built the place. It was falling down when they bought it. I got them set up with a bedroom and bathroom, fixed up the kitchen a little, and I converted all those stables into rooms. That was what they were going to do. Run a bed and breakfast. An air hotel or something. I don't know."

"The place is a bed and breakfast then?"

"Well, the stables are. Nearly ready too, they are. But the house will take some doing. Run out of money. I said they would. Said they should get the place liveable, then focus on the business."

"Sorry, Cyrus, who is *they*? Who are you referring to?"

"Emma and Jason," he said. "Who else would I be talking about?"

"Sorry, who is Jason? Is that Emma's husband?"

Cyrus looked incredulously at Anna, almost dumbstruck by

what she had said, as if she should have known the inside and out of his back-to-front story already.

"Jason is our son. Jason Cross. Emma, bless her, was his girlfriend."

"Do you happen to know where he is?"

"Of course we don't know where he is. Why do you think my wife is sitting here bawling? We're worried bloody sick about him."

"Okay," she said, finding some semblance of calm in her tone. "Let's get finished up here, then perhaps we can focus on finding Jason? You went to deal with the chickens–"

"I was just helping her out. Showing her the ropes."

"And when you got there, you found Emma."

"It was quiet," Cyrus said. "Too quiet for my liking. I thought I saw something move. In the paddock. About a hundred yards from the house. The fog was in, so I couldn't be sure. So I went closer, and spooked the birds–"

"Birds?"

"Ravens," Cyrus said, nodding as he recalled the memory. "That's when I saw what I did. I called out for Jason. Even had a look around for him. But the truck was gone. I ran all the way back here to call you lot, and that's when you turned up."

"So you didn't take a mobile phone with you?"

"Don't have one," he said with pride. "And they don't have a house phone yet either. Supposed to be installed later this month. Don't suppose there's much point in any of it now."

"How well did you know Emma?" Anna asked.

"A little. She was alright. Helped him a lot. Helped Jason. Had some problems, he did."

"Problems? What type of problems?"

"Oh, you know, mental health or something. No doubt some know-all came up with a name for it. Everything seems to have a name these days. In my day, they called a spade a spade. When things got on top of you, you just got on with it. All sorts of nonsense now."

"I see. I'm trying to build a picture, and you're being very helpful, so thank you. Let me see if I understand this correctly. Your son Jason was working away–"

"Cornwall," Cyrus said. "That's where he was. Too far for us to get down too often. Must be nearly eight hours in a car. I'd be stopping every chance I got to use the lavatory."

"And that's where he met Emma, is it?"

"S'right, yeah. She grew up around these parts. Fate, they called it, that the two should meet so far away. She'd been down there a few years. Anyways, he had a funny turn, see. Wanted to be closer to home. Said he wanted to do something more empowering."

"He's ever so strong-minded," Mary Cross said, trying to pull herself together. "I always said he'd do well. Didn't I, dear?"

Smiling affectionately at his wife, Cyrus nodded, and then found Anna's stare.

"He said he wouldn't mind starting a bed and breakfast. You know? So he can work from home. Be his own boss. Well, as luck would have it, that plot was up for sale." He nodded at the French doors and through the net curtains.

Anna could just make out some activity at the top of the far field.

"Is that...?"

"That's it," Cyrus said. "I knew the fella selling it. Used to keep sheep there. I had a word, and before you know it, they were back here setting up their bed and breakfast. I mean it all happened so fast."

"So they were one month from opening their bed and breakfast and this happened? How tragic," Anna mused. "What a wonderful life they must have had."

A moment of silence fell over the room, the catalyst for Anna to excuse herself.

"I'll just need to make a call," she told them both as she stood and slipped her phone from her jacket pocket. "Let's see if we can't find Jason, alright?"

"Course, it weren't all plain sailing," Cyrus continued, raising his voice to reach Anna, who by now was in the adjacent kitchen staring up at two white-suited crime scene investigators in the distance. "Not since the court case, at any rate."

She ignored Kieran's messages and found DI Bloom's number on her phone. Dialling it, she had just placed the phone to her ear when Cyrus' statement registered in her busy mind.

She stepped back into the doorway.

"Which court case is that, Cyrus?" she asked, keeping her voice calm and low, while inside, her mind was racing.

He turned, set his tea down on the tray, and peered at her over the wing of the armchair, adopting that same expression that implied she should have known the ins and outs of a duck's backside.

"Emma's court case, of course. How many court cases do you think we have around here? Killed a man, she did."

"She didn't kill him," Mary corrected him. "Manslaughter, or something."

"Yeah that's it. Manslaughter. She was a carer. That's what she did in Cornwall. That's how she met Jason. Anyway, when money began to run out, she had to find work to pay for the bed and breakfast. I don't know what happened. I heard so many different versions, I couldn't tell you what was truth or lies. But the old man she was looking after died in her care. The family said she was negligent. Pressed charges, they did." As Cyrus ventured deeper into the story, he became more and more animated. His hands waved, and his face became elastic with expressions. "She did near a few months in prison, on... What's it called? You know, when they're held until the trial?"

"Remand?" Anna said, guessing at where he was going.

"That's it. Three months, Jason was on his own while she was banged up. Anyways, she got off with it in the end. But they were never the same since then."

Dumbfounded, Anna stepped backward until she bumped into the sink. She turned and gazed out of the window again, at those two white dots on the horizon.

That was when she heard DI Bloom's irritated voice calling her name from her phone.

CHAPTER SIX

Freya tapped the red button on her phone to disconnect the call, and stared at the house at the far end of the field. Through the window, she could just make out Anna, who said she had been standing in the kitchen. From there, a person might see all the way up to the house. From there, if inclined, an individual might keep a watchful eye on their son and his girlfriend. Or they might just keep a watchful eye on their son's girlfriend.

A few metres away, Michaela snapped a hard case closed and dropped the equipment beside the rest of her pile.

"All done," she called. "I'll have a stab and guess you'll want the results fast-tracked?"

"What a funny turn of phrase to use," Freya replied, returning from where she had been lost in thought.

"There was nothing meant by it, I can assure you that," Michaela replied, and she bent to collect a few cases. Even with her assistant, it would take a few trips to load the car.

"I'm sorry," Freya said, and she shook off the residue of thoughts that had begun to form the puzzle. She approached the younger, taller, and slimmer woman, and stared down at the body of Emma Blanch. "It's not been a great morning for any of us. Is there anything I should know?"

"What you see is what you get with this one, I'm afraid. Although, there are two leads I'm hedging my bets on." She pointed to the trail of little flags that led from Emma's body toward the fence. They were one metre apart, clearly identifying the path that somebody had taken. "If we can get a clean mould, we may be able to get the size and model of the footwear. It's too boggy here, so we've extracted the cleanest one and taken casts, and we'll take a sample of the resident's prints from somewhere to cross check against. We'll get to work on those in the lab. Secondly, take a look at the wound." Lowering herself to a crouch, Michaela retrieved a pen from her breast pocket and held it over Emma's throat. "I can't claim credit for this theory. It was Doctor Saint who suggested it. But this is a slice, not a stab. It's precise, and was performed with a very sharp blade."

"A scalpel?"

"No, larger than that. A scalpel is short and would merely nick the skin, unless the killer used the full range of motion their shoulder would allow. That's just unnatural, and highly unlikely given that the victim wouldn't exactly be standing still. Also, the thickness of the blade and angle of the leading edge are wrong. No. This blade was six-inches long at least, and thick like a hunting knife or something. It's hard to say. The pathologist will pick up on it, I'm sure."

"Thank you, Michaela," said Freya, as the taller woman stood and collected a few cases. Freya remained crouched beside the body but watched her walk away. It was the second time Freya had encountered Michaela Fell. The first was when the body of a woman had been discovered in some woods a few miles away in Woodhall Spa. Freya got the impression from Michaela's makeup that her appearance and encounter with Ben were not a coincidence. Michaela stopped to greet Ben, and Freya imagined she might be conveying the same message to him, albeit an abridged version.

He was a handsome man, Freya thought, and not for the first time. He was broad, tall, dark, and his features were distinct. The sharp nose, square jaw, and piercing eyes were near perfect. Clearly, Michaela noticed it, too. She placed a case on the ground to free a hand, and in the past twenty seconds had swept her hair behind her ear at least three times. Then four. And she gave a fake laugh, finishing with a bite of her bottom lip.

It was a ritual mankind had played out for millennia. It started with a physical attraction, then pheromones and hormones came into play. And should the perfect blend of magic be concocted from that chemical lust, then who knows? That was the fun part, for most. Swiping right on a dating app didn't have the same romantic appeal. It was as if the time-served method of two people finding a shared appeal simply took too long for modern man. Especially for those who had, for some reason, felt compelled to send Freya lewd photos of certain body parts, or in one case, of somebody else's oversized body parts.

The interaction ended, and Ben appeared oblivious to Michaela's chemical calling card. He approached Freya, hands in pockets and hair swept back by the incessant wind.

"We all set?" he asked, and glanced over the body of Emma Blanch.

"Why is she out here, Ben?"

Freya stood from her crouch, and felt her knees click. She wrapped her coat around her, and her hangover reminded her she wasn't free of its powers just yet.

"You okay?" Ben asked, and he reached out to grab Freya's shoulder.

"Yep, head rush, that's all."

"You need fluids, Freya. Come on, let's find Anna and see what she has to say."

"I've spoken to her," said Freya, and she gestured at the house at the far end of the field. "That house belongs to Mr and Mrs Cross."

"Cross?" said Ben. "The boyfriend?"

"Yep, that's his mum and dad's house. His dad came up to feed the chickens this morning. Found her out here."

"So we should speak to him."

"No. No, Anna can handle it. There's a chance the son is responsible for this, and they know it. Anna will stay there for the day, at least until Gillespie finds the car. I don't want to go in heavy-handed on them. Not yet anyway. There's more to the story that I'll tell you later, but trust me, we need the father on our side."

"Fair enough," Ben said quietly. "And in answer to your earlier question, your guess is as good as mine. The call came in at what, five-thirty? First of all, the chickens are on the far side of the house, and secondly, are those flags the path the killer took?"

"Somebody went that way. Not necessarily the killer," said Freya, as her phone began to vibrate. She glanced down at the screen and recognised the number. "I need to take this. Let's get out of here. Let them take her to the mortuary. All we're doing is treading over the crime scene. I'll see you at the car."

CHAPTER SEVEN

They drove in silence. It was as though, while Ben had waited by the car after talking to uniform to arrange the cover, a new Freya had returned – a distressed Freya, lost in thought, silent and brooding.

At the station, he parked and tried to rouse her, but she refused to meet his eye. In the building, Ben climbed the flight of stairs ahead of her, while she walked slowly, reading a message on her phone.

"How's Martin doing?" Ben asked without looking back.

"It's not Martin, it's somebody else," she said, then realised her mistake. "Mark, I mean. Oh, just give me five minutes. I'll be right behind you."

Smiling to himself, Ben entered the first-floor corridor, where CID were based. Immediately, he heard a rabble coming from the incident room. Raised voices, and what sounded like fraying tempers.

He passed DSI Harper's office, which was empty, as he expected. He hadn't been in of late, and even DCI Will Granger was being cagey about his superior's whereabouts.

Ben approached the incident room and peered through the window in the door. The door was renowned for having the loudest squeal in the history of doors. So he waited to get a feel for the affray.

He was both relieved and sorely disappointed at what he witnessed.

"Kit Kat," DC Jackie Gold said, leaning back in her chair. Her voice was loud, and she seemed almost carefree in the absence of any authority, the way a schoolgirl might wreak havoc while the teacher took a comfort break. "Many have tried to beat it, and all have failed. It is the king of chocolate bars."

"No way," DC Cruz argued. "It's a Twix. The best chocolate bar by far. It is definitively the perfect blend of chocolate, caramel, and biscuit. Forget your wafer, and your nougat—"

"Kit Kat's don't have nougat."

"No, but those other ones do. Double Deckers. It's like chocolate makers only have a choice of four ingredients – biscuit, caramel, nougat, and nuts. They've got no imagination."

"How can you say that? What about Turkish Delight?"

"You have got to be kidding me," a third voice said. At the far end of the room, Ben was surprised to see DI Standing strolling into view, a man who held the same rank as Freya and was held in high regard by Will Granger. "Turkish Delights should be banned. They're just too different. And why are they so bloody expensive? They're half the size of a regular chocolate bar, for crying out loud."

"What about Toffee Crisp?" another voice said, and Ben was even more surprised to see the usually introverted and well-behaved DC Chapman raising her opinion. "Those are my favourites."

"They've got rice crispies in. That's like baking my mum's chocolate cornflake cakes and marking them up by five thousand per cent. She can knock them up in the adverts halfway through

Coronation Street and still have time to make a cup of tea before the second half. No way. If chocolate companies want to win the battle, they'll have to do better than bloody rice crispy bars."

It wasn't that Ben was angry at the lack of work taking place. The team worked hard, and rarely did anybody moan. But Freya had descended into a mood, and if she walked into that racket who knows what she might do.

He pushed open the door slowly to maximise the squealing hinge, and the room fell silent. He shot Chapman, Cruz, and Gold each a warning stare, and they returned to their work.

DI Standing, however, remained resolute.

"Here he is, Lincoln's answer to Dirty bleeding Harry," he said, but the only person who laughed was DC Phil Moray, and he was so far at the other end of the room that Ben hadn't even noticed he was there. "I see you're not happy stealing Cruz from me. You need Gillespie and Nillson too now, do you? What is it, one to make the coffee, the other to bring the biscuits?"

Ignoring the comment, Ben moved into the room, letting the door swing closed. He always found it odd that the squeal was never reversed, as it should have been in his mind. It sounded the same in either direction. He sat behind his desk, shook the mouse to wake the laptop, and then entered his credentials.

"You know how to bring a party down, Savage, don't you?" Standing growled, then addressed the room, "You don't get none of this silence malarkey in my team."

"DI Standing, I'd thank you for getting out of my way and leaving my team to work, if you please," Freya said. She had burst into the room so fast that even the door had been too scared to make a noise.

"I was just telling–"

"I said bugger off, Standing," she yelled, then tossed her bag onto a nearby desk, freeing up both hands.

It was the first time Ben had ever heard Freya use bad

language, and by the looks on their faces, it was a first for the entire room. Her middle-class, privileged accent shone through, and Ben thought it added a certain weight to the words. It did the trick though. DI Standing eyed Ben one last time, then slunk off to his half of the office. There was no formal line that divided the space, just the configuration of desks and white boards that provided a kind of unwritten demarcation, which Standing had tastelessly likened to an ongoing war in the Middle East. Annoyingly, the door was close to Ben's desk, so every time Standing entered or left the room, he was forced to endure the sanctimony of the insufferable man.

Chapman, Gold, and Cruz shared concerned expressions and looked to Ben for an explanation. But with almost no idea as to why Freya's mood had altered, he shrugged, and waited for her to finish writing on the whiteboard. All would become clear, of that he was sure.

And it did.

She spoke calmly and with reason, taking extra care not to demonstrate any hint of aggression in her tone. She stood with her feet together and the whiteboard marker in her hands, waiting patiently for everyone to sense the silence, stop working, and then turn to face her.

"Thank you," she said, quietly, so that Ben had to edge closer to hear her. The white board behind her showed the usual configuration of names, some of which Ben was familiar with, but there were a few he was not. She circled Emma Blanch's name. "Twelve months ago, Emma Blanch worked as a carer for this man." She circled a name Ben had yet to hear of. "Harry Garland. Ninety-one years old. Survived World War Two, the recession, and the decline of aristocracy. You name it, he survived it. He deserved care. Emma Blanch was that carer. That was until, for one reason or another, she left him unattended in the bath, and he drowned. Three months on remand and a gruelling trial later, Emma is handed a not guilty verdict. Enough for her to get back on with her life. Fast forward to five-thirty this morning. Emma and her boyfriend, Jason, have bought a property in Wasps Nest, which they are renovating into a bed and breakfast. Jason's father, Cyrus," she said, stopping to circle the names of the Crosses then continuing almost without breaking breath, "went there to help her with the chickens and the last of the building work. He found Emma's body lying in the field they had earmarked to grow their vegetables."

The room was silent as the team digested the information, and Freya allowed them just enough time before carrying on.

"Cyrus Cross, Jason's father, is at home now with DC Nillson, who, as you may or may not know, began her career as a family liaison officer. So, DI Standing, if you're wondering where she is, and why she isn't answering your calls, it's because she's in an extremely volatile situation and I've instructed her to ignore all calls except the ones from me."

Out of Freya's sight behind the board, Standing shook his head, but said nothing.

"In the house, we found a suitcase packed and ready to go with Emma's belongings, and their car is missing. Also missing is Jason Cross, the boyfriend."

"Have we tried ANPR?" Chapman suggested.

"Gillespie is on it, thanks, Chapman. The vehicle was last seen heading south on the B1189 near Timberland," Freya advised. She reached for a blue file in her bag and slapped it down on a desk. "Gold, make copies and have the notes typed up, please. Everyone else, familiarise yourself with the facts. I'll brief you all in one hour when we know more."

"Ma'am," Gold said, raising her hand as if she was still at school. Freya looked up at her, and the room waited with bated breath. Gold was about to poke the sleeping bear.

"What was the cause of death?" said Gold.

"Her throat was sliced from left to right," said Freya, and she held Gold's stare. "She bled to death."

"Brutal," Cruz added quietly.

The interest sparked a slight shift in Freya's demeanour. She sat on the edge of the nearest desk and folded her hands in front of her lap.

"What does that tell you, Gold?" she asked. "Last time you were asked to assess a crime scene, I believe you were one hundred per cent accurate."

"The throat was sliced, ma'am?" Gold said. "Seems personal to me. I mean, stabbing is one thing, but slicing a throat takes some doing."

"And you, Cruz?" Freya said.

"Just hatred, ma'am," he replied. "It's very personal. But if she had that trial before, there might be lots of people out there who wanted her dead. Who's to say they won't strike again now they have a taste for it?"

"Let's hope not, Cruz," she said. "Let's hope not."

The team waited for a prompt. Nobody dared to rouse Freya's temper. Nobody except Steve Standing.

"That's a tough one, Bloom," he called out, his voice filled with mockery. "Dead girl. Missing boyfriend. It's hardly rocket science, is it?"

"Now I know why DS Gillespie was so fast to make assumptions," Freya said, by way of a retort. But that was all she offered him, choosing instead to distribute the workload. "Chapman, find Emma's next of kin. We'll need to notify them before we do anything. Then see what you can find on the trial. Check newspapers, the internet, and local forums. Let's start working on a list of people who might have held a grudge against the victim. Gold, you're putting the notes into some sort of order for me and distributing them. Gillespie is working on the missing vehicle and the boyfriend. When he gets back, we'll have a few more avenues open. Anna is with Jason Cross' parents, and Ben, you're with me. I want to hit the mortuary this afternoon. I don't want the pathologist holding us up. That just leaves you, Cruz."

Detective Constable Gabriel De Cruz leaned back in his chair and let his head fall back in dismay.

"Oh, don't tell me, I'm door knocking again," he said. "I'm supposed to be in the office today, boss. Duty sergeant asked me. Maybe someone else can go and knock on some doors?"

"Why do you need to be here?"

"I don't know. A new phone system or something. I just have to stay and keep an eye on the engineers."

"We don't need a new phone system," Ben said. He picked up a handset, dialled three numbers, and Cruz's desk phone rang.

"DC Cruz," the young detective announced when he answered. He collected a pen from his desk and dragged his notepad closer.

"There's nothing wrong with this one," said Ben, and it took Cruz a few moments of looking between Ben and the phone to realise his mistake. "See, we don't need a new system."

"We do if we want to spend the budget, Ben," Standing said from the far end of the room, and the team all turned to find him leaning back in his chair, listening in. "Besides, it's a county-wide rollout. Every station will be getting them."

"It's a top-notch system apparently. We'll be able to transfer calls to our mobiles if we want. All the conversations will be recorded, too. I read the pamphlet. We'll even be able to dial from our laptops if we really can't be bothered to extend our arm all the way to the phone," Cruz said, excited at the new technology.

"Why would we want to record all the conversations? We can do that already, can't we?"

"With some help from the tech guys. But we need to record them all, apparently," Cruz answered.

"It's a compliance regulation," Freya said. "They rolled them out in the Met when I was in London. Looks like the hype has spread."

"That's it. Compliance," Cruz added. "It's like a cloud telephone or something. I can't wait, personally."

Freya appraised the young DC, who seemed pleased that he had managed to squirm his way out of going door-to-door and gained himself a day in the warm office.

"DI Standing?" Freya called out.

"Oh Christ," he groaned. "What?"

"Can you please assign one of your team to stay in the office to oversee the installation?"

"I have," he said. "Cruz."

"Cruz is on my team until this investigation is over. Somebody else. What about Moray?"

"Eh?" Moray said, with a mouthful of bacon sandwich.

"You heard," she said, then turned to Standing. "Do I need to go and get DCI Granger's approval, or can we work this out ourselves? We are, apparently, mature, empowered adults. In fact, I'm sure he'd also love to hear about your favourite chocolate bar, if he didn't hear you. I heard you from the bloody stairwell."

"Alright, alright," Standing said, and nodded to Moray who slapped his sandwich down in disgust.

Turning back to Cruz, Freya caught his expression. He clearly wasn't happy with the result.

"See Sergeant Priest and ask him to assign a uniform to assist you," she said.

"I bloody hate door knocking," Cruz muttered under his breath.

"And that's exactly why you're doing it," Freya said, then addressed the room. "Any questions?"

"Any point?" Cruz said, rolling his eyes, at which Freya strode toward him, placed her hands on his desk, and leaned in close.

"None at all, DC Cruz. Not only do I want to see a plan of the target residences, I want you to spread your wings a bit. Are there any cameras anywhere? Local businesses, traffic cameras, anything?"

"I don't know. I'm not that familiar with the area to be honest. It's off the beaten track."

"So, get familiar. Make a plan. You're in my team for the time being, so you need to think for yourself. Now get to it, or I'll send you back to Team Neanderthal, and you won't be able to chat to the girls about your favourite bloody chocolate bar."

CHAPTER EIGHT

THE WASHROOMS AT THE END OF THE CORRIDOR WERE EXACTLY
the reason she tried to avoid taking comfort breaks at work. Of
course, it was unavoidable to use them at least two to three times
a day, but she made a conscious effort to limit her visits. They
weren't dirty as such, more tired. The floors were bleached every
night, and she knew the seats were cleaned, but it was the corners
of the cubicles where a mop couldn't get to that put her off. It was
a tiny thing, and she knew it. But she couldn't get past it. Which
meant that every time she was in there, she subconsciously sought
other reasons to justify her irrational behaviour. Such as the ring
of grime around the base of the taps and the stains on the ceiling
tiles.

Carefully, she splashed some water on her face, then leaned on
the sink and studied herself in the mirror. Where had all those
lines around her eyes come from? And the fine down on her top
lip hadn't been so visible before, had it? She dried her face with a
paper towel, then reapplied the makeup that had been disturbed.
There was no point going out looking like an old clown.

Her phone buzzed once in her pocket, and she knew who it
was. She also knew that a single vibration was a WhatsApp

message, as opposed to the double vibration that signalled an email, or the continuous vibration that signified a call.

She selected the cubicle which, in her mind, was the least bad of the three, closed the toilet lid, and sat down. The message was short and to the point, and she was considering her reply when somebody entered the room. Habitually, she glanced at the cubicle lock, then eyed the space beneath the partition wall to see if she could identify the visitor by her shoes.

"You can't hide in there all day, Freya," Ben said.

"What the bloody hell are you doing in here?"

"Checking on a friend."

"I could be doing anything."

"No. You've been in here for more than five minutes. You're never more than three."

"What?" She leaned forward and unlocked the door, then pulled it open with her foot. She remained seated the whole time. "You time me in the washroom?"

Ben was leaning on the sinks with his arms folded, just as he might stand at a bar. He looked down at her perched on the toilet seat.

"Not time you, but, you know... You get a feel for who takes how long. Take Jackie, for instance, never less than five minutes, never more than ten. While Steve Standing–"

"Always more than fifteen."

"You're getting it."

"I don't come here to read the paper or check Facebook."

"No, you come here to read personal messages. Are you going to tell me what's wrong?" Ben asked. "I can stand here all day. It's much cleaner than the gents."

"I can't believe you would actually dare to come in here and harass me."

"That's a bit strong. I did tell Jackie to make sure her and Chapman keep their legs crossed for a while. So, it's just you and me, boss. What's happened? We've established it wasn't Martin who upset you."

She sighed, and some tiny part of her found the funny side to it, and then she warmed to his concern.

"It's Greg," she said, and found herself staring at the dirt around the pedestal. All the cleaner had to do was get the corner of a cloth around it. A bit of elbow grease.

"Your husband? I thought you were getting divorced?"

"Divorces take time. Although I'm not sure why. But it wasn't about that, it's something else."

"What then? I didn't even know you still spoke to him, to be honest. You never talk about him, or his son, for that matter. What was his name?"

"Billy," Freya said softly. "His name is Billy. And I know I don't talk about them, but that doesn't mean I don't think about them. I spoke to Greg this morning. It's Billy. He's not going to let me see him for Christmas."

"Were you that close? I'm sorry, Freya. I know you've mentioned him, but I had no idea—"

"I raised him, pretty much. Not from a baby, he was already walking when I met him, but I watched him grow. I don't know, Ben. There's something about children. When you witness them develop, when you pick them off the ground, and when you hold them at night, even if they're not your own, you care. You really care about them. I've done everything I can to put myself in a position where nobody else matters, where I can focus on myself and my own problems. And now I find myself drawn to him, and Greg won't let me see him," she said, and felt the warm sting of tears. "He said that Billy has been through enough. He doesn't want to confuse him. Am I so selfish that I didn't even stop to consider how Billy was doing during all this time?"

"You've been through hell, Freya. It's not selfish. You're still healing. You've been here how long? A few months? A few months, after what you've been through? Sometimes you have to be selfish to get through the hard times."

"Why am I even sitting here on the bloody toilet talking to you about it? I should be in the car. I should be on the motorway already. I need to fight to see him. I've become a coward, Ben. A selfish coward who wakes up with strange men in their house and can't remember their name. Someone who's afraid of their past. That's not me."

"Cut yourself some slack, mate."

"Mate? Since when do you call me mate?"

"Since we're in the girls' bogs, and calling my boss, *boss* while she's sitting on the toilet seems a bit off-kilter to me."

"You came in here," she muttered, then sighed. "I know. You're right. I'm being stupid. I'm not sure if I'm worried about Billy, or worried about what he thinks of me."

"Let me talk to him?"

"What? No."

"I'll do it," Ben said, without thinking. "I'll pretend to be your boyfriend, Martin."

"Mark," Freya corrected him, and for a moment, there was hope and humour in her eyes. "And he's not–"

"Ah, whatever. Greg won't know, will he? I'll tell him you're indisposed or something."

Freya stood, straightened her outfit, and tried to see her reflection in the mirror, hinting for Ben to step aside.

But he didn't. At least, not until there was a gentle knock on the door. He leaned over and opened it a fraction, just enough to see Chapman standing outside in the corridor.

"Is this your office now, Ben?" she said. "Suits you."

"Ha ha," Ben replied, and she slipped him a piece of paper. "Thanks."

He let the door close and opened the folded sheet while Freya straightened her hair and checked her makeup.

"Where did you say Greg's house is?"

"You mean, *our* house?" Freya corrected him, then added, "South London."

"I thought you relinquished any part of it when you drove off in your motor home?" Ben said. Should anybody else have uttered those same words, then Freya might have exploded. But somehow, over the course of the past few months, she had come to know when his off-the-cuff slants were malicious and when they were meant to raise a smile.

Her smile was not raised but her amusement was roused enough for her to look him in the eye with a straight face.

"It's still half mine. Until we get the divorce, I'm stuck–"

"In my dad's poky little cottage?" Ben said. "Could be worse."

"Yes, it could," she agreed.

"Well, here you go then," Ben said, handing her the piece of paper. "Emma Blanch's parents live in Kent. You can kill two birds with one stone. Visit them and break the news, then go and see Billy."

"I'm leading the investigation, Ben. I can't just go off on a jolly because it suits my personal circumstances."

"Take a day or so," he said, ignoring her complaint. "I'll cover for you if anybody asks where you are."

CHAPTER NINE

It was mid-afternoon by the time Ben and Freya reached the mortuary in Lincoln County Hospital. It was Freya's third visit to the wretched place, with its whitewashed walls and floors so thick with bleach that the leather soles of her boots seemed to stick fast with every step she took.

"You called ahead, right?" she asked Ben, as they entered the long corridor. "I can't stand waiting around in this place."

"You don't want to stand still too long here. Doctor Bell will have you bagged and tagged in a heartbeat. Pun intended."

The mention of the doctor's name reminded Freya of her first encounter with the slightly off-the-wall pathologist, and she exhaled, long and slow, rolling her eyes as Ben grinned at the memory, savouring it with apparent delight.

"You should have warned me what she was like."

"Oh, I see," Ben replied. "What was I supposed to say? Oh, by the way, be on the lookout for a female IC-one, five foot nothing with bright blue hair and a face full of piercings?"

"You could have just mentioned that she was…"

"Was what?"

"Different."

"Ah, now I see," Ben said as they reached the double doors. "We were standing right here, and you heard whatever it was she was listening to–"

"Chopin," Freya said.

"Right, Chopin. And you said, *now this seems like my type of person*," Ben said, mimicking her posh accent. "You made a judgement based purely on the music she was listening to while she worked."

"It was a backhanded inference to your friends."

"Yeah, inferring that they're somehow less civilised, or lower in society, because they don't listen to Chopin."

"Ben, their names are Snowy and Squawk for crying out loud."

"That's not their real names. And besides, they're not really my friends. They just drink in the same pub as me."

"Right, like you're not really my colleague, you just happen to be there wherever I go. Even the bloody washroom. I can't do anything without you looking over my shoulder."

"Why do you always do this?" Ben asked.

"Do what?"

"Why do you always have to get spiteful when you're stressed about something?"

"I don't. I'm not stressed," Freya said, just as the door to the mortuary opened and Doctor Bell stood there gazing at her with her huge, brown eyes, and bright pink hair.

"Hey. How about keeping the noise down a little, eh?" she said, allowing the rhythm of her Welsh accent to carry the weight of her stare. "Some of us are trying to work in here, you know?"

"How you doing, Doctor Bell?" Ben said.

"Right," Doctor Bell said, her face still stern. "You two having a barny, are you?"

"No, we're just–"

"Well, take it some other place, won't you?"

"Doctor Bell, we've got an appointment. I called ahead."

"Oh. Right. Sorry, yeah. Now I remember."

"We're here to see the girl who was brought in this morning," Freya explained, and touched her throat to indicate the wound Emma Blanch had suffered.

"Ah, the girl who was brought in this morning. Right. Yes. Follow me then. Let's get you suited and booted," Doctor Bell said, and she led the way into the huge room and showed them where the disposable masks and sterile jackets were kept. "Emma Blanch, wasn't it?"

"That's her," Freya said, and Ben caught her attention, quietly smiling at Doctor Bell's odd mannerisms. It was true, the pathologist was a character, but the smile also indicated that their argument was over. No hard feelings. She winked at him in reply, smirking as Doctor Bell collected a clipboard as she passed a workstation and began to spin it like basketball. Freya wondered how long she had been practising that move, and a small part of her willed her to drop it, just to knock her down a peg or two. But she didn't. They approached a stainless steel bench. A blue sheet had been pulled over a body, which Freya could only assume was Emma Blanch.

Doctor Bell laid her hands on the mound gently and calmly.

"Exsanguination," she announced, raising her voice the way a headmistress might bring order to a school assembly. She seemed to break the word down to articulate each syllable as if it were a word on its own. Then she lowered her voice, and looked between Freya and Ben. "Bled to death. Terrible way to go."

"That's confirmed, is it?" said Ben, somehow managing to get past the pathologist's strange ways. "No sign it could be–"

"Anything else?" Doctor Bell said. "Not that I can see. Haven't had time to get to the nitty-gritty yet. But there's nothing to suggest otherwise. Organs are fine and healthy. Strong respiratory system. Non-smoker. All looks dandy."

Ben shifted on his feet and folded his arms, a sign he was uncomfortable with something.

"How about–"

"Sexual interference?" Doctor Bell said, and her gaze fell to his groin, lingering there for far too long. "No. Not this one. I'll swab to be sure, but I can usually tell."

"Doctor Bell," Freya began, and the pathologist made a show of giving her undivided attention.

"Won't you call me Pip?" she said. "It's not like we just met."

"I'd prefer it if we kept some formalities," Freya said, still a little unsure of the doctor.

The doctor seemed a little taken aback at first, then shrugged it off and waited for Freya to continue.

"The wound. Peter Saint, the FME, suggested it might be a hunting knife. In fact, the crime scene analyst said the same thing. If we could get an idea of what we're looking for–"

"Fat blade," Doctor Bell said, almost spitting the words. "You see, look here. The leading edge of a blade is kind of V-shaped. You know?"

They both nodded, allowing her to state the obvious in order to get to the point.

"They call it the profile," she continued. "An ordinary Stanley blade will have a shallow profile and will be symmetrical, whereas a kitchen knife will be asymmetrical. The cut is sided, usually by design, or to suit a right or left-handed user."

"And what do we have here?" Freya asked.

"Oh, this is a symmetrical profile. And the V," she said, forming a V with her hands, then expanding them, "is wide. As wide as ever I've seen. Like an axe or something. But it wasn't an axe."

"What type of knife would do this, then?" Freya asked. "I presume this is enough to make an assumption on the weapon?"

"Next we have the length," Doctor Bell said, ignoring Freya's question, but she nodded in response as if to say, *I'll get to that, but first you need to listen to me.* "The blade that caused this wound was at least seven inches long, with a nick on the leading edge, somewhere close to the hilt. Look here, see," she said, and she carefully slipped the sheet from Emma's face, taking care to keep her shoulders and chest covered. "See this secondary tear here? That's a signature. You find the blade with that nick, and you find the bastard that did this."

She glared at them both, before covering Emma once more.

"What are we looking for?" Ben asked.

"I've been looking into it," Doctor Bell replied, and she headed over to a nearby bench. Freya and Ben joined her, where she began spreading out printed images of potential weapons. Each printout was of a different type of knife. "Not these two," she said, and she shoved them to one side with little to no grace. "Nor this one either. Far too fine," she said. Then she rested her hand on the centremost piece of paper, covering the image with a tattooed hand. From the side, Freya thought Doctor Bell's face was almost as much metal as it was flesh. Her ears had at least ten piercings in each, and her left eyebrow contained a row of different coloured rings.

She removed her hand.

The image was of a large knife with some kind of fixture or fitting on the handle, and a metal hoop on the back a little larger than a two-penny coin.

"What you are looking for, boys and girls, is a Lee Enfield Land Bayonet. They were used in World War Two, but not many were produced. Less than two hundred thousand, according to the database."

"You have a database of knives?" Freya asked without thinking.

"No, I have access to a database of blades, profiles, and what-not. You don't think I memorised every single blade, do you now? I'm not Carol bloody Vorderman, you know."

"How can you be so sure this is the blade?" Ben asked.

"Ah, easy," she said. "From the blade profile and the blade length, I was able to narrow it down to these," she said, and waved her hand over the mess on the bench. "But Emma told me which one I was looking for."

Freya rolled her eyes just as Doctor Bell looked her way and caught her. She feigned a yawn to disguise her ill-manners, then cursed herself inwardly at the move.

"Look here," Doctor Bell said, and she pulled the sheet back from Emma's body again. A ring light hung above the stainless steel table, and Doctor Bell pulled it down, shining the bright light on Emma's neck. "See that, do you?"

"The red mark?" Ben said, then stepped aside for Freya to have a look.

"It's a bruise," Freya said. "Made from the ring on the back of the bayonet. The part that I'm guessing the rifle muzzle slips through."

"Bingo," Doctor Bell said, and covered Emma again. "Now what do you make of that then?"

Freya imagined the scene. She closed her eyes, picturing the field, the house, and the fog that Cyrus Cross had mentioned. She saw Emma Blanch in her mind's eye. She was standing there in the field.

Then a hand reached from behind her, clamping her mouth shut. She fought, but stilled at the touch of the cold blade against her neck.

"Emma had a choice," Freya said. "The killer. He gave her a choice."

Doctor Bell cocked her head to one side, as a dog might at the mention of the W-word. Ben simply stiffened. Neither said anything, intrigued as to what Freya had to say.

"The ring on the bayonet is on the back of the blade. The red bruise on the right-hand side of Emma's neck. He came behind her, and pressed the blunt edge against her throat. He knew the blade was razor-sharp, because he'd sharpened it, and if he didn't have to hurt her, if she said the right thing, then he wouldn't."

"A random killer would have just used the sharp edge," Doctor Bell said, and Freya nodded.

"He asked her something. He gave her a choice. A question. Like, I don't know what, but he made the decision to kill her right there."

"And if she gave the wrong answer then she would die," Ben said, following her narrative with ease.

"He simply flipped the blade around, and..." There was no need to say those words. But the vivid images Freya imagined came to mind once more. She indicated to the place on Emma's face she was interested in. "Her mouth," she said to Doctor Bell. "The killer came from behind. He placed his hand over her mouth to stop her screaming. When she was quiet, he asked her the question."

Doctor Bell's eyes were wild with fascination and respect.

"Leave me to it," she barked. "I'll get right onto it. You'll have an answer today."

"It'll be a handprint," Freya said. "I need–"

"Measurements, fingerprints, and some kind of demographic," Doctor Bell finished for her. She gazed at Emma's Blanch's face, lingered for a moment, then met Freya's stare. "If it's there, ol' Pip'll find it."

CHAPTER TEN

THE SKY WAS ALREADY DARKENING BY THE TIME THEY LEFT THE hospital, and a few houses had their Christmas lights on. Through some tinny speakers, a man's dull voice sang the opening lines of *In the Bleak Midwinter*, which was thankfully drowned out by the wind as they walked away from the main entrance.

"How are you feeling now?" Ben asked, as he stopped beside the machine to pay for the parking. "Have you decided what you'll do?"

"I could send Jackie down there. If my child died, then I'd want someone like her to break the news. She did well last time."

"But you can't send Jackie to check on Billy."

"I know. I'm debating whether or not I should even respond. I mean, I'm not part of his life anymore."

"That's you making excuses again. Can I tell you what I think you should do?"

"Will I be obliged to do it?"

"No. No, you do as you wish. Just some friendly advice. It helps to see things from a different angle."

"Go on then. Let's hear how you think I should approach my future."

"Go. We're in town. Grab him something from the shops. Make it memorable. You know? Something special."

"Then cut my ties?"

"Well, not quite as severe as that. But ease yourself away. You came here to start again. To start a new life. If Greg makes you feel like this every time he calls or texts, then you're just straddling the two lives. One foot in each camp. And while that may please Greg, and anybody else, it's not really doing much for your head, is it?"

"I guess," she said softly, and Ben collected the ticket from the machine and gestured for them to continue walking.

"I don't want to overstep the mark here, Freya. But you came here to sort your head out. So, sort your head out."

"Is everything so black and white in your world, Ben?"

"Crap or get off the pot. That's what my dad would say."

"Ah, yes. A man of action. And what would you do while I'm gone? If I go, that is."

"I'll drop you in town and wait for you. I might do some research into that bayonet."

"Research? I could help."

"You need to buy Billy something. I don't need help. Unless, that is, you're scared," Ben said.

"What?" Freya snapped, her tone bitter and sharp.

"You're scared," Ben said as he clicked the key fob to unlock the car. He stopped at the door and leaned on the roof. "You're scared of letting go. You're scared of having both feet here."

"You have no idea how I feel."

"It's nothing to be ashamed of. I would be, too."

He climbed into the car, closed the door, and hit the button to start the engine, adjusting the climate control for maximum heat in the footwell. The seconds passed and Freya was still leaning on the roof of the car. All Ben could see was her jacket pressed against the passenger window glass, but he could imagine her scathing expression. It had been a calculated risk, and he was prepared for the consequences. He lowered the passenger window.

"I'm sorry if that's not what you want to hear, Freya. I'm just being honest with you."

She didn't move. Perhaps he really had overstepped the mark. He sighed audibly, and still, she didn't move.

"Freya, it's make your mind up time."

Again, she didn't budge.

He pushed open his door and climbed out, then turned to face her over the car. And to his surprise, in place of the scathing and bitter expression he had expected, there were tears. Genuine tears. He'd finally done it. He'd broken the strongest woman he had ever met.

"I'm sorry," he said. "I said too much. It's your life, I shouldn't–"

"No," she said, somehow managing to sound strong. "No, you're right. I need to face him. It doesn't matter what Greg thinks. I need to..."

She paused, her mind clearly a muddle.

"Crap or get off the pot?" Ben said, hoping to inject a little humour into the mix.

She didn't smile. But there was something in her eyes that told him she was grateful for the attempt.

"I'll be in and out as fast as I can," she said.

"It's Christmas. Prepare for hell."

"If I can handle DI Standing, then I'm sure I can handle a few Christmas shoppers."

CHAPTER ELEVEN

"I'LL PICK YOU UP HERE," BEN SAID, AS HE STOPPED THE CAR AT a pedestrian crossing outside House of Fraser. "Just call me when you're five minutes away."

A swarm of people crossed the road to the monotone tune of the crossing. Freya thanked him, then climbed out, bracing against the cold.

A car horn honked behind her, and she turned to find Ben waving through the open passenger window.

"Something memorable," he said. "Special."

"Memorable," she replied, and a passer-by gave her a questionable look, clearly interpreting her as a mad woman shouting in the street.

Ben laughed to himself, raised the window, and as the driver of the car behind leaned on his horn, Ben pulled off.

The entrance to the store was thirty metres away, and in that short space, a middle-aged woman with two children in tow exhaled a cloud of cigarette smoke for Freya to walk through. Her nausea was roused, and she was glad that the first department she came across in the store sold makeup and perfume. She sampled the most expensive perfume she could find, and checked her reflection in the mirror. Then, happy that the smell of smoke was at least quenched, she appraised the shop, and made her way to the children's section.

There were rows of Disney toys, some soft, some plastic, and some that were just plain bizarre – alien-looking things that would do better in a Halloween display. In the next row, a child, who was too short for Freya to see over the shelves, activated several toys and a cacophony of nursery rhymes bellowed out, aggravating Freya's headache that was now just a dull thud in time with her pulse.

She sighed and walked away, spying a jewellery section at the far end of the floor. The glass counters glittered and sparkled, and a weary shop assistant eyed her, clearly wondering when the best time to intervene was. Typically, Freya loathed being sold to, managed, led, or coerced in any way, shape, or form. But her guard was down, and the girl opened with what she assumed to be a friendly statement.

"I usually end up buying something for myself too," she said. "I'm so much easier to buy for."

She had a local accent, which Freya had grown to love. Her name tag read Tanya and was pinned to her black, long-sleeved blouse.

"It's just a little calmer here," Freya said, making eye contact for the first time. "How do you cope with the racket?"

Tanya laughed and shrugged.

"I'm blinded by sparkles and deafened by Disney," she said.

"A sensory overload. I imagine you lock yourself in a dark room when you get home."

"If I could, I would. I'm just doing this to get through uni."

"Oh really? What are you studying?" Freya asked, purely out of habit, and she regretted asking before she'd finished speaking.

"Graphic design, actually. Although, whatever I end up doing, it won't be standing in a shop, I hope. I'm not really cut out for it."

"There's nothing quite like conveying job satisfaction to warm up a customer," Freya joked, but the jibe was lost on the girl.

"I have to fend for my little brother. So it's not like I begrudge doing it."

Freya raised an eyebrow.

"He's only six. We live with our gran. So I like to help out, you know, financially."

"That's very admirable. What's his name?"

"Damon. He's a sweet boy. Hasn't a clue what's going on, but if he smiles, then…you know? It's worth doing this."

"I see," Freya said. "And what do you plan on getting him for Christmas? Something special?"

"He's just into toys. Lego mostly. But we can't afford too much of it. He'll have little bits and bobs."

"But if you could afford anything, what would you get him?"

"Just something to remember Mum by, I think," she said, nodding her head as she considered it. "Maybe a photo of her in a frame, or a locket. Something he could keep forever, you know?"

"I do, yes," Freya said, and she spied a pendant beneath the last row of glass. "Do you gift wrap, by any chance?"

"Of course. Although, if I'm honest, I'm not the best at it."

"Then I'll take that one," Freya said, pointing at the item she had spotted. "I'm sure your wrapping is better than mine. I'll just have a mooch while you do it. I might see if I can find something else."

She left the girl to wrap the pendant, wandered back through the children's section, and then took the escalator to the ground floor, where most of the men's clothing and accessories were. She passed the shirts and sweaters, all of which were nice, she was sure, but not enough of a statement for what she had in mind. At the far end of the shop, she found a section displaying items suitable for the country gent – quality Wellington boots, winter jackets and gilets, and fine tweed sports jackets. She found what she was looking for on a small Barbour display beside a leather belt, a couple of wallets, and classic leather holdalls.

Two minutes later, she was back upstairs. She walked with purpose along the row of children's toys she had perused before, snatching an oversized stuffed dog off the shelf, and she placed the three items on the counter.

"No need to wrap these ones," she told Tanya, who was just adding a bow to the wrapped pendant. As she expected, it was wrapped beautifully. "But I might take some of that ribbon," she said.

Seeing why Freya had asked for the ribbon, Tanya cut a length from the roll, then tied a neat bow around the stuffed dog's collar.

She paid, and wished Tanya a happy Christmas, suggesting that firstly she might give herself more credit for her wrapping skills, and secondly, that she might stop to enjoy time with her brother. "Time is the most precious gift you can give a child," she said. "Trust me. You'll wish you spent more time with him when he's older."

Tanya wished her well, and as Freya rode the escalator to the ground floor, she called Ben. A strong wind rasped across the phone's microphone, and Freya had to pull it away from her ear.

"I'm just leaving now. Are you close?" she called, aware that her raised voice had alarmed a few other shoppers, one of whom tutted and shook her head but refused to make eye contact.

"I had an idea," Ben said. "Head up Steep Hill. There's a curiosity shop on the right-hand side. I'm in there."

"I've lived here four months, Ben, and this is my first, and hopefully my last, shopping trip in Lincoln. Where is Steep Hill?"

"Well, if you're out of breath when you're walking up it, you're on the right road," he said, and she heard in his voice how pleased he was with his poor humour and vague directions. "I'll see you in about two minutes."

CHAPTER TWELVE

FREYA REGRETTED HER IMPULSE TO BUY ALMOST IMMEDIATELY after she had left the store. With one arm clutching the stupid stuffed dog, and the other holding a paper bag, she had no free hands to fasten her jacket, which she had unbuttoned when she had entered the shop and been hit by the heating. But armed with just two clues, Freya felt compelled to solve Ben's childish riddle. He was less than two minutes away and on a road called Steep Hill.

Approximately thirty seconds later, she was sure she was on the right street. The going was getting harder and, ahead of her, the hill was getting steeper. The road was obviously ancient and not designed to be walked on with three-hundred-pound heeled boots, which caught on the cobbles with every other step. The shops were getting quainter though, which she enjoyed, and the addition of Christmas lights added a certain romanticism to the experience. There was an old sweet shop, model shops, and a second-hand store; when Freya peered through the window, an antique looking dressing table caught her eye.

She made a mental note that should she ever find herself having to kit out a home, she might like to peruse the area more.

A hundred yards later, Freya saw an old shop that appeared to be a converted cottage. The sign on the ancient brickwork read Curiously Classic, and had been painted in some kind of scripted font to give the shop that antique feel.

A bell rang out when Freya pushed open the door, and it was then she realised how noisy it had been outside. Her cheeks flushed, and her shoulder ached from carrying the dog, but she walked further into the shop, growing curiouser with every step.

The place was an Aladdin's cave. There had been no attempt made to open the space up into a shop, and the layout still resembled that of a house. In the front room were a few tables, each with old brass items and trinkets. A row of fireplace tools stood in a line beside a box that was overflowing with old shoes. Around the walls, clothes rails were filled to capacity, but the clothes were not modern in any way. There were woollen coats from the sixties and seventies, much like the one Freya was wearing, only they appeared to be less comfortable. There were dresses and shirts and trousers, all of which looked itchy and unforgiving. Above the rails, old paintings in gilded frames and brass lamps filled the walls.

She entered the next room, turning sideways to squeeze the dog through, and knocked a coat stand so that it rocked and threatened to fall. As she reached out, the bag she was holding slammed into an antique framed advertisement for Pears soap that was leaning against the wall. It rocked once, then fell forward, and seeing the calamity, Freya stuck out her foot to stop it from hitting the floor, but inadvertently kicked it into the next frame, an advertisement for Bovril showing a woman in Victorian clothing playing golf. Freya had just enough time to subconsciously read the headline – *for health, strength, and beauty* – before it too fell forward and slammed on the floor.

Freya was sure she heard the glass crack.

She froze.

Her cheeks burned and she prayed to a god she only called

upon in times of desperation that the earth might open up and swallow her whole.

A head poked around the corner.

The ground did not open up, nor was she swallowed whole.

"Now then," the old man said, who seemed to have more hair in his ears than on his head. But he said nothing else. Instead, he waited for Freya to offer some kind of explanation with a look of utter perplexity on his face.

"I'm sure there's some kind of rule about fire exits being kept clear," she said.

"Is that right?" he replied, and before he ventured into the argument that was already playing out in Freya's mind, Ben stepped into view.

"There she is," he said, glancing at the ridiculous dog. "I see you managed to find something small and memorable."

"Did you find what *you* were looking for?" Freya asked, still wedged in the doorway, but riding out her embarrassment with as much style and grace as she could salvage.

"Upstairs," Ben said, and he nodded toward a staircase so steep and narrow that Freya doubted she could get up it in her heeled boots, even without the dog.

"You can leave that down here," the old man beside Ben advised. "Perhaps leave me a few pictures on the walls."

The smile Freya gave him was tight-lipped and as disingenuous as she could muster. She stepped over the fallen frame and let the dog fall from her arm onto an uncomfortable looking seat. Ben was still visibly amused, and waved his hand in the direction of the stairs. "After you."

The staircase creaked under her weight, and where it turned, Freya had to turn her foot sideways as the steps became narrow. But she made the ascent without ripping anything off the walls, and cringed at yet another room with no visible wall space and nearly every inch of floor space covered in World War Two memorabilia.

The clothes rails on one side of the room were lined with military uniforms, while the rails on the other side offered fashion garments of the era. There were hats on moulded heads, which sat on old typewriter boxes, which sat on tables, which sat on old rugs. And boots, dozens of boots, lined up against the foot of one wall like a row of soldiers facing a firing squad. Flags adorned most of one wall, torn and tattered, while helmets had been perched wherever they would hang.

"Through here," Ben said, and he touched her elbow before leading her through a doorless arch that, due to the clutter in both rooms, Freya hadn't even registered as a doorway.

The last room held only smaller items. There were three glass-topped counters, which Freya sized up in her head, and wondered how the owner had managed to get them up the rickety, old stairs. On display were old compasses, whistles, little stoves, and anything small enough and valuable enough that an avid collector might slip into his or her pocket. The owner slipped behind the next counter, where Ben waited patiently for Freya to join him. He tapped his finger on the glass, and there, beside a row of hand grenades that Freya assumed would have been made safe, were three bayonets.

"The top one," Ben said, singling out the savage looking blade. It was straight as an arrow with a fat blade profile, and on the back was the steel hoop for the muzzle of the rifle to pass through.

"And this is a land bayonet, is it?" she asked the man behind the counter.

"That's a number seven, mark one. Quite rare and in great condition, considering."

"Considering what?" she asked.

"Considering it's eighty years old," he replied.

"How long have you had it?"

"This one? A few months. They don't tend to hang around. Quite collectible, you know."

"Are there many collectors of this sort of thing?" She waved her hand around the room, and beyond.

"Thousands," he said. "Most of it gets sold online now. My son takes care of that. But we get a few who like to come and see before they buy." He leaned in closer. "Come for miles, they do, some of them."

"Interesting," Freya said. "So presumably there are hundreds of shops like this up and down the country?"

"There's a few, yes. Used to be more, mind. Most of them have gone online-only now. Less overheads. I dare say if it wasn't for where we are, we might have to."

"So you still get a lot of foot traffic? That's good to hear," Freya said. "I think it's sad when a shop closes down. Even if it has an online presence, it's still sad. The internet has no charisma, don't you think?"

"Couldn't agree more," he said. "I've been here twenty-something years and couldn't imagine not coming here every day. My son jokes that the only reason I'm still here is because I put my keys down somewhere twenty years ago and haven't managed to find them since."

She smiled at the joke, then focused on the bayonet.

"What can you tell me about this model?" she asked.

"What can I tell you? Well, over the past two decades, I've seen all sorts come in here. I know people, see. I can count on my one hand the amount of times I've had someone like you come looking for something like this."

He stared at her, not with any malice, but with a certainty and joy in being right.

"People like us?" she said.

"Police," he replied.

"Ah. Very astute, sir," said Freya. "How many more of these do you have?"

"That's it. It's genuine, and you'll be hard pushed to get one in such good condition."

"I'm not looking to buy it."

"Two hundred and fifty pound, to you," he said.

"We don't really need to buy one, sir. We need to know if you've sold one recently. And if so, do you keep records?"

"Yes," he said, after making a point of visibly conveying his disappointment. "And for blades and whatnot, I'm obliged to keep records."

"Can we see them?" Freya asked.

"Like I said, in all my years here, I've had a few police officers come by. Every single one of them remarked how nice it was that an old shop like this is still going."

"It's quaint," Freya said.

"And not one of them put their hand in their pocket. Not one. Free information. That's all you want. Free this, free that. It's a wonder I don't put a sign on the door to keep you lot out."

Freya sighed and glanced at Ben who, judging by the look on his face, found the interaction mildly amusing.

"How much is the Bovril picture?"

"The broken one?" he said, cocking his head to one side with interest.

"The broken one," she replied, nodding.

"Fifteen quid."

"I'll give you ten."

He pondered the offer, then relented. "Right. Ten it is."

"Done," said Freya.

The old man reached below the counter and produced a records book, which he laid on the glass countertop. "You have been," he said with a smile. "Now then, let's see what we've got here."

CHAPTER THIRTEEN

After collecting the car from the multi-storey car park, they joined the queue of traffic vying to get onto Pelham Bridge. Christmas shoppers and commuters alike, all bustling to escape the city. Freya reclined the passenger seat a little and closed her eyes, just for a moment. Just to rest them, and dream of the following day when her hangover would be gone. The day after a hangover was always the best, and it was always a time when Freya swore never to drink in large quantities again, knowing full well that the very next time she stumbled on a particularly nice wine, she would forget her promise to herself, and drain the lot. Then she remembered that despite the next day's promise of feeling healthy, she had to undertake a long drive and two harrowing events – events that she did not relish at all.

"It's funny, isn't it?" Ben said, as one lady in a dark coloured Mercedes hugged the rear bumper of the car in front of her to stop Ben joining the traffic. "If we were driving a liveried car, all of these drivers would have their hands on their steering wheels, that man wouldn't be on his phone, and we'd be all the way up there by now." He pointed to the far side of the bridge, then let his hand slap back onto the steering wheel dejectedly. "But in an unmarked old Ford Focus, you get to see how people really drive."

"And how rude some members of society really are," Freya added.

A pair of headlights flashed once allowing Ben to pull out, and he waved his thanks to the driver.

"We need a plan," he said, verbalising exactly what Freya was thinking, but which the dread of the following day was prohibiting.

"My thoughts entirely," she replied. "What do you think? And why the bloody hell haven't we heard from Gillespie? Not that I relish hearing what he has to say."

Ben tapped the little screen on the dashboard and began to browse the contacts stored in his phone. He found DC Gold's desk phone and hit dial.

"It's a quarter to five," he said while the dial tone began. "We'll never make it back before five-thirty at this rate."

"DC Gold," Jackie said, when she answered the call.

"Jackie, it's Ben. Who's there with you?"

"Denise Chapman, DC Cruz, DC Nillson, and Gillespie," she said. "DCI Granger was here a while back. He was asking after DI Bloom."

"I'll pass on the message," Ben said, with a sideways glance at Freya.

"Listen, Ben. Sorry about earlier."

"Earlier?"

"You know? The whole chocolate bar thing, we–"

"It's okay, don't worry. No harm done."

"I mean, how were we supposed to know she would be in a mood?"

Freya sat forward, adjusting her seat to be more upright.

"It's okay, Jackie. Let's just drop it, yeah?" Ben said, clearly sensing where she was going.

"What was up with her anyway? She had a face like a slapped arse."

"While you were debating the qualities of chocolate bars, I spent the morning staring down at a woman your age, DC Gold, who had her throat slashed open like she was just a piece of meat," Freya said calmly. "I was wondering who on earth could do such a thing and why. They call it police work. So, if I had a *face like a slapped arse*, as you put it, I can only apologise. Next time I have to witness such horrors, I'll endeavour to adopt a cheerier disposition."

The silence that followed was long and uneasy.

"Sorry, ma'am," came Jackie's reply eventually. "I was just a little concerned, that's all."

"I want you to get everyone around your desk with everything they've found out so far. I want a full debrief. Call us back in less than two minutes," Freya said, and she reached forward, hitting the button to end the call.

Another silence ensued, during which time Freya retrieved her notebook and pen from her bag.

"She's okay," Ben said. "She didn't mean anything by it."

"I know that," Freya said. "And you know that. But I find it's often healthy to re-establish the status quo."

The dashboard screen lit up. The words *Jackie Desk* flashed up on the screen and the speakers issued a shrill dial tone. Ben hit the green icon to accept, and nodded for Freya to run the call.

"Are we all here?" she said.

"Yes, ma'am," Jackie replied. "And listen, I'm sorry–"

"Forget it, Gold. You should hear some of the things I call you behind your back," said Freya, and smiled inwardly at Ben's wide-eyed expression. "We'll need to keep this brief until we're all together, so I want bullet points from each of you. No monologues. Is that understood?"

There was a pause during which Freya imagined the team looking at each other and perhaps nodding.

"That's fine, ma'am," Gold said, keen to make amends.

"Fine by me," Gillespie, called out. Judging by his voice, he was further from the phone than Gold, but somehow he was just as loud, if not louder.

"DC Chapman, what do we know about the Emma Blanch manslaughter enquiry?" Freya asked.

"Erm, it was back in June, ma'am. The man's name was Harold Garland. He was ninety-two years old. Apparently he died in the bath. The pathologist report says he suffered a mild seizure which could not have been avoided. However, had Miss Blanch been in attendance, then he wouldn't have slipped under the water."

"Surely people die in the care of others all the time?" Ben said. "I mean, if someone vulnerable has round-the-clock care, the odds are pretty high that when the time comes, a carer would be present, or at least in the house."

"I thought the same," Chapman continued. "But the family raised the issue of money and property going missing. Which led to an enquiry, and subsequently, a dispute."

"And that's why Emma Blanch was held on remand," Freya said, reading between the lines. "That makes sense. Who are the family members that were involved?"

"Mr Garland's son mainly," Chapman replied. "Alex Garland. Fifty-five years old. Lives a few minutes away in Potterhanworth."

"Any previous?"

"Only driving offences. Nothing of note."

"Good," Freya said. "Anything else to add?"

"I've typed up my notes in full. I'll email them across to you highlighting the detail. But that's about the size of it so far."

"DC Gold," Freya said. "Have you put the files together like I asked?"

"Yes, ma'am," she replied. "They're on your desk ready for you."

"Good. Email me a copy of everything. I'll be travelling so I'll read them while I'm away," Freya said. Then before Jackie could let loose her tongue and inquire as to where Freya was going, she pushed the briefing on, "Cruz, how's that plan looking?"

"Yeah, not bad," he replied, sounding like a stroppy teenager whose video games had been taken away until his homework had been completed.

"Is that it?" Freya said, and she looked to Ben for support, who simply shook his head.

"Gab, it's Ben. Have you studied the location and identified residences and businesses to approach?"

"Yeah. I did that this morning."

"Okay," Ben continued. "Have you asked Sergeant Priest for a uniform to help you?"

"Yeah, I did that, too. He's given me Amanda Fuller. Some new girl."

"Well, then I suggest you use the opportunity to demonstrate the leadership skills you picked up from DI Standing," Freya said, knowing full well the idea would be lost on the young detective constable.

"Eh?" he said.

"Show her the ropes, Gab," Ben said, as he indicated to take the turning that would take them east toward the station. "Time to step up, mate."

"Oh right. Yeah, of course. Oh, I also had a look into cameras. There's nothing connected to the police network, but there's a huge farm down there. I reckon they might have a camera."

Slightly astonished that the young man had actually put some thought into the task, Freya was a little taken back as she said, "That's good, Cruz."

"Thanks," he replied, again like a teenager, but one who had his video games returned as a reward for doing his homework.

"Gillespie, where have you been all day?" Freya said.

"Where haven't I been?" he replied, his voice brash and aggressive in contrast to Cruz's light tone. "I've been down to Sleaford. Spoke to the local police. I've been bloody everywhere.

There's no sign of Jason Cross or the pickup anywhere. It's like he upped and vanished like a fart in the wind."

"He's somewhere," Ben added. "Chapman, can you help DS Gillespie? Get onto his bank. See if his cards are being used. Check Emma Blanch's, too. He might be using those."

"Gold, you can help them here," Freya interjected. "I want you to look at their social media profiles. See if they have any other friends or family in the area. Somebody close. He'll need somewhere to stay."

"Will do, ma'am," she said.

"In the meantime," Freya continued, "I'm heading to Kent to speak to Emma's parents–"

"You, ma'am?" Jackie said, with both an element of confusion and worry in her voice.

"Is there a problem with my decision?" Freya asked.

"Well, no. I mean, you're the boss."

"I'm glad you recognise that."

"But last time, you sent me. I was just wondering if–"

"If you somehow did something wrong, other than offend me?"

"I can't help but think that."

"You're too sensitive, Gold. I'm heading down there first thing in the morning as I have something else to deal with. In the meantime, DS Savage is in charge. You all have jobs to do."

"What about me, ma'am?" said DC Nillson. "Shall I go back to Mr and Mrs Cross?"

"No. Go to the station in the morning. You'll be spending the day with DS Savage piecing all of this together. Doctor Bell has identified the weapon as a World War Two bayonet. British Army issue. We have a lead, so you'll be helping him with that. Now, is everyone clear on what they need to do?" Freya asked.

"Yes, ma'am," Jackie Gold said, still keen to make amends.

"Aye," Gillespie groaned, then muttered, "clear as a fart in a fog."

"Good," Freya said, her finger poised over the button to end the call. "One last thing."

The team waited, and Freya enjoyed a brief moment imagining them all staring at each other, waiting for her to grill them for the chocolate bar incident earlier that day.

"Good work. I'll see you all in two days' time."

She ended the call.

"You know how to work a crowd, don't you?" Ben said. "It'll be weird not having you around."

"Breathing down your neck, you mean?"

"Exactly," Ben said, making it clear by his tone that he was, in fact, joking. "Freedom at last."

"Don't get too comfortable. I'd hate to disappoint you when I get back."

Ben said nothing, although it was clear by the way his mouth hung open that there was something he wanted to say.

Suddenly, he indicated, slowed, then pulled into the car park of The Red Lion pub.

"What are you doing?" she asked. "I have to get back and prepare."

"Prepare for what? You'll be gone for one day. Come on. I'll buy you a beer."

A beer was the last thing on Freya's appetite following the previous night.

"No," she said. "Honestly, the thought of a drink is making me heave, especially in this hole."

"What do you mean? It's fine."

"It was probably fine a hundred years ago when it was built," she said, as Ben climbed from the car. "Ben? Ben, did you hear me? I'm not going in there."

"Come on. You'll feel better. Trust me."

"Ben, I can't."

"Okay then," he said, closing the driver's door. He turned and walked toward the entrance, taking the keys with him, and leaving

Freya alone in the dark car park. Almost immediately, the heat began to give way to a damp chill.

"Ben?" she called.

He turned at the entrance with one hand on the old, wooden door.

"Hair of the dog," he called.

She scanned the car park, suddenly aware of how an onlooker might have perceived them as an arguing couple, and she as a wife who had just lost an argument with her husband. The car park was in need of resurfacing. Heavy brewery lorries had created a series of large potholes in the mud and gravel, and pools of water had formed in the holes that reflected the bright moon in the bleak sky above.

A white van had been parked close to the pub entrance, and beside it was a row of three family-sized cars, each of them at least five years old. The BMW, which was parked at the front of the building, Freya guessed, belonged to the landlord, John Sinclair, a man she had met just once and had taken an immediate dislike to. Not for anything he had said, but for his old-fashioned beliefs that his bar staff should be young, pretty, and not afraid to flash the flesh.

A car passed the pub somewhere close to the fifty-miles-per-hour speed limit, and the red taillights meandered into the distance. Freya let her head fall back onto the headrest, resolute that she would not give in to Ben. In her mind, the argument they would have played out in several forms. She won in every one of them.

A car approached from the direction in which the previous car had been travelling. Having spent more than five years in uniform identifying target vehicles by their headlights, she had formed a habit that she had continued subconsciously. Mostly as a means of passing time while being a passenger. But occasionally, the habit paid off.

The headlights that approached were not common. They were

round, like a Volkswagen Golf, but the shape of the car was all wrong, and the lights were riding higher than a standard hatchback car. It rolled into view, far slower than the previous car, perhaps forty miles-per-hour, leaving enough time for Freya's sleepy mind to wake up, and kick into gear.

CHAPTER FOURTEEN

THE FIRE WAS RAGING, THE AIR WAS THICK, AND THE SALOON bar was relatively quiet save for a middle-aged couple in the booth, a pair of teenagers of questionable age, and three regulars at the bar, who Ben was expecting to see.

"Now then, Ben," Snowy said, killing their previous conversation. "Bit early for you, m'lad. What's up? Been a hard day, has it?"

"Half a pint of Summat Blonde, please, Franky," Ben told the barmaid, as he settled in to lean on the bar. He eyed the barmaid's thong that was mostly on show as she leaned down to collect a fresh glass, before responding to Snowy, "When is it never?"

"It's a thinking game. That's what that is," said Rob, the larger of the three men who were all perched on weathered and worn bar stools. "The old grey matter needs a break once in a while."

"It's not my head that needs the break, mate," Ben replied. "It's my body. Starting with my feet."

Franky placed his ale down, then offered the card reader for him to swipe his credit card.

"That muck won't help," Snowy said, and he brandished his Guinness. "What you need is stamina, my friend."

Raising his glass in a silent toast, Ben sipped at the pale ale and savoured the cleansing of his throat.

"It's local ale, and I'm local," Ben said. "I didn't know you were Irish, Snowy."

"On my father's side," said Snowy. Then he added in jest, "Apparently anyway. Never met him myself. You all set for Christmas then, are you?"

"All set? If you mean, have I bought all my presents, then yep. Did everything from the comfort of my own desk. Not a Christmas shopper or a queue in sight."

Rob scoffed audibly. "If we all did that, they'd be no shops left. It's all part of the fun. You know? The queues, the crowds, the hot dog stand in St Marks Square. Finish up with a pint in The Magna Carta. That's what Christmas is all about. You surprise me, Ben, with your modern ways."

"You're a plumber, Rob, right?"

"Right."

"You work for yourself?"

"Always have done," he said defensively.

"So you can take a morning off to go into town, to rub elbows with the crowds and catch the flu. Some of us have work to do. And you know what? If there were no shops, and we all had no reason to go out, then perhaps my job would be a damn sight easier."

"Wow," Rob said in mock awe. "A genuine Ebenezer Scrooge."

The three of them laughed at Ben's expense, and Squawk, the youngest of the three, and Snowy's budding young apprentice-slash-skivvy, spoke up for the first time.

"What did you get then?" he asked.

Ben shrugged. "Oh, this and that. Bought myself a new electric razor. Got the same one for my dad and my two brothers. You'd think they would have done me a deal for buying four of them."

"You bought four of the same thing?" Squawk said, slightly astonished.

"Yeah. Why make it complicated?"

"And that's your Christmas shopping done?"

"Yeah," Ben said, taking a larger mouthful of his ale. "There's a lot to be said for singledom, boys."

"What about the girl you were with before?" asked Rob. "I say girl, but she was more of a..." He paused to think of a polite way to describe her.

"Milf?" Squawk suggested.

"Milf?" said Ben. "Who?"

"Her?" Snowy said, and he pointed to the doorway.

Ben turned to find Freya leaning into the bar, her expression one of urgency. She said just two words, both of which hit Ben like shots of adrenaline in each leg.

"Ben. Truck."

CHAPTER FIFTEEN

"Which way?" Ben called as he chased her across the car park, being mindful of the deep potholes that were filled with rainwater.

"Back towards Lincoln," Freya replied, as she pulled the door open and jumped inside.

The Ford's wheels spun in the loose gravel and mud, and Ben was already changing to second gear by the time they hit the tarmac. He pulled on his belt and clipped it into place as Freya found a number on her phone and hit dial.

She held the phone to her ear, and Ben lined up the questions in his mind for when she had finished.

"Gold?" she said. "Volkswagen truck spotted on the..." Freya paused, and looked across to Ben.

"B1189, heading west through Timberland," he said.

"Did you hear that?" Freya asked Jackie, and the fact that Freya did not repeat the road number or the name of the area told Ben that Jackie had heard and was making arrangements. "Get the word out to all local units to be on the lookout."

"If he doesn't turn off, we can block him at the junction with Sleaford Road," said Ben. "If he does turn off, then we'll lose him."

"Keep me informed, Gold," said Freya, and she ended the call.

"Are you sure it's him?" Ben asked.

"Positive. I caught the tail end of the number plate. GVO."

"You memorised the number plate?"

"No, just the last part. Something I learnt in uniform."

"All *I* learnt was that I didn't want to be in uniform," he joked, but Freya didn't react. She remained stoic.

"Don't think I won't forget about that little antic, you know."

"What antic?"

"Leaving me in the car like that. You didn't even leave me the keys so I could keep warm."

"I honestly thought you'd come in after me," Ben said, and for a moment, he felt a pang of guilt. "I thought you were just being stubborn."

"You really don't know me, do you?"

"Clearly," Ben said. "You didn't miss much, anyway. Except the fireplace."

"And the three stooges?"

"All present and correct. They send their love," Ben said, a slight fabrication of the truth, but one which he was sure they would appreciate.

"I'm sure they do," Freya said, though her tone offered little in the way of sentiment.

Before Ben could argue their case, Freya's phone rang out, and this time she put the call on loudspeaker for Ben to hear.

"Ma'am, it's DC Gold."

"Go ahead, Gold."

"We've got one unit making their way to the junction with Sleaford Road. ETA two minutes."

"Should be fine," Ben said. "As long as he doesn't turn off."

"There's nobody else about. There's a huge drive to catch drink drivers coming out of the city, being Christmas and all that."

"Bloody Christmas," Freya said. "Right. One will have to do. Make sure he has the details. We're about three minutes behind."

Ben applied more pressure to the accelerator, taking them up to sixty-five miles-per-hour. They both silenced with every bend he navigated, hoping to see the red taillights in front. Still on the line, Jackie was tapping away on her keyboard.

They passed the turning to Woodhall Spa, then slowed as they approached the village of Metheringham and drove through the level crossing.

"We're coming up to Meg, Jackie. If he came this way, we'd have him by now."

"Where's Meg?" Freya asked.

"Metheringham," Ben explained. "Meg is short for Metheringham."

A few seconds passed.

"Why?"

"I don't know. It just is. It's been called Meg for as long as I can remember."

"Does everything have to have a bloody nickname here?"

"Jealous?" he asked. "Frey?"

"Do not ever give me a nickname," she mumbled, and stared at the dashboard screen waiting for Jackie.

They heard her talking to somebody else on another call, her tone dejected.

"Are you still there?" she asked eventually.

"We're here," Freya replied, as Ben reached the junction with Sleaford Road. It was a T-junction. Turning right would lead them to Lincoln city, and left would take them to Sleaford. A U-turn would take them back to Timberland and beyond to Billinghay. A marked BMW estate was parked in a layby near the end of the road. Lowering the passenger window, Ben slowed to a stop beside it, and the driver, a mature man with glasses, followed suit. "Sit tight, Jackie, we're pulling up beside him now. Call you back in five."

"DS Ben Savage," Ben said, and showed his ID, though it was too far for the officer to read. "Did anything come through?"

"No pickups," he said. "And no Volkswagens. You're lucky I was in the area. I'd just finished a roadside breathalyser."

"I presume the driver passed the test?" Freya said, making a show of glancing into the empty back seat of the car.

"Yeah. Can't win them all."

"Are you heading back into Lincoln?" Ben asked.

"No, I'm based out of Coninsby," he replied, indicating that he would be turning around and heading back the way they had come.

"In that case, do us a favour and keep your eyes peeled. We know he's taken this road before. He might be going back to wherever he's holed up."

Freya unfastened her belt, opened the door, and passed a card through to him with her phone number and email address printed on the front, below her name and rank.

"Could you call us if you see him?"

"I'll keep an eye out," he said, exhaling loudly, like the favour he would be doing them was of significance.

"He's involved in a murder enquiry," Freya said, to add a little more weight to the request.

He nodded and made a show of dialling Freya's number.

"Got you on speed dial," he said. "I'll take the long way back. Can't promise anything, mind you."

"It's appreciated," said Ben, and he went to pull away, raising Freya's window.

"Wait," Freya said, and she lowered her window again, getting the officer's attention. He raised an eyebrow, waiting to hear what Freya had to say. "If you see him..."

She paused, hoping she'd said enough.

He nodded to indicate he had understood, but an overwhelming sense of responsibility tugged at Freya's mind.

"He might be dangerous," she added.

"Appreciate the warning," he replied. "I'll be mindful. You have a good evening."

Ben indicated right at the top of the road, and watched the marked BMW indicate left as Freya stored the uniform's number.

It was Ben's phone that rang next. It sounded over the Bluetooth system, loud and obnoxious in the moment.

"Jackie?" he said, answering the call before the first ring had finished.

"Ben, I've just had word from Chapman. She's been on to Kent Police about Emma Blanch's parents."

"Right," Ben said, sensing some bad news.

"Firstly, they didn't live in Kent. They moved to Lincolnshire in two thousand and one."

"That could have been a huge mistake," Freya said, shaking her head in disbelief.

"The father was killed in an accident more than a decade ago, which caused the mother to have a stroke. She lasted another four years. The address that Chapman found was an old driving license that hadn't been updated. It wasn't Denise's fault."

"What type of accident?" Ben asked, brushing over the blame for the misinformation.

"I found the story in the newspaper archives. It looks like they bought some land, and he had some kind of machinery accident in their barn. It doesn't really say much else."

"That changes things," Freya said with a huff.

"Did Emma have any brothers or sisters?" Ben said, conveying his disappointment for Freya by way of a tight-lipped smile.

"One brother. Thomas Blanch. Lives in Boston, about an hour from here."

The tone of Jackie's voice suggested she was waiting for something. Freya glanced across at Ben, then nodded.

"Okay, find him and deliver the news," she said. "I'd like to know how Emma ended up in Cornwall, where she met Jason Cross."

"Yes, ma'am," Jackie replied, without hesitation, but weirdly pleased with the responsibility of undertaking the worst task in the entire investigation. "It kind of makes sense that she'd leave, though."

"What makes you say that?" Freya asked.

"Think about it. Emma would have been eleven or twelve when her father died, and eighteen when her mum died. She would have been angry with the world. Maybe she just upped and left? You hear about it, don't you? You know? People just leaving when they get bad news. A complete life change. She moved as far away as she can possibly get."

"Maybe her family holidayed there?" Ben said.

"Right. To start a new life," Gold continued. "The poor kid had been through a lot, only to then be accused of negligence when someone she was caring for passed away. It's just blow after blow."

"That's life," Freya said. "Blow after blow. Some of us get back up, some of us don't."

"And which type was Emma Blanch?" Ben asked her.

To which she paused, pondered the possibilities, then replied, "That's what we're going to find out."

CHAPTER SIXTEEN

The morning heralded a new day, and a clear head for Freya, although that was where the elation ended. Three messages were waiting on her phone, and a killer still roamed free.

By the time she had showered and dressed, she had considered her reply to Greg's text message, and by the time she had finished applying her makeup, she had reconsidered what she might say, and then slunk back into denial. As for both of Mark's messages, she would pretend she hadn't seen them at all.

The morning wind off the fields was biting on her exposed ankles, her tights proving to be less than adequate. But with a limited wardrobe, and a strong message to convey, she would need to call on her A-game. The main road from the farm to the station was fast-moving, despite a fog creeping in off the fields. Twice Freya had to brake harder than she would have preferred to avoid a collision; both times had been a result of people driving too close to the car in front. If she was honest with herself, Freya had to admit that she had been guilty of that in her early days of driving. But a career in any of the emergency services was enough to quell the temptation. Too many times, Freya had seen the results of road traffic accidents, and too few times had a driver with such bad habits walked away unscathed.

Calming her driving had somehow calmed her nerves, and she climbed the steps to the first floor in a completely different state of mind. She was focused. She was sharp. She was–

"DI Bloom," a voice boomed along the corridor, just as she was about to enter the incident room, and DCI Will Granger stepped from his office ahead. "I could recognise those heels a mile away. My office, please. When you're settled."

She entered almost immediately, still clutching her bag, and stood waiting by the door.

"Come in. Sit down. I don't bite," Granger said. "Did you get a coffee yet?"

"I'll get one when we're done," she replied. "I'll probably only get one today. I'd like to sit and enjoy it if I can."

"Over to you," Granger said. "I'll get to the point then, seeing as you're so eager to get started. I've had a complaint about you from a senior member of my team. I don't like complaints. I don't like disruption in my team, and I don't like having to be a school dinner lady breaking up arguments. Do I make myself clear?"

"Absolutely, guv," she said. "Am I to assume the complaint came from DI Standing?"

"You are, indeed."

"And may I ask the nature of the complaint? I'd like to address the issue completely."

"Surely if you know who made the complaint, then you'll be aware of why they made the complaint?"

"If it's DI Standing, it could be for a number of reasons. I just want to make sure I'm dealing with the right issue."

"Is there a problem between the two of you, Bloom? If there is, then I need to know."

"There's no problem from my side, guv," she said. "Which I imagine you would be aware of, seeing as I wasn't the one knocking on your door telling tales."

"Don't be smart," Granger said. "I'll be honest with you. He made more than one complaint."

"One of which will be something along the lines of *she's stealing my team*."

"Correct."

"You told me yourself to use any resources I need."

"Do you really need Ben, Gold, Chapman, Anna Nillson, Cruz, and Gillespie?"

"Who does that leave Standing?"

"Just DS Moray and DC Vaughan."

"I'll take them too if they're going. Did you read the file on Emma Blanch?"

"I did. It's still early days," Granger said.

"There was some development last night. I'm going to need to split the team and bring in some more uniforms."

"Split the team? But Gillespie told me it's an open and closed investigation? I saw him here early this morning."

"Early? Gillespie? He doesn't normally arrive until nine-fifteen."

"Well, he was here early today. Full of beans and raring to go. So was DS Cruz, come to think of it. Have you said something to them? Warned them or something?"

Freya smiled at the thought of both taming Gillespie and bringing Cruz up to speed, and without her even trying. She shrugged, feigning all knowledge.

"You must be doing something right, Bloom, though I dare not hazard a guess as to what that is."

"So what else did DI Standing have to say?" Freya asked, moving the subject on. There was no real need to highlight Standing's flaws. That kind of thing was usually made evident with very little intervention from a third party.

"He felt you belittled him in front of the team. He said you were throwing your weight around. He's never complained before, I might add."

"Strange," Freya said. "Did any of the team mention it? Did they complain at all?"

"Not yet."

Freya said nothing. She raised her eyebrows, as if to say, 'And the problem is?'

Granger sighed and sat back in his seat as if he had been the last one to get the punchline of a joke.

"It sounds to me like DI Standing is upset that I'm leading the Blanch investigation," Freya continued. "He's also aware that I'm here on secondment, and is looking to shorten my stay. Shall I talk to him, guv?" she asked, knowing full well that she had returned Standing a backhand he would have to work his arse off to return.

"Leave him with me," Granger grumbled. "Talk to me about the development in the investigation. Bring me up to speed."

"The missing pickup was spotted last night. DS Savage and I saw it on our way back from the city. Whoever it is, he's mobile and still local. That tells me he hasn't finished what he set out to do."

Nodding his agreement, Granger sat forward again, invested in what Freya had to say. "I noticed we haven't instructed Kent Police to pay the victim's parents a visit. We'll need the body formally identified. All I've heard so far are plans to catch the killer. We do need to keep to protocol here."

"Understood, guv. I was planning on going down myself. I had some unfinished business at home. I was going to kill two birds with one stone."

"Had some unfinished business, or have some unfinished business?"

She paused, reflecting on the question. Such a slight change in verb made all the difference in whether Freya still needed to go or not.

"Had," she said, hoping the pause did not raise any doubts.

"But?" Granger said. "I sense a *but* coming."

"DC Chapman and Gold worked late. It seems that not only did the family move to Lincolnshire in two thousand and one, but Mr Blanch died nearly eleven years ago. Machinery accident, apparently. His wife suffered a stroke shortly afterwards and died four years later."

"Any other next of kin?"

"A brother. Jackie is delivering the bad news. But add to that the choice of weapon, a World War Two bayonet, and the fact that Emma Blanch was recently found not guilty of negligent manslaughter, and we've got the beginnings of a very complex investigation, guv."

"You need more bodies?"

"Detectives, please. One body is enough."

"We're maxed out. It's Christmas, and you've got ninety per cent of the team working on this case. You'll have to make do. Use uniform if you need more. Sergeant Priest will see you alright."

"Will that be all, guv?" she asked.

He stared at her, as if there was a reason for him to be angry at her and it was on the tip of his tongue. But whatever it was, it had gone from his mind.

"Good work," he said. "Have Gold give me an updated report. The press are going to be all over this, and it'll be me who delivers the Christmas joy. Again."

CHAPTER SEVENTEEN

THE INCIDENT ROOM DOOR SQUEALED OPEN, AND THE FACES OF seven individuals looked up from their desks. The first six either nodded or voiced their tired greetings to her, while the seventh, Standing, who was on his own at the far end of the room, scowled in defeat at the lack of shouting from Granger's office.

She set her bag down on her desk and scanned the room. The hum of voices that had dimmed when she'd entered returned. They were busy. They were working. They were invested.

"Gillespie," she said quietly, so as not to cause too much disruption.

"Aye?" he replied, twisting in his seat to look at her. He seemed fresh-faced and actually looked a lot better than she remembered him ever looking.

"You shaved," she said.

"Aye, well, yeah. It happens from time to time."

"You look good. Keep that up."

"Ah," he said, like he just had to make a noise of some description, but couldn't think of a suitable comeback.

"You started early today," she said, loud enough for Standing to hear. "You too, Cruz."

"We figured we'd get a head start. That bastard's still out there," Gillespie said on behalf of them both.

"Well, you should both know," she replied, raising her voice another decibel or two just to reach the far end of the room, "DCI Granger noticed. He's impressed. Well done. Keep it up."

They shared surprised yet pleased expressions.

"Thanks, ma'am," Cruz said with that boy's charm.

"Aye," Gillespie concurred with that brash and aggressive tone of his. "Nice one, boss."

"Do you want coffee?" she asked, adjusting her seat to witness the look of utter incredulity on Standing's face at the far end of the incident room. Not only had two of her team members been paid a compliment by the DCI, which to Freya's knowledge had never happened before, but she hadn't been given the shot across the bow Standing was hoping for.

"Does a bear crap in the woods?" Gillespie said. "I'm fading fast. The last time I was up this early, I was on nights."

There was a joke in there somewhere, and Freya offered him a smile in return but nothing else.

"Good. Get everyone's order and call it in. If we spend more than ten pounds, they'll deliver for free."

"You mean from the coffee shop down the road?"

"Where else would I mean?"

"I thought you meant from the kitchen, like."

"That's not coffee as I understand the definition," Freya said. She looked up at Standing who had lowered his head and was keeping quiet. No doubt he was planning his next attack on Freya.

"Steve," she called, "Gillespie is getting the coffees in. My shout. What are you having?"

Standing raised his head, then checked his watch, though Freya didn't understand why. "From the coffee shop up the road?"

"Aye," Gillespie said, clearly keen to maintain the dialogue between himself and his actual line manager. "Real coffee. I'm having the works. Pumpkin latte with a wee squirt of whipped cream and three sugars."

"That's actually disgusting," said Gold. "How on earth do you have any teeth left?"

"Because normally I'm only allowed a flat white, and if I want sugar, I have to bring it myself," Gillespie said, and then realised that Standing was listening. "I get it though. I mean, it's confusing, right? One person wants a latte, the other wants a cappuccino..." He stopped himself, realising that the more he spoke, the less positive the light was that shone on Standing. "Anyway, who's having what?"

While the team gave their coffee orders to Gillespie, Freya took the opportunity to venture into Standing's half of the office, something she had done only once, and she had been met with a barrage of underhand insults.

"A word?" she said quietly, then sat down on the seat closest to him before he had a chance to respond. She held her hands up to him in surrender and stared him in the eye. "I'm offering one chance. If you don't take it, then don't ever go behind my back to Granger and accuse me of doing what you should have been doing in the first place."

Being a smart man, Standing understood exactly what she meant, despite the sentence being convoluted. He laid his pen down, sat back, and folded his arms, but said nothing.

"A line in the sand. You and me. From this day, if you have a problem with me, you come to me. I'll do likewise. No more flinging insults across the room for everyone to hear. No more backhanded comments trying to raise a laugh at my expense. No more us and them. What do you say, Steve?"

"I say you're a stuck-up cow and you're full of it," he growled, his voice a deep rumble. "I say you purposefully set out to undermine me. Well, I'm not one to sit back and watch you climb the ranks with your smart mouth and cheap perfume."

The cheap perfume slant was a new approach, and one Freya

guessed he had thought of on the spot. But he had made his view clear, and Freya hers.

"Don't say I didn't try to make peace," she said, and she stood, knocking the chair back into the desk. She was going to add a finishing comment, a final blow to his masculinity, and she even leaned in to say it. But she stopped herself from speaking, rapped her knuckles on his desk, and simply smiled sadly, before leaving him to his own devices.

"Right, listen up," she said, loud enough for the whole room to hear. She strode back to the team, leaving Standing behind, and clapped her hands three times to gain everyone's attention, in case they hadn't responded to her calling. Only one individual was still writing, his eyes down and his attention elsewhere. Freya lowered her voice, "Cruz?"

The entire room was deathly silent, and Gabriel Cruz looked up, blushed, then set his pen down.

"Thank you," she said, then let the silence hang over the room a few seconds longer. The lack of noise meant she could speak quieter, an old trick used by management to keep the audience on the hook. "Emma Blanch did not have a family of her own. Her parents died some time ago, leaving just her and her brother, Thomas Blanch. Jackie, as I mentioned last night, please find her brother. Make the arrangements for him to formally identify her body with Doctor Bell."

"Ma'am," Jackie replied, and made a note of the task.

"Yesterday, we gathered facts. We assessed the situation. Emma Blanch was killed with a World War Two bayonet. Her boyfriend, Jason Cross, is missing, and so is their truck. Emma served three months on remand accused of negligent manslaughter for the death of Harold Garland. Alex Garland, Harold's son, was behind the prosecution, claiming that a large sum of money was missing from his father's house."

The room followed as Freya strode back and forth, allowing her heels to click loudly on the floor.

"We are not here to decide if Emma Blanch was guilty or not. That bird has flown. We are here to understand why Emma Blanch was killed. Do I make myself clear?"

"Ma'am," said Gold.

"Aye," Gillespie added.

The others nodded, and Freya found Ben studying her every move from his seat.

"Alex Garland has no real previous, but that doesn't mean he isn't angry. Chapman, find out all you can about him and Jason Cross. Build me profiles. I want to know what they do. Who Garland lives with. What car he drives, and I want to see bank statements and phone records for both."

"Yes, ma'am," Chapman replied.

"Cruz, I read your plan last night. It's clear and detailed, so well done. It's time to execute it. I want a detailed report at the end of the day, but obviously if you hear anything of significance–"

"I'll call you," Cruz said, and he stood, knocking his chair back into Gold's desk. He began packing his little rucksack with his belongings, his notepad, phone, and a warm hat.

"Cruz?" Freya said.

"Ma'am?"

"Not now. Wait until after the briefing."

"Oh, right. Okay."

He sank back to his seat with his arms half in his jacket, and his complexion took on the colour of a beetroot.

"Good. The area is quite remote, so there aren't too many doors to knock on. You should have plenty of time to complete it. Nillson, you're with DS Savage hunting down the weapon. Ben, do you need anything from the team?"

"Not yet," Ben said. "Although, Gab, our man might be a collector of World War Two artifacts. When you're knocking, keep your eye out. You know? Anything hanging on the walls, that type of thing."

"Will do," Cruz said, who had managed to slyly slip his hands free of his jacket.

"That just leaves you, Gillespie," Freya said.

"Aye. Suppose I'll be out hunting down the boyfriend again?"

"Not the boyfriend, Gillespie. Although he would be a bonus. Try finding the truck. It's a bigger target."

"Ah, I spent all day looking for it. It's gone. We'll probably find it torched somewhere in a field."

His desk phone rang, and he suddenly straightened at the thought of coffee, but dared not answer the call while Freya was talking to him.

"We saw it last night. He's still local."

"The same one?" he said, and the phone continued to ring.

Freya took a step forward, reached down, and hit the speaker phone button, nodding for him to take the call.

"Aye?" he said to the caller.

"DS Gillespie?"

"Aye," he said again.

"Your coffees are at the front desk. The girl wants paying. It's nineteen pound thirty-four."

"Aye," he said, Freya still holding his stare. "I'll be down shortly."

"Next time, have them call you from outside. I'm not a receptionist, you know?"

"Aye," he said, and the call ended.

"Truck, Gillespie," Freya said.

"Aye."

"Aye, what?" Freya said, keeping her voice low and calm.

"Aye, boss."

"Gold, when you're done talking to the brother, you're with me. We're expecting the lab report this morning. I need your help collating all the information for a press release," Freya said, wrapping up the briefing. "Does everybody else know what they're doing?"

They voiced their collective responses, all of which were positive, and Freya beckoned for Jackie Gold to join her. She pulled an extra seat across for her to sit beside Freya at her desk, and opened the file.

"Erm, ma'am?"

"Gillespie?" she said, without looking up.

"Can I have twenty quid to pay for the coffees?" he replied.

CHAPTER EIGHTEEN

BEN OPENED HIS LAPTOP, LOGGED IN WITH HIS PASSWORD, AND then began the usual five-minute wait for the computer to become usable. If he tried to use it before that, he'd be hit with the spinning wheel of death, which only a reboot would fix, and then, of course, he would have to endure the obligatory five-minute wait from the beginning.

Dragging a chair behind her, Anna Nillson took the desk opposite him, and set her laptop down. It was already open, and Ben had noted that either her laptop wasn't as groggy in the morning or she had already endured her five minutes and was ready to work. She smiled at him and glanced at his laptop, and he shrugged it off.

The incident room door squealed open and Gillespie came in backwards, carrying two recycled cartons, each holding four coffee cups.

"Coffee's up," he announced, and he bent gracefully in front of Jackie for her to remove the top tray and take her coffee. They set them down, and while he had the audience, Gillespie took full advantage of it. "Black, no sugar."

"That's me," Chapman said, pushing her chair along the floor backwards a few feet, until she could just reach the coffee he was holding out.

"Latte."

"Me," Ben called, and his coffee was passed from Gillespie, to Jackie, to Anna, and then finally to him.

"Cappuccino. Very Continental. That must be Anna's," Gillespie said, passing her drink along the same route. "Another latte. I'm guessing that's you, Cruz. And..." He paused, unable to bring himself to say it out loud.

"And?" Jackie said, as each of them stared at him floundering.

"A flat white," he said quietly. "Not boring at all."

From her desk beside the window, Freya eyed him with a neutral expression, which only Ben knew well enough to be her poker face.

"I'm glad you approve of my taste in coffee, Gillespie," she said, as he walked it to her desk, set it down, and returned to his own coffee without making eye contact with any of them. He took the opportunity to distract the team from his embarrassment by bringing their attention to the remaining drink.

"And finally, the creme de la creme, the king of caffeine, the morning glory," he said, as if he were introducing a show or a wrestler at the beginning of a fight. "A pumpkin latte. Blended from the finest hand-picked Ethiopian beans. Milk from the milkiest of cows. Topped with the squirtiest of squirty cream. And made with the love and care of Sarah from the shop down the road."

He tipped up the eighth and final cup, and a handful of sugary sachets fell to the desk. He selected two, tore them open together, and poured them into his coffee.

"The elixir," he whispered, in awe of what was in his hands. He held the coffee in the air as it were the FA Cup and he was the winning captain.

"Hopefully, now we can all do some work," Freya said. "That should keep you going all day."

"If he doesn't have a heart attack," Jackie added. "That's about two thousand calories."

"Aye. Two thousand calories of pure delight," Gillespie agreed. "Right, then. I'd better go and find this pickup truck. Did you say it was seen last night, Ben?"

"DI Bloom and I saw it passing through Timberland heading toward Meg. Gold arranged for a unit to wait at the end of the road. You know the junction with Sleaford Road?"

"Aye, I do. I'm guessing he turned off then?" Gillespie said, and he strode over to the map of the area which was pinned to the wall. He found the road in question and traced it with his finger. "There's not many places he could have turned off though. He either headed toward Woodhall Spa or he came off at Metheringham and used the back lanes to get back to Nocton."

"Or Wasps Nest," Ben added. "Uniform were out in force last night on a drink driving clamp down. They couldn't spare anyone else in time. Freya and I took a drive through on our way home, but the roads in Nocton were empty. It's a quiet enough place at the best of times, but if word got out about the murder, which it probably has, most of the village would have stayed at home and locked their doors."

"I'll take a swing by the house. Was it locked down?"

"Priest assures me that one of his team oversaw the crew padlocking the doors. Fraser, I think. You'll have to check with him for the code."

"Fraser?" Gillespie said, pulling a face. "Is he the one with the face like a bulldog chewing broken glass?"

"You really do have a way with words, don't you?" Freya said, stopping whatever she had been saying to Jackie. She lowered her voice, "It might be for the best if you stop referring to people by their physical appearance. Especially if it's derogatory. I heard DCI Granger pull someone up on it a while ago."

"Really? Who?" Gillespie asked.

"Walsh, I think his name was. He's one of the dog handlers."

"Walsh? You mean Welsh. The bloke with the big ears and eyes like saucers? He's a fine one to be pointing out people's deformities."

"They're not deformities. It's just the way he looks. He can't do anything about it."

"Aye, right. It's just the way he is, boss," Gillespie said with more than a hint of sarcasm. Then, as he was collecting his bag and coffee from his desk, he added, "Looks like a character from the bar scene in Star Wars, but it's fine. It's just the way he was born."

"Gillespie?" Freya said, her voice not rising in volume but sharpening in tone.

"Aye, right. I'm going, I'm going. You all have a nice day in the nice, warm office. While some of us out there freezing our–"

"Just go," Freya snapped at him, and as the incident room door squealed shut behind him, she caught Ben grinning, offering a little smirk of her own.

They shared a moment while the others got their heads down to work, silently amused by Gillespie's Celtic charm and the humour he brought to the team. Then the moment passed, and the reality of the case returned.

"Doctor Bell suggested the murder weapon was a World War Two bayonet," Ben said by way of an opener to Anna. He took his seat, and leaned forward, showing a printed image of a similar item. "The blade profile matches. And do you see this ring here, where the rifle connects? This matches a bruise found on Emma Blanch's neck."

"I bet those are valuable," Anna said, taking the image off him. "An ex-boyfriend of mine used to collect war medals and stuff like that. He even had a grenade. It was made safe, but still. He used to keep it on the mantelpiece until I told him it had to go. Couldn't watch a film and relax with that thing staring at me."

"That's the good news," Ben said, happy she was familiar with the market for memorabilia. "These things are out there, and they're rare."

"And the bad news?" she asked.

"Is that these things are out there, and they're rare. Luckily, I found a shop that sold one recently. You know the little shop on Steep Hill?"

"Oh yeah. That's where he used to go. Couldn't go into town without him having a mooch in there."

"We spoke to the owner yesterday," Ben said, and he handed Anna the slip of paper the owner had written the buyer's details on. "See what you can find out about this guy. Is he local? Is he a dealer? Does he have previous? You know? Build a profile of him, and we'll take it from there."

"Gotcha," Anna said, then held the piece of paper at arm's length as she tried to read the old man's writing. "Edward Pope? Is that right?"

Ben nodded. "That's all I could read, too. There can't be many Edward Popes who are into this stuff. See what you can find, alright?"

He stood from his desk and made his way over to the white-board. Then stepped back and studied what Freya had written the day before. He was adding the names Harold Garland and Alex Garland to the board, creating a hierarchy to show the relation-ship, when the incident room door squealed once more.

It was the remainder of DI Standing's team arriving for work. Detective Constables Phil Moray, a grumpy, middle-aged man who said very little and contributed even less, and Cheryl Vaughan. They stopped in their tracks when they saw the activity in the room. As if on cue, Moray pulled his sleeve back to check his watch, and Vaughan glanced at her phone, both checking the time.

"Eight thirty-five," Freya said, using the clock above the door. "Nice of you to join us."

Sheepishly, they headed through the space between the desks

and into Standing's end of the room. There were a few exchanged grunts and feeble greetings, and Ben glanced back at Freya, who didn't show how pleased she was, but Ben knew the truth. The battle between Standing and Freya had, up until now, been silent guerrilla warfare, with Standing responsible for most of the attacks. But whatever she had said to him earlier had marked a change. Somehow, she had managed to weaken his defences. The whole coffee debacle had been a prime opportunity for him to engage in a public attack, and yet he had remained sullen.

One thing was clear, the end of the war was a long way off, and there would be more battles to come. But for the time being, he sensed Freya had the upper hand.

"Ma'am," Jackie said, breaking the near silence, "I've got the brother's address. Shall I–"

"You know what to do, Gold," Freya said. "Do you need one of us to come with you?"

"I'll be fine," Jackie replied. "I'll take a uniform. Everyone's needed here."

Freya nodded her appreciation, and then turned to Ben as a phone began to ring. "Ben, how far have you got with Edward Pope?"

"Ben?" Jackie called from her desk. "Doctor Bell on the phone. Shall I pass her through?"

"Yep," he replied, and he reached for the phone on the nearest desk, hitting the speaker phone button as soon as the screen lit up.

"Doctor Bell?" he said, glancing at Freya to make sure she was listening in as well.

"Now then, Ben," she said, her Welsh accent fluid like a lullaby. "Sorry it's late. I got caught up with a motorcycle accident last night."

"Oh dear. I don't envy you having to deal with that," Ben said. Most of them in the room had seen the horrific results of motor-cycle accidents. Nobody said a word.

"I know," she continued, her voice saddened. "Some bastard knocked me off on the new bypass. Can you believe it? Bent my brake lever, dented my fuel tank, and scratched my new helmet. Bloody drink drivers, I tell you."

Freya rolled her eyes, and everyone in the room who had come to the same conclusion as Ben sighed with a little relief.

"Are you okay?" Ben asked.

"Well of course I'm okay. I wouldn't be here talking to you if weren't, would I?" she said, with her weird sense of logic. "Anyway, I told you I'd get back to you about the Blanch girl. I've got some good news and some bad news, I'm afraid."

"What's the good news, Doctor Bell?" Ben said.

"Well, I swabbed her, and I'm certain there was no sexual interference. The killer was in and out, no pun intended, by the way."

"And the bad news?"

"Well, you can tell your boss, DI Bloom, that she was absolutely spot on. Brilliant, she was. Whoever killed Emma Blanch placed his hand over her mouth from behind."

Freya's eyes lit up in anticipation.

"Definitely a male?" Ben asked.

"Definitely. Whoever did this is a large man. No doubt about that."

"What about prints?" Freya called out, as she stood to join Ben.

"No, I'm sorry. He might be a big man, but he's not a complete oaf, whoever he is. He wore gloves."

"Damn it," Freya said. "That would have given us something to go on."

"I know," Doctor Bell said, sounding uncharacteristically sympathetic. "I have managed to do some calculations of my own, though. He's somewhere between one hundred and eighty-five and one hundred and ninety centimetres tall. I can tell, see, from the angle of his handprint on her face."

"So we're looking for a tall man with hands?" Ben said, hoping Doctor Bell would see how vague her news had been.

"There's no need for that, Ben," she said, clearly not appreciating his comment. "I did find something else though."

"Go on," Freya said. "Right now, anything you can tell us will help."

"Well, he might not have left any fingerprints, but I did find traces of something on Emma's face." There was a rise in Doctor Bell's voice, as if she was very pleased with herself about the news she was about to deliver.

"Traces of what, Doctor Bell?" Ben asked, and the room hushed in anticipation.

"Dimethicone, Aloe Vera, and Cyclomethicone," Doctor Bell said, and waited for them to respond.

But nobody said anything.

Freya stared at Ben, who stared at Jackie, who shrugged. It was the least likely person of all that provided the answer – a gruff voice from the far end of the room.

"I know what that is," Standing said, as he stood and walked slowly towards them. "Pip, it's Steve Standing here. How you doing?"

"Oh, alright, Steve? Been a while since you darkened my doors, you old devil, you."

"I know, I've been picking up scraps for the past few months. Did you say you found Cyclomethicone?"

"That's right. All over her face, it is."

"That's gun oil," Standing said. "The killer had gun oil on his gloves."

"That's right," Doctor Bell said, her voice high in pitch. "First prize. I smelled it at first. Unmistakable, it was. Aloe Vera. So, I did some analysis this morning."

"It's definitely gun oil, Doctor Bell?" Ben asked, as Standing took a step back toward his own space.

"Undoubtedly. I even have the name of the brand for you. I'll email you the details."

"Doctor Bell, you're a diamond," Ben said.

"Yes, thank you for your effort," Freya said. "You've been a great help."

"You're welcome. You know where I am should you need anything else. Ta-ra now."

The call ended and the screen on the phone dimmed.

From his end of the room, Standing was staring at Freya. He nodded once, then turned and left them to deal with the lead.

CHAPTER NINETEEN

"Gun licenses," Freya said, raising her voice. "Chapman–"

"Already on it, ma'am," she said, without looking up from her screen.

"Good, thanks. We'll need to crosscheck the list with any names of dealers," said Freya. "Anna, what's the name the owner of the shop gave Ben last night?"

"Edward Pope, ma'am," Anna replied.

"Chapman?"

"Checking now," she said. "Give me two minutes."

Freya clapped three times to rouse the team. "This is good news, people. This is a break. Let's keep it going. We're getting names. We like names. Names are good. Names are opportunities. Opportunities open doors. We get the names. We vet the names. We build profiles. Could they be Emma's killer? Do they have the means? Do they have the motive? Next, we get evidence. In this instance, we're looking for gun oil. We're looking for gloves. We're looking for a specific World War Two bayonet. Everything we need is laid out for us. All we have to do is bring the pieces together. Gold, how do we do that?"

"Ma'am?" she said, suddenly sounding very timid.

"Come on, Jackie, we have all this information. We have Jason Cross, the boyfriend. Maybe he was angry at Emma wanting to leave? Maybe he didn't want anyone else to have her? We have Cyrus Cross. The man who discovered the body. The boyfriend's father, who perhaps would do anything for his son's happiness. We have Alex Garland. Surely he's a prime suspect? Emma Blanch was very nearly convicted of being responsible for his father's death. He lives two minutes from the scene of the murder. Lastly, we have Edward Pope. A man known to have recently purchased the exact same World War Two bayonet. Why would he have killed Emma? What's the link? Is there a link? These are the things we need to know. These are the things I need you all to be looking into, to be voicing, to be querying. So, in answer to my own question, Gold, how do we bring the pieces together? We eliminate the implausible. Four men. Maybe none of them did it. Maybe one of them did it. Or maybe all of them did it. We have to eliminate people from this list."

"Ma'am," Chapman said, "according to the firearms register, there's no mention of an Edward Pope. I double checked with his National Insurance Number as well in case he uses a different name."

"Good. Does that cross him off our list?"

"No, ma'am," Anna said, with a confidence that Freya always enjoyed hearing from the usually quiet members of the team. She was tapping away at her keyboard, then stopped to read something. "DS Savage asked me to build a profile on Edward Pope. Chapman's right. He doesn't have a gun license. But he has got a previous for assault. No convictions, but he's had cautions."

"Who were his victims?" Ben asked.

"There's one name on all three reports. Female. Karla Rebane. I think it's a girlfriend or something. It was all a few years ago. He's had nothing since."

"But he's no angel, that's a start," Ben said. "Where is he living?"

"Just off Dixon Street in town."

"That's thirty minutes away," Ben said, and watched for Freya's reaction.

"Want to pay him a visit?" Freya asked. "At the very least, he might be willing to show you the bayonet. If you ask nicely, that is."

"I'll ask DCI Granger for a warrant," Ben said. "I'll take Nillson just in case."

"No," Freya said, and Ben froze. "I mean, yes, by all means take Nillson. It'll be good exposure for her. But there's no need for a warrant. Not yet anyway. We'd be hard pushed to get one out of DCI Granger on the back of what we have on Edward Pope so far. I'd prefer to wait until we have something solid. Just pay Pope a visit. Get a feel for who he is. We'll go from there."

Nodding, Ben stood and pulled his heavy jacket over his shoulders.

Anna Nillson stowed her files and phone in her bag, grabbed her jacket, and stood by the door waiting for Ben, who looked back at Freya.

"Keep me informed, boss," he said.

She nodded, grateful to have an engaged DS on her team. Gillespie was a good detective, but he let humour get in the way of results, and there was a strong chance he had picked up a few bad habits from DI Standing. Ben, on the other hand, took himself too seriously.

The door squealed open and closed, and the remaining detectives winced at the racket.

Freya took a step forward, collating the information in her head. Not only did she have to think of the investigation as a whole, but she had to know what each member of the team was working on, and when the information was likely to start coming in.

She took another step, and another, staring at the floor as she did.

"Chapman, talk to me about Alex Garland. What do we know?"

"Alex Garland, ma'am," Chapman said, as she flicked through her paperwork. She selected the sheet of paper on which she had made her notes, then turned in her seat to read them out.

"Bullet points, please," Freya said. "Let's keep the momentum going."

"Alex Garland," Chapman repeated. "Sixty-two years old. Owns a joinery firm. Has done for most of his adult life. Not married." She skim-read a few of the duller points, then found what she had been looking for. "Ah, this is where it gets interesting. Alex Garland is the only child of Harold and Hilda Garland. Both deceased. However, in his day, Harold Garland..."

She paused.

"What?" Freya asked.

"It looks like Harold Garland was a wealthy man. I thought I recognised that name. He was one of the wealthiest men in the area."

"It takes all sorts, Chapman."

"I mean, like, serious wealthy, ma'am. As in, lord of the manor wealthy. The Garland family are well-known. Well, they used to be. Old money, my dad would call them."

"But aren't anymore?"

"I don't know," Chapman replied. "I'm not really up on local gentry."

"Me neither," Freya said. "But if his son had to start a joinery firm, then it suggests they aren't so well off as they might once have been."

"Alex Garland also has a firearms license," Chapman added.

"Does he indeed?" Freya said, just as Jackie's phone rang. "Why don't you and I pay him a visit? Get your things together. You can give me some more detail on the way."

"Ma'am," Jackie called out from behind Freya's desk.

"Are you still here, Gold? We'll be locking up the girl's killer before her family have been made aware at this rate."

"I'm sorry. The phone keeps ringing," Jackie explained. "There's someone at the front desk to see you. They didn't give a name."

"Thanks, Jackie," Freya said, and she collated all of her papers into a single pile which would need to be put into some kind of order later. "Chapman, meet me in the car park in five minutes. Gold, when you're done with Thomas Blanch, finish off what you can on the press statement and send it through to me. We're paying Alex Garland a quick visit."

Freya left the room before Jackie had time to reply. The door squealed and slammed, and Freya whirled her coat around her, fastening the buttons as she walked, processing information, pre-empting questions and problems, and most of all, thinking about what she could give to Granger in the form of a press statement. She flashed her ID at the door receiver to access the waiting room. A loud buzzer sounded, announcing that the electro-magnet had disengaged and that officers should be vigilant in those few moments in case somebody ran out, or in some odd cases, ran inside the station.

"DI Bloom," she said, announcing herself to the members of the public who waited on the plastic, blue chairs. Her choices consisted of a woman with a child, whose eyes bore dark rings suggesting she was either a drug user or deeply upset. Freya guessed the latter. There was an old man who clutched a piece of paper in his hand, on which, even from the other side of the room, Freya could identify the DVLA logo. Whatever the problem was, Freya was sure it couldn't be resolved at the police station. At the end of the row of seats, perched on the edge with legs outstretched, was a young man with a baby face. He looked up when Freya introduced herself, then stood and approached her, his hands thrust deep into his pockets.

He was tall enough that Freya could look him in the eye,

which made him shorter than the average man. But he was stocky, which he somehow used to make up for being vertically challenged. For a brief moment, Freya imagined how Gillespie might describe him, then banished the thought.

"Can I help you?" Freya asked.

"I'm not sure. I asked to speak to somebody."

"About anything in particular?"

"My sister," he said. "I think something has happened. I can't reach her."

"Okay, what's your name?" Freya asked, stepping over to the front desk. "Perhaps we can find someone to help you."

"It's Tom," the man said. "Tom Blanch."

— — —

CHAPTER TWENTY

— — —

THREE KNOCKS WITH THE FLAT OF DS SAVAGE'S LARGE HAND were enough to disturb the neighbours on either side of Edward Pope's house. A light flicked on in the hallway of one, and in the other, a curtain twitched.

"The neighbours may have heard us, but Pope certainly hasn't," Anna said, taking a step back to admire the man who stood in front of the doorway, apparently fearless. The potential was there for Pope to tear open the door, and then Ben's throat, yet Ben stood with one hand in his pocket, slamming the palm of his other against the UPVC doors like he was a schoolboy knocking for his mate to come and play football.

"I'm going to try the back," Ben said, and before Anna could contest, he had slipped into the alley in a flurry of coat tails.

Making a show of vying for a better view to the top windows, Anna stepped back to the public footpath. There was now four metres between her and the front door, enough time for her to hit the panic button on her radio and scream for DS Savage to get back should the need arise.

The street was average looking with average cars. Respectable people. It wasn't one of the rundown areas with bins spilling over and rusty, old cars on the driveway. It was the type of street where kids could play in the road like she used to do, and call "car" to pause the game, only for it to resume when the vehicle had passed. A nice road. Not the type of road that Anna aligned with the requirements of a killer.

But that was being judgemental. That was stereotyping. That was wrong.

Ben emerged again in a hurry, his jacket flowing behind him, and he strode to the front door, forced the letterbox open, and dropped to a crouch.

"Edward Pope. I know you're in there. Open the door. It's the police. You're not in any trouble," said Ben, then waited and watched. "We just want to talk to you."

Nothing.

"Maybe we should get a warrant," Anna said.

"I know you're in there, Mr Pope. I saw you through your back window."

"You saw him?" Anna said quietly, to which Ben turned to look at her over his shoulder.

"Long hair, five foot ten, average build?"

"Sounds right," Anna said. "That's what his Instagram profile picture looks like anyway."

DS Savage pushed the letterbox open once more, just as the curtain in the window next door twitched. It fell closed again when Anna looked.

"Okay, Mr Pope, we'll be off then," Savage called, as Anna strode up the neighbour's path and gently knocked on the door. Twice. Polite yet formal.

Ben was either staring at her or he was putting his ear to the letterbox to listen for movement. Anna wasn't sure which. The neighbour's door opened on the security chain, and half a man's face peered through the space.

Anna reached for her ID in her pocket, opened the wallet, and held it up for the man to see.

"Hello," she said, in a voice as warm and friendly as she could summon. "I'm DC Nillson. Do you happen to know who lives next door?"

"Is he in bother?" the man said.

Then a voice from behind chirped up, "Who is it, dear?"

"It's the police. She's asking about next door," he replied, turning away from Anna.

"I told you it was the police. I said it was, didn't I?" the wife replied.

The man turned back. "That's the Pope house. Is he in bother, is he?"

"No, no," she said, which wasn't technically a lie, yet.

"Pope," Ben yelled through the letterbox, "if you don't show yourself, I'll come back with a warrant and drag you out on your knees."

"Not yet anyway," Anna said.

"What's she saying, dear?"

"It's young Edward. They want to talk to him."

"So you do know him?" Anna asked.

"Of course we do. We've been here thirty years. Seen it all. They've all come and gone, they have."

"And how long has Edward lived here?"

"What's she saying, dear?"

"She's asking how long Edward has lived here," he said, turning away from the door again, only to reappear a moment later.

"All his life," his wife said. "I remember when he was born. Tell her, dear. Tell her I remember when he was born."

"I heard," Anna said, offering her most patient of smiles. "Do you happen to know where his parents are? Do they still live here?"

"His parents? No. They died. Long time ago." He turned back to his wife. "When did George and Mary go?"

"George and Mary?" she said. "Must be five or six years now. I can check if she wants. Tell her I can check, dear."

"There's no need to check," Anna said. "We weren't aware that he had inherited the house, that's all."

"Is there a problem with the house?"

"No, no. No problem with the house."

"Well, what's he done then? He's never been any bother to us. Has he, dear?"

"Has he what?"

"Been any bother?"

"Who?"

"Edward. He's never been any trouble, has he?"

"Edward? No. He's a nice lad. Tell her. Make sure she knows he's a nice lad."

"We don't even know he's there most of the time," the man said, returning to the gap in the door again.

"Right," DS Savage announced. "That was your last chance, Pope. I'm arranging a warrant now."

He stood and walked to the road, retrieving his phone from his pocket.

"Well, thanks for your help anyway," Anna said, hoping to cut the conversation short. "I'd better be off now. Cheerio."

"Alright then," the old man said. "Cheerio."

"Cheerio?" Ben said. "Have you been making friends, Anna?"

"Ah, give them a break. I learnt a lot actually," she said, as Ben searched his contacts on his phone. "Pope inherited the house. He's lived here all his life."

"Well, he'll be living somewhere else soon. I'm calling Granger. He's definitely in there, and he's scared."

Ben hit the dial button and held the phone to his ear. Anna looked up and down the street, noting the growing number of twitching curtains.

"Guv?" Ben said, and he began to pace up and down. Three steps one way, then three steps the other. "I'm at the property of one Edward Pope. That's it, guv. Ah, Freya told you, did she? That's right. He's refusing to come out. Yes, guv."

Anna heard a click of a lock and the metallic sound of a security bolt sliding open.

"No, guv," Ben continued, turning to pace in the other direction.

Another metallic click, and Pope's front door began to open.

"DS Savage," Anna said, but he was too engrossed in his conversation.

"Yeah, I know it's just a lead, guv. But we've identified the weapon, and they're rare. We just wanted to chat with him, but he's definitely scared of us. Something isn't right."

"DS Savage," Anna said, a little more forcefully, and he looked up, with just a flash of anger in his eyes.

She nodded at the front door, and his whole body spun.

Standing in the open doorway, Edward Pope was a picture of shame and guilt.

"I'll call you back, guv," Ben said, and he ended the call. "Edward Pope?"

The young man nodded.

"I think we'd better have a few words with you."

CHAPTER TWENTY-ONE

"Am I in trouble or something?" Tom Blanch said. He glanced around the bare walls of the interview room, finishing on the heavy, closed door.

"Not at all," Freya said. "I'm sorry it's not the most welcoming of rooms. Most of the people we talk to aren't as forthcoming as yourself, as I'm sure you'll understand."

He nodded, but his expression belied his understanding.

"Somethings wrong, isn't it?" he said, suddenly suspicious of his surroundings. "Is she in trouble?"

"No, no. She's not in any trouble, Mr Blanch."

He was older than Emma, and by more than a few years, too. He leaned on the desk in front of Freya, using one thumbnail to pick at the other. Rough skin lined the sides of his index fingers, and there were signs of dirt or grime beneath his nails. Above all, emanating from his clothes was the unmistakable smell of cigarette smoke.

The door opened and Chapman leaned into the room, slightly perplexed at the change of plan.

"The front desk called me," she said, then spied Tom Blanch sitting at the desk. "Oh, apologies. Shall I come back?"

"No, come in, Chapman. Actually, Tom, would you like a drink? Tea? Coffee?"

"I want to know what's going on," he said. "I came here because I can't get hold of my sister. I went to her house and it's all cordoned off. There's something you're not telling me, so please–"

Freya gestured for Chapman to take a seat. She waited for the disruption to finish, then placed her hands on the desk, interlocking her fingers.

"Tom, I'm afraid I have some bad news. A young woman's body was discovered yesterday morning. We have reason to believe it's Emma."

Silence.

Tom's mouth hung open, and he looked from Freya to Chapman and back again in disbelief.

"What?" he said, while his mind dealt with the news.

"I'm sorry, Tom," Freya said. "I know it's a lot to take in."

"She can't be... Not Emma. Emma Blanch? You must have it wrong."

"I'm afraid she was identified by a man named Cyrus Cross."

"How then?" he said, and his breathing became heavier. "How did she..."

"She died from a knife wound," said Freya softly.

"A knife wound? She was stabbed?"

Freya shook her head. "I'm sorry, but under the circumstances, I see no reason to conceal the details from you. I only wish my response could be different."

He stared at the wall behind her, then at Freya's lips, where he seemed to be lost in thought.

"Tom, when was the last time you spoke to Emma?"

"What?" he said, seeming to come around from his thoughts. "I don't know. A few days ago, I guess."

"And where was this?"

"I went to see her," he said, and switched his wide-eyed gaze to Chapman. "In town. We met. Where's Jason? He'll tell you."

"I'm afraid we've been unable to locate Mr Cross. Perhaps you can help us there?" Chapman suggested.

But Tom shook his head, and looked down at his fingers. The thumbnail he was using to pick the dead skin off his other thumb had made progress. A piece of white flesh hung from the side of his digit, and he dug harder.

"Is that a no you won't help us? Or no you can't help us, Tom? It's important we find him."

"We don't talk. Jason and me. We..." He paused, and as that tiny piece of dead skin fell to the desk, he looked up at Freya sorrowfully. "He doesn't like me. Says I'm no good for her, or something, I don't know. He said I should have been there for Emma. You know, when Mum passed. But I wasn't. But what does he know? He wasn't even with Emma then. Didn't even know her. He don't know how hard it was for us. He don't know what happened to us."

"What did happen?" Freya asked.

Tom sighed, and reverted to beginning a dead skin project on his other thumb.

"Tom? It's okay. You're not in any trouble. We're doing all we can to find out what happened. So if there's something you need to tell us?"

"There's nothing," he said. "It's all in the past."

"Tell me about the past. Tell me about your parents."

"There's nothing to say, really."

"Was it a happy household? Did you have a good upbringing?"

"I guess so. I mean, as good as any. There was always a split in the family, but I think that was just the way we were."

"A split?"

"You know, boys versus girls. It was always me and Dad, and Mum and Emma. When they argued, Dad would take me off somewhere."

"Did they argue often?"

"I don't know," he said, with a shrug and a sigh. "It's in the past, isn't it? Mum always won. She always hit him in the heart."

"And your dad let her win?"

He nodded. "It upset him. You could see it did. But he always tried to put a brave face on. Anyway, Dad died and things got messy. You know, arguments about the insurance money and whatnot. Mum paid the house off with it. But we still had nothing. So I left. I had to. I didn't have Dad to team up with. I was on my own. I couldn't go on like that. It was killing Mum, too. Breaking her heart, you know?"

"I see," Freya said, aware that regardless of how empathetic she could be, there was no way anybody could truly understand how families cope under those circumstances. "It must have been a difficult decision to make."

"I'm older. Older than Emma anyway. She wasn't working, so if one of us had to go, then it had to be me. We didn't speak for years. Not even at Mum's funeral. I stayed out of the way. Paid for it and that, you know? I did the right thing. But, when it came to the day, I just couldn't bear to cause a scene. Not then. I didn't want her to be remembered that way. That was Mum's day."

"I understand," Freya said, and she waited for Tom to continue.

"After that, we went our separate ways, Emma and me. Didn't hear from her. Didn't see her. I was living out near Boston. Not far, but far enough that our paths never crossed. Then, about, I don't know, six months ago, something like that, I saw her in the paper. I saw the way they were treating her."

"Who?"

"The press. Made her look like some kind of monster. We may have had our differences, but there's no way she would have done what they said."

"What did they say?" Freya asked. "She was accused of negligent manslaughter."

"She nursed my mum day and night. That's what she does. She cares for people. Even when she was young, she was always bringing animals home, to care for them, you know? There's no way she would have left a man to die, and there's no way she would have taken anything neither. She isn't like that. Not Emma. She was good."

"Forgive me, Tom," Freya said. "But you said that Emma and you didn't see eye to eye. That you didn't speak. When did that change?"

"Went to see her, didn't I?" he said, his expression solemn. "When she got out. Weren't hard to find her. Not with all the press and whatnot. She wouldn't see me at first, and Jason chased me off. He means well, but he don't know. Not really. So I waited. Took a few days, mind, but she came eventually."

"You waited? Where?"

"Nearby. Up the road. In my car. But it was worth it," he said with vigour. "It was so worth it. I had to get her on her own. Anyways, being all confined and that, she had to get out. That's when we spoke. I told her I was sorry, and so did she. I told her that I'm her big brother, and that even though I hadn't done a good job of it so far, I'd like to try and be one again. Make amends and all that."

He shrugged and stared down at the second piece of skin on the desk, then brushed them both onto the floor and adjusted himself in the seat.

"I'm glad I did," he said, and his lower lip began to tremble. "I'm glad that if what you said is true, then she knew how much I loved her. I only wish the same could be said of my mother. I didn't get that chance."

"Tom, I have to ask you a question. Please do not read anything into it, but it's important. So think about your answer, okay?"

He shrugged again. "Whatever you need. If I can help then–"

"Tom, where you were the night before last? I'm sorry, it's insensitive, but we need to eliminate you."

"Eliminate me?"

Freya nodded.

"I was at home. In Boston. I was there all night."

"And can anybody vouch for that?"

"What do you mean?" he said, beginning to panic. "Here, don't go looking at me for trouble. I came here, remember? I came here looking for her. I didn't ask for any of this, I–"

"It's okay, Tom. Please. It's just a formality, that's all. If you say you were at home, then that's fine."

"I was. You can ask my neighbour. Came knocking telling me to turn my TV down. He'll tell you I was home."

"We'll have that checked," Freya said, and glanced once at Chapman who was already making a note.

"What happens now then?"

"What happens now, Tom, is that we continue with our investigation. We'll need to take your details, in case we need to contact you."

"But what about a funeral, and..." His lip began to tremble again. But he held fast to his emotions and cleared his throat. "Can I see her?"

"Of course," Freya said. "We'll make the arrangements for you to see her. As for the funeral, we'll need to wait for her to be released. Someone at the hospital will help with you with that. DC Chapman will be in touch shortly."

"You reckon you'll catch him?" he asked, and there was an anger in his voice so far away from the innocence he had shown until now.

"Catch who, Tom?"

"Jason," he said, as if the answer was obvious. "You said you can't find him or something. Do you reckon you will? I mean, it's obviously him who done it. Either that or that Garland fella."

"We're doing everything we can to find Emma's killer, Tom.

Now, I'll let DC Chapman see you out. If you need anything, if you need to talk to anybody, you call me, okay?" She slid a card from inside her file, and laid it on the table in front of him. He collected it up and studied it. On his thumbs, there were two dots of blood from the skin he'd picked off. "Tom, you're not going to take matters into your own hands, are you?"

"Eh?" he said, looking up from the card. He scratched his face, and inadvertently wiped a tiny smear of blood on his cheek.

"I need to know you're not planning on looking for Jason Cross," Freya said. She motioned for Chapman to pass her the box of tissues that had been left on the desk. She pulled on the topmost tissue, making it easier to pull out, and then slid the box toward Tom with a nod at his hands. "Leave this to us, okay?"

He nodded, and pulled the tissue from the box, slightly embarrassed, and Freya hadn't the heart to tell him about the smear on his face. He was a big boy. He'd work it out.

Freya gave Chapman the nod to escort him through the security doors, and when she returned, she leaned on the door frame casually.

"What do you think?" she asked.

"I think he's a traumatised man, and it's fifty-fifty whether we see him back in here for an altogether different discussion," Freya replied with a sigh. "Ask Sergeant Priest to have this room cleaned and disinfected thoroughly tonight, please. We're going to be in here quite a lot over the next few days, and I for one cannot get the image of Tom Blanch's dead skin out of my mind."

CHAPTER TWENTY-TWO

"Do you want to do this out here?" Ben asked, and he glanced around at the twitching curtains. "I'm happy to, if that's what you want."

Pope peered into the street. He wore light grey jogging bottoms with white socks and weathered slippers. A little, dark patch on his groin indicated that he had recently used the bathroom, and carelessly. His t-shirt was olive green with the words *Born to Kill* printed on the front. The font was made to look worn and tarnished with bullet holes.

He stepped to one side, his head hung low.

With a glance toward Anna, Ben stepped inside first. It was no indication of poor manners, merely a protective instinct. It would not have been the first time Ben had entered a house and come under attack from a suspect.

"How's your hearing, Edward?" Ben asked.

"Fine," the young man said, as he closed the door and followed them into the small lounge. "I was in the bathroom."

"I saw you from the back window," Ben said. He shoved his hands into his jacket pockets and exhaled. "After I'd knocked twice."

"I mustn't have heard," Pope said, and turned his attention to the floor, a dirty mess of crumbs, stains, and all kinds of unimaginable things. "Do you want to sit?"

Ben looked about the room once more. The settee had clearly belonged to his parents, unless the twenty-something year old was into floral patterns. There was nothing wrong with that. But if the floor was setting the standard, then sitting on the couch would be out of the question.

"Not really," Ben said, to which Anna appeared relieved. "Have you any idea why we're here, Edward? Why we waited for you to come to the door for so long?"

He shrugged, but failed to make eye contact.

"No," he said quietly, then scratched at his unshaven chin with a long, bony finger, pulling his face into a strange grimace as he did.

"No idea at all?" asked Ben. "Have a think about that for a moment. The more you tell me, the less questions I have to ask. Everyone wins. But know this, I'm not going anywhere until I have all my questions answered."

"Don't you need a warrant or something?"

"We're here on your invitation, son. There's half-a-dozen neighbours out there who'll back that up."

The boy said nothing.

"Okay. I'm going to ask some questions, and you're going to answer them. Is that understood?"

He nodded.

"How old are you, Edward?"

"Twenty-three."

"Twenty-three? Living alone. You haven't had it easy, have you?"

Pope shook his head.

"Yet look at you. Your own place. Responsibility. Do you have a girlfriend? Someone to share it with?"

"No."

"Friends maybe? You must have friends round from time to time?"

"I talk to people. On the internet."

"Oh, you're into gaming, are you?" Anna said. "I have a friend who does that."

There was a softness to Anna that Ben appreciated, as well as the fact that she was a little more in touch with the things Ben wasn't. Gaming wasn't even a thing when he'd been young.

"A friend of mine had an Atari when we were kids," said Ben. "I couldn't get into it. My dad wouldn't have bought me one, even if I had. Have you always been into computers?"

Pope shrugged, nodded, and for the first time, he looked up and held Ben's gaze.

"Spend a lot of time online, do you?"

Pope said nothing. His breathing became faster, and suddenly he appeared uncomfortable, shifting his weight from one foot to the next. From the corner of his eye, Ben saw Anna glance at him, then return her attention to Pope.

"What else do you do online, Edward?"

He shrugged again, and looked from one of them to the other.

"Do you mind if I look around?" Ben asked, sensing that the chat Anna had started was going in an altogether different direction.

It took less than a second for Pope to glance at the front door then back at Ben. And it took another for him to make the worst decision he could have made.

He bolted.

He made the door in three steps, wrenched it open, and pulled a small shelving unit to the ground as he left the house. Jumping up after him, Ben clambered over the pile of letters and directories, then kicked the shelves to one side so he could open the door far enough to get through. Outside, Pope was running as fast as he could in his slippers. By the time Ben had taken two long bounds to the footpath, he was already two houses behind.

Cursing out loud, he gave chase. But it was Anna Nillson who, for the second time that day, surprised Ben. She had vaulted the small fence beside the front door, and was heading Pope off diagonally, making use of the open driveways of the neighbourhood.

For a moment, Ben thought her efforts were in vain, but at the last minute, with a sudden rush of energy, she closed the distance, shoulder tackling Pope to the ground. Out of breath from the exertion, Ben caught them up and restrained Pope's flailing arms while Anna cuffed him.

"You do not have to say anything. But it may harm your defence if you do not mention when questioned something which you later rely on in court. Anything you do say may be given in evidence. Do you understand?"

Tears streamed down Pope's face, and he whimpered something intelligible.

"Let's get him to his feet," Ben said, and hauled the boy up by his wrists.

Leading the shamed Edward Pope back toward the house with one hand, Ben handed Anna his phone with the other.

"Get uniform here to bring him in. I don't want him soiling my car."

She made the call, and while they waited for support to arrive, Ben shoved Pope back onto his couch.

"Stay there," he said, then turned to Anna. Had it been Gold or Chapman with him, he would have been hesitant to risk leaving him. But Anna, with all her five foot five inches and fifty kilos could handle a boy like Pope.

Ben strode up the stairs, being careful not to touch anything. He toed the first bedroom door open, enough to peer inside. The place was a mess. Clearly, at some point, the room had belonged to Pope's parents. But now it was his belongings that were strewn across his mother's dressing table. And it was his clothes that were piled on the floor. It was also his cups and plates that filled the surfaces of both bedside tables and his laptop that was poking out of the space below the bed. Carefully, Ben retrieved it. As far as laptops went, it seemed to be a decent one. It was better than the one the force gave him to use anyway, but then that wasn't difficult. An etch-a-sketch would have been more useful than his laptop sometimes.

He tucked the laptop under his arm and entered the next room. During his career, Ben had been in dozens and dozens of bedrooms. He'd carried out searches, spoken to victims of abuse who refused to leave the house, and even helped a lady find her missing cat. But never in all Ben's years had anything prepared him for the room he had just entered.

"What the..." he said loudly.

"You okay, boss?" Anna called out.

He took a moment to digest what he was seeing, then called back, "I'm fine."

Above him, hanging from all four corners of the ceiling by steel-eye bolts and draped across some kind of heavy-duty tent frame was a giant net, green in colour, with fake foliage spliced between the holes to serve as camouflage. A dim, red bulb hung from the centre of the room, and as Ben stepped inside, the shape of a man emerged on his right. He jumped forward out of the man's reach and turned only to find a full-sized mannequin dressed in full UK military combats, complete with webbing, camo-paint, and army issue boots. The room had the smell of old clothing like his father's wardrobe. Around the room, boxes stored similar items. One contained various pieces of fifty-eight webbing, kidney pouches, bum rolls, ammo pouches and yokes. Another contained more up-to-date webbing, some backpacks, and random ponchos. Another box was filled to the brim with army issue boots, and lining the shelves were boxes of gators, ankle twists, camo-paint, Zippo lighters, folding stoves with hexamine tablets, and packets of water-purifying tablets.

"It's a war room," he said to himself, incredulous of the effort that Pope had clearly invested. Even the wallpaper had been painted over with crude images of distant forests and exaggerated sunsets. One of the walls had a Vietnam feel to it, with a few silhouetted Bell Hueys in the distance. "He's a war nut."

The only piece of furniture in the room was an old, pine desk, which of course had been painted olive green. In the foot space, a few steel ammo boxes had been stacked, but the desk itself was clearly Pope's workbench. He could imagine the boy sitting up there all alone, dressed from head to toe as GI Joe, sharpening his knife, or eating his dinner from one of the mess tins.

Ben opened each drawer, finding nothing of any interest, then retrieved the ammo boxes from the floor space below the desk. Placing the laptop on the desk, he unhinged the lid of the first box, and tipped the contents onto the floor.

A pile of random war medals fell out, some with ribbons, some without. Ben picked one up and studied it for a name. But it bore no inscription. He reached for the next box. He unclipped the lid, but even by hitting the box, it wouldn't open. The contents rattled around inside, heavy, hard, and metallic. He tipped the box upside down and banged on the base. The lid gave way under the third hit.

Three bayonets fell to the floor.

CHAPTER TWENTY-THREE

"I WONDERED WHEN YOU LOT WOULD COME KNOCKING," THE man said, as he opened the door and appraised Freya and Chapman with a roving eye that swept up and down each of them, from their feet to their eyes. His wandering gaze finished on Freya, and a single eyebrow raised in anticipation.

Freya held out her ID.

"Alex Garland?" Freya said.

"That's me," he replied.

"Detective Inspector Freya Bloom. This is DC Chapman. We'd like to ask you a few questions."

"Like I said, I thought you might."

"May we come in?"

"Well, if I refused you entry, I'd look even guiltier, wouldn't I?" he said, and he stepped to one side, welcoming them with a sweep of his arm.

The house, which Freya presumed to be Georgian due to its architectural symmetry, was seated in fabulous yet modest grounds. The frontage, a mere quarter-acre of low-maintenance lawns, hedges, and gravel driveway, bore enough grandeur and prestige that when

Freya entered the large hallway, her expectations were already high. The hallway reminded her of a friend's house in London's Grosvenor Square, with its prominent staircase, high ceilings, and mouldings.

But that was where the glamour ended.

More than thirty big, black bin liners were piled in a heap, each one overflowing with rotten wallpaper, pieces of wood, and broken glass.

"We'll go through to the sun room," he called out to no-one in particular, and his voice echoed from all directions. "Apologies, you've caught me in a state of renovation."

"Renovation?" Chapman whispered to Freya. "It's bloody empty, ma'am?"

Freya nodded her agreement, and followed Garland through to the rear of the house.

He led them directly through the centre of what Freya presumed had once been a magnificent home, but now was in ruin. Catching a glance through an open doorway, Freya had expected to see a gentleman's library, quintessentially grand with rows of leather-bound books and a gleaming Chesterfield couch. Instead, she saw an empty room with peeling walls, a tarnished wooden floor, and a pile of dusty tools.

"Have you just moved in?" she asked, as she followed Garland, noticing Chapman taking the opportunity to peer into other rooms. The look on her decidedly unimpressed face suggested Freya wasn't missing anything.

He was at the entrance to the kitchen when he stopped and turned, pondering on how he might respond, then said, "Second time around."

He walked on, and Chapman gave Freya a quizzical look.

"I gather by that statement that this was your family home?" said Freya, as she entered what was possibly the largest conservatory she had ever seen fixed to a residential house. "It must hold a lot of memories for you."

"It does," he said thoughtfully. "However, they aren't all to be cherished."

"We all have memories we'd forget if we could, Mr Garland."

"Naturally," he said with a poor attempt at a smile. He offered them a rattan bench and took the matching armchair.

"You must have had a privileged upbringing," said Freya. "I'll bet this place was spectacular in its day."

"In its day being the optimal phrase. Sadly, it's been left to decay over the years. Neglected, you might say," he added, seeming pleased with the link to his father's death. "Nothing lasts forever. I'm both old enough to remember this house in all its glory and old enough to have witnessed my father losing everything he had. Those final years of his were not his fondest, of that I'm sure. All he had was the roof over his head, canned food, and a girl who tended to his every need. Most of the time, anyway."

"We're not here to discuss the death of your father, Mr Garland. I appreciate it's still fresh in your mind, however—"

"However, nothing. My father's death is very relevant to this conversation. The fact remains that if that little hussy had cared for him with the diligence she was paid for, instead of rifling through his belongings, he would still be here today, and I wouldn't have felt obliged to seek some sort of recompense. Which means that you wouldn't have come knocking at my door, and I could go about my day restoring the house. So, please, don't perceive me as if I'm some kind of backstreet layabout, missy. I may not have lived the life I was destined to live, but I have not lost the Garland tenacity." He sat forward in his seat, pointing his index finger at Freya to add weight to his statement. "If anything, being the first generation of Garlands to work for a living has made me even more tenacious."

"You're angry. I understand that, and I dare say you have every right to be. I know very little about the investigation into your father's death. But if you want to talk about facts, here's a few for you. Fact one. Two nights ago, Emma Blanch was killed in cold blood. Fact two. You have a clear dislike for the girl. Fact three. You are on very dangerous ground. So if you want to prevent me from having twenty officers and a crime scene team here in the next hour, I suggest you shut up and listen to me. Do I make myself clear, Mr Garland?"

"Bring them," he said, and offered a confident smile that, had Freya been raised to a lower standard, she may have leaned over and wiped off his face for him. "You'll find nothing here," he said. "So, if it pleases you to tear my house apart, you'll be doing me a favour."

"Where were you, Mr Garland?" Freya said. "Two nights ago. The night Emma Blanch was murdered. Where were you?"

"Here," he replied. "With a cheap bottle of Pinot noir, having sold the contents of my father's wine cellar. The bottle is out there in the hallway if you'd like to check, and I dare say I have the receipt somewhere."

"Have you sold everything your father owned?"

"Very nearly. It's of no use to me, and restoring this place is quite the money pit. Still, it'll be worth it one day."

"Would you like to help me in my investigation, Mr Garland?" Freya asked, trying a new tactic.

"Would I what?" he replied, appearing disgusted at the sound of it.

"Help me. Help us. We're trying to solve a murder. Perhaps you'd like to help us?"

"How, exactly?" he asked, suspicious of where Freya was leading him.

"You can start by providing a list of every item you've sold, and any details you have of the buyers."

"That's preposterous. Why on earth would you want to see that? It would take me days to collate the information. What a complete waste of my time."

"I'll give you five hours," Freya said, and she passed him another of her cards as she stood. "I'm sure you're aware that, in these circumstances, I could quite easily bring in investigators to tear every inch of your life apart. We'd take your computers away and we'd question anybody who knows you, not to mention arrest you on suspicion of murder. If I don't have a full list of everything you've sold by six o'clock tonight, you'll find that restoring this place is the least of your concerns."

Dumbfounded, Alex Garland sneered but said nothing. Freya stopped at the door and turned back to him, visually appraising him the way he had appraised her and Chapman, only with less of a sexual appetite.

"It's funny to hear you talk of honour, and love, and family, Mr Garland. The girl you accused of being a hussy, a thief, and of being responsible for your father's death nursed her sick and grieving mother day and night for four long years. She gave up everything to be by her mother's side. What is it you did for your father?"

He stared back at her with resentment.

"Good day to you, Mr Garland. We'll see ourselves out."

CHAPTER TWENTY-FOUR

Ben drove while Anna completed her notes, and somewhere behind them in the throng of Christmas traffic, Edward Pope sat in the back of a liveried car.

"Do you have any plans for Christmas?" Anna asked, folding away her notebook.

"I thought you were making notes?"

"It's too dark and too bumpy. I'll do it later. Plus, I always get a bit traffic sick looking down at my notepad while someone else is driving. Do you get that?"

"No, not really," Ben replied. "But to be honest, I don't look down at my notepad often enough."

"What do you think about Pope? Do you think he did it?"

"You know what? If I saw him in the street, I'd say no. Not capable. But after seeing that room, I'm not so sure. You should have seen it, Anna. It's like the guy is preparing for Armageddon or something. Like one of those preppies who live their lives like the whole country's going to fall to bits tomorrow."

"Preppies? Do you mean preppers?"

"Is that what they're called?" Ben asked. "The guys that want to eat squirrels and do their business in the woods and whatnot."

She laughed. "He could be one of those. Disaster preparation is a growing community, and let's face it, the country fell to bits a long time ago."

"Ah, don't abandon it yet, Anna. We still have running water and the internet. It can't be that bad. Besides, I don't get them."

"Preppers?"

"Yeah. They spend their entire lives preparing for something that might happen. Hoping that when it does, they'll be the ones with power, control, and sustenance, or whatever. We did all that on the farm. My dad has solar panels on his roof, we've got enough crops to last us a lifetime, the barns have a backup generator. Do you know what I mean? We even have boreholes for fresh water, and you don't see me running around like Rambo with camo-paint over my face and hoarding weapons. It's mental."

"If that's what people want to do though, you can't knock it," Anna said, always the voice of reason. "Your dad's farm doesn't exactly represent the majority of society, does it? Most people don't have acres of land. But, I'll say this, now I know how prepared you lot are down there, I know where me and Keiran will be coming when it all goes wrong."

"Yeah, you and most of the station, no doubt," Ben said. "Getting back to Pope. He doesn't exactly strike me as capable. He's weak, and the way Emma Blanch was killed, that took strength. Mental strength."

"He did run."

"Oh yeah, I mean, he's guilty of something, and he's definitely not all there upstairs. Is he a killer though? I don't know."

Ben indicated and pulled off the main road into the quiet lane that led into Potterhanworth. Anna glanced at him, as if wondering where he was taking her, but said nothing until they entered the long, narrow lane toward Wasps Nest.

"Are we going to the crime scene?"

"You haven't seen it yet," Ben said. "It might be good for you to get a feel for the place. Forensics have finished doing what they have to do, and it'll be a while before Pope is processed. We'll let him stew in a cell for a while. Soften him up a little. We'll need his laptop sent to Lincoln, too. Remind me when we get back, will you?"

A few minutes later, they pulled into the driveway and Ben cut the engine. Neither of them moved. Instead, they both stared out at the gloomy house. Daylight was falling fast, and a light fog was already forming, rolling in off the fens, smothering everything in its path.

"Not my choice of location," Anna said decidedly. She unclipped her seat belt and, to Ben's surprise, was the first out of the car. She was already peering through the front windows by the time Ben had locked the car and followed. He fastened his coat against the chill, and while Anna took a look around, he turned and faced the road. The view was quite spectacular. The night was calm and silent, and the air was fresh.

The sound of Anna's footsteps fading away roused him. She was making her way round to the rear of the property. He followed, eyeing the padlock on the front door and the pair of woman's Wellington boots that had been kicked off and left for the mud to dry. He came to the corner of the house, and stopped to admire the view across the fields as Anna entered the padlock code and pushed open the back door. But any joy the view once held was now tainted by the horrors of what had taken place.

"It's the right code," she whispered.

"Don't touch anything," Ben whispered back, and he watched her enter the house, taking a moment longer to imagine the scene. What had Emma been doing out there? The footprints in the mud, marked by little, white flags in the ground, indicated she had walked into the field, and hadn't been dragged or carried. The white flags showed a one-way journey, while a red set and a blue set of flags indicated two round trips. One marking the path of the killer, and the other, Mr Cross.

It had been a foggy morning. Ben remembered waiting outside

Freya's house, which was less than a kilometre from his own home and usually visible across his father's fields. But the fog had been heavy, and he wondered what reason Emma Blanch had for being out there in the early hours of the morning.

He was lost in thought, mesmerised by the ever-changing cloud that masked the world, when a shape passed through it from left to right. Ben blinked and tried to focus, recalling what he had seen. It had been a man, of that he was sure. He glanced across to the back door, feeling an acute responsibility for Anna who was inside. He strode to the fence and placed a foot on the bar, peering into the mist, trying to see it again, to reassure himself that perhaps it had been his imagination.

Then he heard it. The distinct sound of a boot on the damp ground. In a heartbeat, he vaulted the fence and paused, poised ready to defend himself, or maybe to reach out and grab whoever was lurking there. He glanced back at the door, mindful that with every step he took, his ability to protect Anna diminished.

With a rough idea of where the sound had come from, he walked, hands out ready to grab, fingers curled, and adrenalin surging through him like a freight train.

That was when he sensed something, or rather, someone. To his left. Creeping toward him just as he crept toward them. He turned and lunged, with only his instinct to guide him through the darkness and the fog, and he felt it. The rough material of a heavy jacket slipped from his fingers. The time for stealth was over. The dark shape slipped from his grasp, and Ben stood tall, catching just a glimpse of the man. He rushed at the spot and he made the connection. His fingers locked onto the man's jacket, and he swept one leg behind his assailant's, leaned all his weight into the move, and pulled him to the ground.

"Help," the voice said, and he writhed in Ben's grip. "Help me."

"Who are you?" he growled, breathless from the suspense.

"Boss?"

Ben stopped.

"Boss? Is that you?"

Every muscle in Ben's body had been tensed. They relaxed in unison, and Ben dropped to his knees.

"Cruz, you bloody idiot."

"Me?" he replied, rolling from Ben's lessened grip. He stood and began brushing himself down. "You're the one that came at me."

"What are you doing creeping about the place? It's a bloody crime scene."

"DI Bloom told me to come. I've knocked on all the doors. There's only about twenty. She said she'd send someone to pick me up. That was bloody ages ago."

"For god's sake, Cruz. I nearly—"

"What?" Cruz said. "You nearly what?"

"Nothing," Ben said, climbing to his feet. He didn't bother brushing himself down; his hands were as dirty as his knees. "In future, make yourself known."

"How was I to know you'd be coming here? I thought it was the killer coming back."

"Why would he come back here?" Ben asked. "This is the last place he'd be."

"Because he dropped this," Cruz said, and he held up a single leather glove. "I found it by the chickens."

CHAPTER TWENTY-FIVE

"Mr Cross?" Freya said, holding her ID up for him to see. Unlike Garland, Cyrus Cross filled his doorway. Naturally, the property was far smaller, and the doorway was of a more standard size, but still, the man was a giant, and his hands were of enormous proportions. "Detective Inspector Freya Bloom, and this is DC Chapman. We'd like a word if–"

"Where's the other one?" he grumbled, cutting her off.

"If you're referring to DC Nillson, then I'm afraid she's busy elsewhere," Freya said. "May we have a few minutes of your time?"

"You found him?"

"No. No, not yet. But we have officers searching for him. That's why I wanted to talk to you. I was wondering if perhaps you know of somewhere he might be."

He looked between them, as if deciding whether or not he should trust what Freya said.

"It's in Jason's interest," Freya added.

He didn't step to one side, as Garland had, nor did he offer a sweeping invitation. Instead, he turned and limped back toward the lounge, grumbling to himself.

Chapman looked at Freya with raised eyebrows, and rolled her eyes, shaking her head at the man's poor manners.

"You get used to it," Freya whispered, then steered her inside.

The house had a classic farmhouse feel – exposed timber beams, open fireplace, and even, noted Freya when she leaned into the kitchen, a flagstone floor, Aga, and copper pans that hung from the mantle. It had been well maintained and decorated to a high standard. It had the type of finish that Freya considered was only achievable with time. Time to manage the upkeep. Time to spend on those smaller areas of the rooms where the spiders like to build webs. Time to scrape the few drops of paint that dripped onto the door handle. Time that was usually only afforded by the rich and the retired.

The Christmas decorations stank of habit, of ritual, of all the things Freya wanted to hate but was jealous of. She imagined Mrs Cross, every year asking her husband to fetch the decorations down from the loft, which would be neat and tidy, so she could put them up almost exactly as they had been the year before, and the year before that. From the old Christmas tree to the mangy, old tinsel on the mantelpiece. It all stunk of happiness, and memories.

Despite the quality finish of the house, there was an over-laying of temporary disarray. Coffee mugs and plates were stacked beside the kitchen sink, a sweater hung over the back of a chair, and, in the lounge, where Freya found Cyrus Cross seated in his armchair watching her every move, a newspaper lay sprawled on the couch, a blanket had fallen to the floor, and a large pair of men's muddy shoes had been kicked off beside the fire and left there to dry.

"Are you alone, Mr Cross?" she asked.

"Cyrus," he gruffed. "Call me Cyrus. You can spare the formalities."

"Okay. DC Nillson mentioned in her report that you live with your wife. Is she around?"

His eyes darted around the room, noting the few items that were out of place. The blanket, the shoes, the newspaper.

"Gone to her sister's," he said. "Can't handle it."

"Oh, I'm sorry. She didn't mention that—"

"Decided last night. Probably didn't help having *her* under our feet all day."

"Will she be back anytime soon?"

"Let's not beat around the bush, Miss…"

"Bloom," Freya said. "Detective Inspector Bloom."

"That's a mouthful. The other girl said I should call her Anna."

"Well then you may call me Freya. May we sit?"

"Don't stand on ceremony. If you're waiting for an invitation, you'll be waiting a while."

Freya took the second armchair. Beside it, tucked out of sight, was a little bag, too cute to belong to the giant who sat opposite her.

"Maggie's knitting," he said, when he saw Freya eyeing it.

Chapman perched herself on the couch, but had to move the newspaper to do so. She straightened the pages and folded them, laying the paper on the arm of the chair.

"I'll be honest with you, Cyrus, Jason could be in a lot of trouble."

"With the law, you mean?" he said, although there was little panic in his voice.

"He's missing, Cyrus. It doesn't look good for him. The best thing he could do is to make contact. If he doesn't want to come in, then he can call me. My first concern is that he's okay."

Cyrus peered at her through his bushy eyebrows, seeming to chew on what Freya had said. Eventually, he nodded.

"He's not the type," he said. "Not to do that. Not my Jason. I said all this to Anna—"

"I read the report. You've been very forthcoming, and it's

appreciated," Freya said. "But I have a feeling you have more to tell us. Tell me about Jason's state of mind."

"Eh? What now?"

"Recently. What kind of mood was he in? Happy? Sad? Positive?"

He stared about the room, a bitter look forming – the furrowed brow, the pursed lips, and narrowed eyes.

"You have to understand," he began, "what he's doing up there. You have to understand that he's sunk everything he's got into that house. It has to work for him. He works day and night. Does what he can during the day. I help him, of course, with the heavy stuff. Then, at night, he ploughs on inside. Painting, sanding, plastering, you name it. My lad doesn't stop."

"You must be very proud of him."

"I am. Of course I am. But..."

"But?" Freya said, and Cyrus sighed.

"It's not without consequences. All that grafting, on top of what Emma did–"

"What Emma did?"

"What she put him through," Cyrus explained. "You know? The court case. It has a weight, all that. On your shoulders. It can bring a man down. And as strong as my boy is, he carries enough weight of his own."

"Ah, yes, Anna mentioned in her report something about that. Jason suffers from depression. Is that right?"

"Same as any other," Cyrus said defensively. "He just had the gumption to say so. You know? To get help. It doesn't make him any less of a man."

"No, it certainly doesn't. We share a similar view there. He asked for help, did he?"

"He did. Reached out to some charity or another. That was when he met Emma. It was her who came to him, see. It was Emma that helped him through it. His mum tried, and, to an extent, so did I. But what does a man say to his boy in those circumstances? He was low. At times, I wanted to shake him out of it. Wake him up, so he could really see who he is. He's special. You know that? He's one of a kind, my boy. He just needs to see it sometimes. Just needs reminding, is all. And he was all the way down there in Cornwall. There's only so much we could do."

"It must have been a difficult time for you all," Freya said.

"That was when he quit his job. I mean, he was on good money, more than most. But it wasn't doing him any favours. I found the house for him, and he and Emma committed. It was good for him. For a while, at least. But he still gets it, you know? The cloud. He still gets it. It still hangs over him."

"But he and Emma were together. Surely she helped him through any dark patches?"

"She did, yes," he said, then his face hardened. "And she put him through them, too."

"Sorry?" Freya said, and she glanced at Chapman to see if she too had heard him say it.

"I said she put him through them, too. She had him round her little finger at times. She could pick him up and make him dance, like a puppet. And she could take him down, too. There was a dark side to that girl, mark my words. Manipulative little cow, she was. I shouldn't speak ill of the dead, but that girl, she could do what she wished with him. We were just powerless."

"A dark side, Cyrus? Sorry, can you explain more? Are you saying that she toyed with Jason's emotions?"

"Like a puppet, I said. Maggie couldn't bear to watch it, and I had to turn a blind eye at times. You know, there's a time when a father has to look the other way. My father probably did the same with us. You can't go interfering in your child's relationship. It just isn't right."

"No," Freya said thoughtfully. "No, you're right. But it must have been hard to witness. How would you describe your relationship with Emma?"

"It was okay," he said. "She knew I had my opinions, but I

think as long as I kept it to myself, and kept my nose out of where it don't belong, she was okay. We got along. For Jason's sake, at least."

"Your opinions?" Freya said. "Do you mean your opinions on the relationship?"

"I mean my opinions on Harry Garland," Cyrus said, his voice rumbling like thunder.

"You believe she was guilty," Freya said. A statement, not a question.

He inhaled, long and deep, preparing to get something off his chest. Something which had been there far too long.

"I don't think she was guilty of manslaughter, detective," he said, and his eyes watered. "I think she was guilty of far worse than that. There. I said it. It doesn't surprise me someone did what they did, as much as it pains me to say it. She had it coming."

"Cyrus, I have to ask you a very difficult question, and I need an honest answer."

He steeled, and nodded, though it was slight. Chapman excused herself, moving into the kitchen clutching her flashing phone, and when Freya looked back at Cyrus, he was watery-eyed.

"Jason is a prime suspect in Emma's murder enquiry. He's in a lot of trouble. In your opinion, is Jason capable of murdering Emma?"

"Capable?" he said. "No. Not murder. Not my boy. There's plenty out there who might have wanted her dead. But not Jason. She was the only one who could bring him out of those dark places. Without her, he'd live beneath that cloud."

"You don't think he could have done it?" asked Freya, seeking confirmation by way of a yes or no answer.

"Not in his right mind," Cyrus said, and Freya caught Chapman's nervous glance in her peripheral.

"Can you tell me where he is? Where might he have gone?"

Cyrus looked at the fireplace. It wasn't lit, but he stared there as if the flames still danced.

"That's one question I don't dare ask myself," he said quietly. "I don't think I could bear it."

"I'm sorry to interrupt," Chapman said, and she leaned into the room from the kitchen clutching her mobile phone. She was clearly undecided if she should say anything. She looked wide-eyed at Freya, conveying a message that not only do experienced detectives understand, but grieving parents also.

"It's him, isn't it?" Cyrus said, and for the slightest of moments, there was hope in his voice. But it had trailed off before he had ended. "Tell me, girl," he breathed.

Freya nodded, giving her permission to relay the message. She would suffer the consequences to put the old man out of his misery.

"They found Jason. He's alive," Chapman said, and that same glimpse of hope came and went like the breeze. "But they don't know for how long."

CHAPTER TWENTY-SIX

The incident room door squealed and slammed, arrogant in the team's combined silence. Freya waited for Gillespie to settle, then spoke.

"Gillespie, over to you," she said, hearing her voice crack from fatigue.

Nobody was sitting. Each of them remained on their feet, attentive and ready to move.

"Aye, well," Gillespie began – his usual slur while he considered what he might say. "There's not much to tell. I've got every local uniform on the lookout for the pickup. I've been to every scrap dealer in the bloody county, and I found nothing. Nothing. Soul destroying–"

"Police work," Freya said.

"Aye, that's what I was going to say. Soul destroying police work. I've been up and down the Sleaford Road more times than the number thirty-one bus, poked my nose into every farm I found, and still, there was just no sign of the bloody thing. Then I got a call from Coninsby nick. Said they'd been called to a car fire out in Billinghay in the morning. They said it might be of interest."

"A car fire?" Chapman said, clearly hoping that Gillespie would repeat what he had said. The man had a knack of talking fast, and his thick accent was often hard to follow.

"Aye, yeah. It was it. The truck, I mean. Torched. I told you it would end up being torched in a field. Should have listened to ol' Gillespie, eh? It was almost unrecognisable when I saw it. Number plates had melted, glass shattered, and all that remained of the dashboard was a bunch of wiring. I couldn't even see what colour it had been. But those VW headlights, aye, they're unmistakable. I knew."

"There'll be no chance of picking up any DNA from inside then," said Freya. "He's covering his tracks. Did you speak to the fire brigade? Did anybody see anything?"

"No," he said, shaking his head. "The whole thing was over before lunch time. It was only when they were dragging it from the field that one of the uniforms recognised it. Said he spoke to you the other night. Tried to call you, but you weren't answering your phone. Big fella. Forehead like a football pitch. Said you'd remember him."

Ignoring Gillespie's habit of picking up on people's physical appearances, Freya pushed him to finish, so she could communicate her plan.

"Anyway, he called it in," Gillespie continued. "I guess whoever I spoke to at Coninsby nick actually remembered me. He gave me a call and I went down there."

"And Jason Cross?"

"Oh aye," Gillespie said, adopting an altogether different tone. One of grim remembrance. "Not at first, mind. The fire service had long gone. They were pulling the truck out of the field, and well, I'd been on the road all day. And that coffee—"

"The Mardi Gras of coffees?" Jackie said.

"Aye," he said, nodding with embarrassment. He grimaced and blushed. "Well, like I said, I'd been on the road, and well—"

"You got caught short?"

"You could say that. I slipped into the bushes out of eyesight, you know? That's where I found him."

"Jason Cross?"

He nodded. "Aye. What was left of the wee fella. Nearly didn't see him he was so charred and..." He shuddered at the memory. "He must have crawled from the fire. I thought he was dead. I don't even know why I checked. Habit, I guess. I..."

"It's okay, Gillespie. He's alive now, right?" Ben said.

"Aye, barely."

"Well then, you saved his life. You should be proud."

"Not that he'll thank me for it if he wakes up. I don't know how a man can survive that."

"Was there any sign of anybody or anything?" Freya asked. "Footprints? Something to start the fire?"

Gillespie shook his head. "If there were any prints in the mud, the firemen would have flattened them. I'm surprised you didn't see the helicopter. Had to airlift the bugger out. There was no way an ambulance would have got to him in time."

"Did you speak to him?" Freya asked. "Or try, at least?"

"He may have had a pulse, boss. But I'll be honest with you. I'd be surprised if he'll ever say anything again." For the first time, Gillespie appeared truly sickened.

"This changes things," Freya said. "Anna, I want you to go to Lincoln Hospital. Find out where he's being treated and stay there. If he comes around, call me. Ben, talk to uniform. See if we can get a round-the-clock presence."

"Eh?" Gillespie muttered. "What for?"

"He's still alive," Freya said, then shook her head. "He's not meant to be. Whoever killed Emma Blanch has made a mistake."

"It's suicide, surely?" Gillespie said. "If someone else did it, why didn't they just slot him? Like they did with Emma."

"Because he wanted to make it look like a suicide," Freya said, thinking hard.

"If you ask me, Jason Cross saw no option but to end it all. But when push came to shove, he couldn't go through with it."

"That may be the case," Freya said. "However, while you were out looking for Cross, we've covered every other angle."

"Eh?"

"Let's take it back to basics," Freya said, raising her voice to the room, and bringing the murmur back to a silence. "Three men. Edward Pope. He had the means, but lacked the motive, and as far as we know it, lacked the opportunity. He's in custody downstairs. Ben, Jackie, he's yours. Find out if there's a link to Emma Blanch. Check his emails, phone records. You know what to do."

"Ma'am," Jackie said, while Ben just nodded, and the two exchanged glances.

"Alex Garland," Freya continued. "Lacks the means, has a questionable alibi, and has what I would deem the strongest motive of them all. Gillespie, you can help me there. I have just the job for you."

"Working with the boss," Gillespie said, seemingly pleased. "You can count on me, boss. You and me. We'll find the bastard."

"It'll be a team effort, Gillespie. I need everyone switched on and communicating. There's one more potential suspect we haven't discussed. Cyrus Cross. Jason's father. His motive is questionable. But he lives next door, so had the best opportunity of them all. Chapman, we'll need your attention to detail. Go through Anna's report. Take Cruz with you. Show him how it's done, please."

"Yes, ma'am," Chapman said.

"Something to note. If you remember what Doctor Bell said, the killer is a large man. Cyrus Cross is a large man. But we can't convict a man on size and location alone."

"What about the glove I found?" Cruz asked. "That was big."

"Where is it now?"

"I had uniform take it to the technicians," Ben said. "If we can get some DNA from inside, we'll be bulletproof."

"Good. So, in the meantime, we're waiting for the results from the glove, we still need the results from the casts of the killer's boot prints found at the scene, and we're waiting for Jason Cross to wake up. That gives us a very short period of time to get everything we can on those three men. One of them killed Emma Blanch. The question is, who was it?"

"Three men," Gillespie said, his voice low and thoughtful. "One with the means, one with the motive, and one with the opportunity."

"That's about the size of it. Are you ready to get your hands dirty, Gillespie?"

"I was born ready, boss. I'll show you."

"Good. Go and see Sergeant Priest before he finishes. You'll need two uniforms to help you."

"Eh? I thought I was helping you?"

"Oh, you will be helping me. Don't worry about that," Freya said, dragging the pile of reports from the team into her file. She checked her watch, then looked back at him. "You said you wanted to get your hands dirty."

"Well, it was a figure of speech, really."

Ignoring Gillespie, Freya addressed the team. "Call your families. Tell them you'll be late home. And if you need anything at all, you know where I am." She turned to Gillespie, who was still looking perplexed. "Meet me by the car in two minutes," she said. "You'll need some gloves."

CHAPTER TWENTY-SEVEN

Edward Pope had been sitting in the interview room for thirty minutes. A single uniformed officer stood guard, and the smell from Pope's unwashed body was thick in the air.

"Thank you," Ben said, as he held the door for Jackie to follow. "We'll take it from here."

The uniform left, and Pope stared up at them wide-eyed. A crop of lank, greasy hair fell over his forehead, which he swept back with a sweaty palm.

Ben took the seat closest to the door, leaving Jackie in charge of the recorder. She wrote the date and time, plus the attendees on the tape's little, white, sticky strip, and slotted it into the machine. Then, clearing her throat, she hit record, announced the date and time, and introduced herself, Ben, and Edward Pope.

Finally, she nodded at Ben to proceed, collecting her pen from the little, elastic hoop in her notepad.

"Can you confirm, please, that you are Edward Pope?" Ben asked.

Pope nodded, slow and unsure of himself.

"For the tape, please," Jackie said.

"Yes," Pope said, leaning in towards the recorder.

There was a naivety about the young man. The deer-in-head-lights expression, the slack jaw, and the lack of social skills all suggested he'd had very little life experience. Nobody to show him the way of the world. It was easy to feel sorry for people like him, Ben thought. Unless, of course, they were hiding something. Which Edward Pope was.

"Do you know why you're here, Edward?" Ben said, kicking off the discussion.

"No," Pope replied with a shrug.

"Edward, you've been arrested on suspicion of murder. You've been read your rights. Do you understand them?"

"A what?" he replied. "A murder?. How? Why? I haven't–"

He stopped to take a few deep breaths, his chest rising and falling.

"You have the right to legal representation, Edward. Do you have a solicitor you'd like to call?"

He shook his head, clearly terrified of his situation.

"We can provide a duty solicitor free of charge, if you like."

"A solicitor?"

"Legal representation."

"Do I need one?"

"If you have anything to hide, then maybe. That's your choice," Jackie said.

"What can you tell me about a girl named Emma Blanch?" Ben said.

Pope looked at the door, as if he was trying to remember the name, then shook his head.

"I don't know an Emma Branch," he said.

"Blanch," Jackie corrected him, exaggerating the L.

"I don't know her. Should I?"

"Okay," Ben said. "How about a man named Jason Cross?"

"I don't know him either. What's all this about? I haven't–"

"Edward, tell us about the room in your house."

"Which one?" Pope replied.

"The war room," Ben said, for want of a better name.

"That's my stuff. That's where I keep it all."

"Is that a pastime of yours? Do you collect war memorabilia?"

"Yeah, kind of. I usually end up selling it though. That's what I do," he said, looking from Ben to Jackie. "I buy it all as cheap as I can. Then sell it on."

"Is that your job? Is that how you pay bills?"

"I wouldn't call it a job. But I don't really like going out. Mum used to say I was a couch potato. I used to sit and watch films all day. I know I'm different," he said boldly. He nodded and swallowed. "I know, you think I'm odd. Everyone thinks I'm odd. I don't do well outside. I feel like everyone is staring at me. I'm safe at home. I like it there."

"Have you heard of a place called Nocton?" Ben asked, and to his surprise, Pope nodded. "Have you been there recently?"

Pope shook his head. "I don't think I've ever been there. Maybe when Dad was alive. He used to take me fishing sometimes. Although, I never did much fishing. I used to just go for a walk. Didn't see the point in catching them and putting them back."

"But not recently?"

"No. I haven't been anywhere recently. Not really."

"So when do you leave the house?" Jackie asked. "You do go out sometimes, don't you? It's healthy to get out and walk."

"Yeah, I go out. Mostly to the post office," he said. "To send my stuff."

"The things you sell?"

"Yeah. I go once a day sometimes. It's not far. I can be there and back in half an hour. Depending on the queue. Tuesdays it's busy, so I have to get there early. But mostly, it's okay. They know me in there. You can check with them. They'll know me. They'll tell you."

"I'm sure they would," Ben said, beginning to understand the boy. The was a layer of maturity to him. On the surface, he came across as a childlike figure, someone who had never really developed mentally. But the more Ben spoke to him, the more he made sense. He knew his own mind and limitations, and lived his life accordingly. Ben respected that, despite the terrible hygiene, poor diet, and bad habits. The boy was living how he wanted to live. It was admirable. "Edward, a few days ago, a young girl was murdered."

"The Branch girl?"

"Blanch," Jackie said, correcting him again.

"Right. Blanch."

"She was killed with a bayonet. A specific type of bayonet," Ben said.

"It wasn't me," Pope began, his voice rising in pitch, and his face dropping into a horrified expression. "I haven't been anywhere. I didn't–"

"Edward," said Ben, holding his hands up to calm him down. "It's okay. We just need to find the weapon. You could even help us."

Nodding, Pope controlled his breathing, but his wide-eyed and terrified expression was fixed.

"We're looking for a…" Ben referred to the notes he had made, flicking through the pages of his notebook. "A British World War Two Land bayonet."

"A Land *Service* bayonet," Pope corrected him.

"Right."

"They're common enough. I come across them from time to time. I don't keep many bayonets, shipping prices are high."

"Why's that?" Jackie asked.

"The weight," Pope said, with confidence. "But I do get them. What one are you looking for?"

Again, Ben looked down at his scribbled notes.

"It's a number seven–"

"Ah, the mark one," Pope said. "Yeah. They're two a penny."

"Two a penny?" Ben said. "I spoke to a man in a shop about them a while ago. He said they were quite rare."

"Of course he did," Pope said. "He probably wanted you to buy it."

"I thought I'd made it quite clear that I wasn't looking to buy," Ben said. "But I could be wrong. In fact, I made it quite clear I was looking for anybody who had bought one recently. Do you know the shop? It's called Curiously Curious. In the city."

Pope said nothing. He stared at Ben but suddenly gave nothing away.

"He told me somebody had bought one online. The details he gave me were yours, Edward."

"I know it," Pope said quietly. "Yeah, I bought one from there a while back."

"Where is it?" Ben asked. "I found three bayonets in your house. It wouldn't take much for me to get a warrant to search your entire house. If it's there, we'll find it."

"You won't," he replied, far too quickly. "It's not there. I sold it. It went last week. I posted it..." He squeezed his eyes closed and appeared to be recalling his movements. "Must be four days ago, now. You said the girl was killed a few days ago. It can't be me. See. I knew it. It can't be me."

"And you can prove this, can you?" Ben said. "I mean, do you keep receipts from the post office?"

"Yeah, I have to. I have a full inventory. I sell everything through eBay, so you can even see my account. I'll show you. Get my laptop. I can show you now."

Ben stared at him, feeling Jackie glance from him to Edward and back again, waiting for him to make the call.

"DC Gold will get your laptop," Ben said. "You can show her."

"See. I told you it wasn't me."

"But, Edward," Ben said, his eyes never leaving Pope's, "why did you run?"

Pope's elated expression faded once more to the all-familiar look of terror.

"What?"

"You ran. You made us chase you, if you remember? My colleague had to tackle you to the ground. You're not going anywhere, Edward. Not until you tell me why."

Pope was sullen. He began fiddling with his fingers, and a tear formed in the corner of his eye. It was the first guilty sign he had shown since the interview began.

"Edward?" Ben said softly. "Do we need to search your house? I can have a team of police officers there in under an hour."

He shook his head, refusing to make eye contact. It was a look of shame.

"Get me my laptop," he said softly, and laid his hands flat on the table, forcing himself to look up and meet Ben's gaze. His nostrils flared, and the tear broke free, leaving a trail across Pope's face. "Get me my laptop, and I'll show you."

CHAPTER TWENTY-EIGHT

FREYA DROVE WITH GILLESPIE IN THE PASSENGER SEAT WHILE A liveried car followed behind with two uniforms.

"Good work, Ben," she said, as he finished the account of his interview with Edward Pope. "It was a long shot, but if the bayonet he bought was in the post at the time of the murder, we can pretty much strike him off."

"That leaves two," Ben replied, his voice loud and clear over the car's Bluetooth system.

"Are we taking bets?" Gillespie said.

"You're not on DI Standing's team now, Gillespie," Freya said. "Ben, I'll call when we're done here. Keep me posted."

"Will do," he said, and ended the call.

The winter daylight had long since passed, and the fog rolled across the grounds of the Georgian house like old souls.

"Creepy," Gillespie said, as if to himself, as they drew closer to the house and the old architectural features seemed to emerge from the gloom. He turned to Freya. "This is Garland's house, is it?"

She nodded, pulling the car to a stop behind Garland's work van, and close to the skip.

"Looks can be deceiving," she said, as she pushed open her door and climbed out. "It's not as glamorous as you might think."

"Glamorous?" he replied, over the roof of the car. "Of all the words you could have used, glamorous is not one. I can assure you that."

"How would you describe it, then?" she asked, though her mind was elsewhere.

"Creepy, terrifying, macabre, sinister, eerie. Not glamorous," he said, keeping his voice to a whisper. "If a pretty woman walked through that door in a long, red dress, I'd expect her to hover down the steps, if you know what I mean?"

"That's quite a description, Gillespie," Freya replied, as the two uniforms approached.

"Aye, well," he replied. "I do have a GCSE in English."

"It's a shame you don't exploit that more often. You might come across less crass."

"Eh?"

"Are we ready?" Freya asked the team as the two uniforms gathered around.

The first was a young man in his mid-twenties. Freya had seen him before, but had never had the opportunity to work with him. The second, however, had proved to be reliable in a previous case.

They all nodded, and she retrieved the folded warrant from her inside pocket, then closed her jacket again, bracing against the cold. She knocked on the door, and had barely replaced her hand in her pocket when the door was opened. But this time, there was no chivalry or grand welcome. Garland, small in the large doorway, scowled at her.

"Hello again, Mr Garland," she said, handing him the slip of paper. "You'll find everything is in order. We have a warrant to search these premises and your vehicle. Failure to comply with the warrant will lead to your arrest."

"You bitch," he replied. "I've just spent two hours compiling an inventory for you."

"Hey now," Gillespie cut in. "You just mind your tongue—"

"It's okay, DS Gillespie," Freya said, her eyes not leaving Garland's. "That's your first strike. I'll give you that one for free. Any more insults or offensive remarks, and I'll have you cuffed and in the back of that car. You can watch us go through your possessions one by one from there. Do I make myself clear?"

"Crystal," Garland said, after appraising each and every one of them.

"Good," Freya continued, as she stepped inside, gesturing for her team to follow. "You'll need lights and gloves."

The hallway was suddenly lit by bright wall lights. Garland, with his hand on the switch stared at her still. "It might feel like the nineteenth century in here, but I do have electricity, you know."

"I'm glad to hear it. Right then, team," Freya said, bringing their attention to the black refuse bags that had been piled at the bottom of the wide stairway, "I want all of these bags searched."

"You'll be tidying up after yourselves, I hope," Garland said.

"Maybe," Freya said, then turned to Gillespie. "You're in charge. Get to it."

Gillespie's face was a picture of disgust. But, to his credit, as crass and immature as he came across in the presence of his colleagues, he portrayed himself as a true professional in front of Garland when the suspect turned to face him.

"Shall we go through to the kitchen?" Freya said to Garland, turning to walk away and leaving him no option but to follow. "I'll take a look at your inventory through here."

She stepped into the once-grand kitchen, placing her bag on the large island countertop.

"Now then. Laptop, please."

He stared at her, a man whose language and tone gave the impression of wealth and power, like an aristocrat, but whose visual appearance was that of an ordinary man. A nobody. He wore jeans stained with paint and soiled with dirt. A once-white t-shirt was torn and sullied with sweat marks.

"You won't find anything," he said. "In there, or on my laptop. I've nothing to hide."

"In that case, it shouldn't take too long then, should it?" Freya replied. "Chop chop, Mr Garland."

The place was a building site, but, with imagination, the potential was there for it to be restored to its former glory.

Whether he had resigned himself to the fact that Freya was not going to give up, therefore making resistance futile, or if he was looking to find favour with Freya by adopting a more personable approach, she couldn't tell. But the change in attitude was welcome.

"I told Dad to do this years ago," he said. "He could have sold it and lived on the profits quite comfortably."

"Stubborn, was he?" Freya said, as Garland opened the laptop for her and entered his password.

"It's a family trait, I'm afraid," he said, then gestured at the laptop. "I saved a spreadsheet on the desktop. Pretty much everything was sold on eBay, except for the few items that were of any real value."

"And where did you sell those?"

"Auctioned. The emails are on there, if you need to check."

Freya opened the file he'd mentioned, and then opened the email application, setting herself up to crosscheck everything. Lastly, she opened the browser and browsed to eBay. In a few clicks, she had found his profile and all the items he had bought and sold in the past twelve months.

"You have been busy," she said. "As I understand it, you own a joinery company, is that right?"

"The first Garland ever to get his hands dirty, I think," he said, and offered a weak laugh at the thought. He looked about the room, then back at Freya. "To think that this place would have had cooks and staff running about, while my privileged ancestors lazed about the house."

"A sign of the times, maybe?" she said. Although she loathed the man, based on her previous encounter with him, she did find a kind of humility with him. An honesty about his heritage that may have been harder to glean under other circumstances.

"Dad lost it all," Garland said. "When I was younger. Poor investments, greed, and dare I say it, laziness. He swore blind that money should work for you, not the other way around. It doesn't always work like that. Sometimes you have to go out and get it."

"And that's what you did, is it?"

"I *had* to. It's not like I was encouraged to. No. Dad actually forbid me at one point. Think of the family name, he used to say. He soon got used to it though. If I hadn't have done that, I'd never be able to do up this place. I'd have to pay for someone else to do it."

"There's honour in that," Freya said. "Do you think he'd be proud?"

"If he were alive?" Garland said. "He wouldn't show it."

"And what do you intend on doing with the place when you're done?"

"Sell it," he said with a shrug, and the comment surprised Freya.

"Sell it? Your family home?"

"It would set me up for life," he explained with a sigh, and then Freya saw the true Garland in him.

"So you can live as your forebears once did. In relative luxury. You genuinely believe you were robbed of a way of life, don't you?"

He stared at her, and whatever humility Freya had witnessed was gone.

"I'll have the life I was born for," he said. "I've grafted long enough."

"Do you mind if I take this away with me?" Freya asked, seeing that the list of sold items on his eBay account was more than ten pages long.

"Do I have a choice?"

"Not really. Is there anything I should know beforehand?"

He smiled, seemingly pleased with himself.

"No, detective," Garland said. Then he added, "Oh, and while you're looking at my emails, you might want to look at the one from the Roadside Lodge in Canterbury. It's the hotel I stayed in a few nights ago. The night Emma was killed, I believe."

Freya glanced through the hallway to the team working through the bags. Gillespie was picking up the contents of a bag he had turned upside down. The light from the hallway lit the front door and the steps beyond, where several bags had already been searched and cast outside.

"You said you were here that night, Mr Garland," Freya said.

"Apologies. I must have got my dates mixed up," he replied, folding his arms and leaning against the kitchen island. "I met with some old friends of my father's. I think you'll find the reservation is in order, Detective Bloom," he said with a grin.

"I should nick you for wasting police time," Freya said with a sneer. But the comment merely raised a wry smile on Garland's smug face. "But I can wait. I know you're involved, Garland. And I'll find out how. You mark my words."

She scooped the laptop into her bag, and left him wondering exactly how she might achieve that, but if she was truthful to herself, she didn't rightly have an answer. All she did know is that he fell into the bracket of people she despised – smarmy, entitled, and downright villainous.

"How are you getting on, Gillespie?" she asked as she stormed through the hallway.

"Aye, just fine. I've got bits of wallpaper in my hair, and I'm sweating in places I never knew I could sweat, but aye, we're getting through it, boss."

Freya stopped at the doorway and caught a glimpse of Garland in the hallway admiring her from behind.

"Good," she said. "When you're done there, tear the house apart. If you find anything, nick him and bring him to me."

CHAPTER TWENTY-NINE

BACK AT THE STATION, FREYA WAS SITTING BEHIND HER DESK IN semi-darkness. She was marvelling at the missed calls and three text messages from Greg, each one more bitter than the last. Yet they all carried the same sentiment as the first.

Stay away from us. We don't need you.

There was one message which Freya was glad to see though, and she read it four times in the space of twenty minutes, the way an alcoholic has just one more drink.

Thanks for the other night. The offer of dinner still stands if you'd like to meet up again. I would. M.

Grateful that he hadn't mentioned the falling asleep thing, Freya read it one more time. At least this one might have manners. Manners went a long way in a day and age when etiquette seemed to be in a state of regression.

Without warning, the incident room door slammed open, crashed against the wall, then closed of its own accord, squealing like a wounded animal.

Ben dumped his file onto his desk, swore, and kicked his chair so it rolled across the room.

"How did it go with Pope?" she said, from the darkness, and Ben startled.

"For god's sake, Freya. What are you doing sitting in the dark?"

"Contemplating death," she said, then waited for him to consider a response, but chose to put him out of his misery. "Not my own. Don't worry. Emma's."

"Well, that's good to hear," Ben said, as he dragged his chair back to his desk. "Why are the lights off? I didn't think anyone was here."

"The lights are off because I didn't switch them on," she said, stating the obvious as a means of avoiding the truth.

Ben stood and took two of his big strides to turn them on.

"No," she said. "No, let's enjoy the peace for a while. There's less distraction that way. Tell me about Pope. I'm guessing he didn't give you the answers we needed?"

"He had a bayonet. The right model. It was him who bought it from the curiosity shop. All that stacks up."

"But?"

"But he sold it. That's what he does. He sells war memorabilia online. I've seen his laptop. He sells bloody tons of it. Medals, clothes, hats. You name it, he sells it."

"And the bayonet?"

"In the post. Second class service to somewhere in Cambridgeshire. Posted it the day before Emma was killed."

"It was a long shot, Ben. Don't beat yourself up about it."

"I know. It's just bloody frustrating."

"So why did he run?" Freya asked. "I'm sure Anna told me he ran."

"He's been looking at porn on the internet. Bloody porn, Freya."

"What? Not..."

"No, nothing untoward. Nothing deviant. Nothing of any significance whosoever. Just regular porn that..."

"That what, Ben?" she said, enjoying him work himself into a corner.

"That normal people watch. That's all."

"Normal people? Here's me thinking you were quite a normal bloke. In fact, I thought I was normal, too."

"You know what I mean," he snapped, but with very little bite in his bark.

"That's not illegal. He's a single man."

"I know," Ben said, his voice climbing in volume and pitch. "He's a bit…" Ben paused, seeking the politically correct way to describe Edward Pope.

"Simple?" Freya said, although she was sure that was not a PC description.

"That's one way to describe it, yes. I would have said naive," Ben said with a sigh. He opened his laptop and tapped the keyboard. Then tapped it again, harder this time. Finally, he shoved it to one side and leaned his elbows on the desk. "So, we're down to two. Garland and Cyrus Cross."

"Make that one," Freya said. "Garland has a hotel reservation in Kent. I called them. It all checks out. He was there."

"I thought you said he was at home on his own that night? With a cheap bottle of wine, you said. I thought he was our man. You're not telling me we're looking at Cyrus Cross?"

"Yep, that's what he told me. Went down to meet a few of his father's old friends. It's a long drive. It makes sense to stay down and drive back the next day."

"And Gillespie?"

"He's there now bagging up Garland's rubbish for him. He played me, Ben. The bastard played me."

"So, one then," Ben said. "Cyrus Cross. If he doesn't check out, then we have to concede that Jason Cross killed Emma, and then tried to take his own life."

"Are you suggesting we start over? That we shift our attention to Jason Cross?"

"Maybe we're looking at this wrong, Ben. Maybe Doctor Bell wasn't right. Maybe the murder weapon wasn't a bayonet? Maybe somebody actually cared enough for Emma to avenge her death?"

"By killing Jason?" Ben said. "That doesn't make sense. Whoever killed Jason took him the night Emma was killed."

"You're right," she said, and let her head fall back over the chair.

"Let's face it, Cyrus Cross lives next door, he wasn't exactly Emma's biggest fan, and from what he said, Emma had Jason by the balls. He couldn't do a thing without her. She could lift him up, and she could drop him from a great height. And when the one you love experiences trauma," Ben said, "starts behaving oddly..."

"That kind of thing can do strange things to a man," Freya said, with more than a hint of a personal anecdote embedded into the theory.

"He fits Doctor Bell's description."

"He does, and he was the one who found her."

"But why would he kill his own son?" Freya said, and the two pondered the question in silence.

"Maybe he was hiding him," Ben said. "You know? Keeping him low, out of sight. Waiting for the commotion to blow over. Maybe Jason had had enough, and Cyrus stepped in to save his son from mental torture?"

"Okay," Freya said, seeing where Ben was heading. "Cyrus would have known about Garland's prosecution. Everybody knew. It's no secret he despised her. So what about if Cyrus Cross hatched a plan to put the blame onto Alex Garland while he was hiding his boy?"

"Set him up, you mean?"

"That's exactly what I mean."

"Cyrus Cross set up Garland?" Ben said. "He's an old man."

"Exactly," said Freya. "So who would look at him? He hides Jason until Garland is charged. Jason could then make a miraculous appearance. Probably feign amnesia or something. If he did it right, Jason wouldn't have even had to know it was his dad. Dark morning. Foggy. Hood over the head. Cyrus Cross is a very large man."

"And the whole Cross family can carry on with their lives."

"What do we have that links Cyrus Cross to Garland?"

"Nothing that I know of. They've both been in the area for decades, so given the tiny community in Wasps Nest, they must know of each other."

"Check to see if there are any previous conflicts between them. Neighbourly stuff, you know. Enough for one to hold a grudge against the other. I also think there's a whole piece we're missing here."

"Such as?"

"Emma. Did she actually kill Harold Garland?"

"I thought we weren't going there?" Ben said. "The force spent a lot of money investigating that."

"So we'll have records. I think that's a job for Chapman in the morning. Let's leave it for tonight."

"I'll get Jackie to look into the Garland and Cross thing," Ben said. "She knows her way around the system better than me."

He sat back in his chair, and not for the first time, Freya admired his sheer size, outlined against the moonlit wall. He was a man's man. Hardened by a life on his father's farm and his arduous career in the force. He had done well to make DS, and would easily have been DI, had it not been for Freya's impromptu arrival in Lincolnshire. He had every right to be mad at her or to hold a grudge. Yet there was a compassion in him that was rare and genuine. He was probably the one person she could count on as a friend.

"It's seven p.m.," Freya said. "I'm going to check in on Gillespie to see how he got on at Garland's place. Chances are that he struck out, but you never know."

"I don't hold much hope."

"No, but it was a good opportunity to see how Garland reacted under pressure. He didn't kill Emma Blanch. Of that, I'm almost certain."

"Almost?" Ben asked.

"Almost," she replied, nodding in the darkness. "He may have taken pleasure from her death, but kill her? No."

"I honestly thought today would go better than it did," Ben said. "We had Garland, Cyrus Cross, and Pope. Three strong leads."

"Three dead ends," Freya said. "Did I tell you her brother made an appearance this morning?"

"Her brother?" Ben said.

"Thomas Blanch. Apparently he's been trying to contact her. Some kind of attempt at making amends."

"What for?"

"Family stuff. Apparently he and Emma didn't see eye to eye after the father died. It was making the mother ill so, being the eldest, Thomas left, leaving Emma to care for her. He saw her trial in the newspaper and found out where she lived."

"Were they on speaking terms when Emma died?"

"Apparently so," Freya said. "After more than ten years of not speaking. She must have been a right piece of work. From what Cyrus Cross says, she was quite the manipulative one."

"Jason Cross suffered from depression, didn't he?" said Ben, and he collected his file, opening it to scan through a few notes, using the light from his laptop to read. "Yeah, here we go. This is from Anna's original report from her discussions with Cyrus. She's written that Jason met Emma when he was going through a difficult time. Emma worked with a mental health charity, apparently."

"Cyrus said something similar to me. He told me that she was the only one with the power to bring him out of a dark spell," Freya said. "But she also had the power to put him in one. She had complete control over his state of mind."

"Sounds like a right bunny boiler," Ben said. "No wonder nobody liked her."

"She didn't have much luck, did she?" Freya said.

"What do you mean?" Ben asked. "She met a bloke with a good job and money, and as far as I can tell, from Anna's report, he gave it all up to buy them a place in the country. I wish someone would do that for me."

"She cared for her mother, who died. She cared for Alex Garland's father, who also died," Freya said. "If that was me, I'd be looking for another occupation."

"How did her father die?"

"Heart attack," Freya said. "When the Blanch family moved to Lincolnshire, they bought a small plot of land out near Horncastle."

"The good life?"

"Not quite. They spent every penny they had. Huge debts. The father was working in the barn on his own when it happened, working some kind of machinery. You can imagine the rest. I suppose it was that one accident that was the catalyst for a whole raft of subsequent events. The life insurance was used to pay the house off, and they moved onto a whole new chapter. Her mother died a few years later. Funny, isn't it? The way one event can alter the paths of so many people?"

Ben said nothing, but she felt him watching, and guessed he would have read between the lines of her comment.

She switched on her desk lamp, took her feet from the desk, and opened her own file, aware that the last time she had collated her papers, it had been a rush job and nothing was in the right order. It was as she set the papers down that her phone flashed once, and a message appeared on the screen.

All your belongings are bagged and boxed. My solicitor will be in touch to arrange a date you can collect them and drop the key off. We'll be out.

"Loving the filing system," Ben said.

She looked up and spied him watching her.

"Sorry?"

He gestured at the pile of papers, but said nothing.

"Don't judge me. Besides, we're not all obsessive. If we were, we wouldn't achieve much, would we? We'd all be alphabetising our records instead of getting out there and talking to people. Catching bloody killers."

Even as she spoke the words, she heard how sharp her tone was, but could do little to stop it.

"That's a bit harsh," Ben said, clearly not hurt by the comment. He had thicker skin than that, thankfully.

She sighed.

"Sorry. I'm just..." She stopped herself from saying what was on her mind.

"Freya?" Ben said, and he sat forward, a genuine look of concern on his face. "What's wrong?"

Freya said nothing, choosing to swallow the emotions that were building up in her throat.

"It's Greg, isn't it?" Ben said. "Has he called you?"

"He won't let me see Billy," Freya said. "So I messaged him to give him a few home truths, and to say that I'd bought Billy something for Christmas. But, because I walked out, apparently I don't deserve the opportunity to see him. He says he's been picking up the pieces since I left, and if Billy sees me, it'll confuse him. Now he's just said that all my possessions are boxed up and he'll arrange a time for me to collect them."

"What a bastard," Ben said, with the same genuine tone. "He bloody cheated on you. What were you supposed to do?"

"I know. I know. The same thing is going round in my head. I need to move on."

"You can't. You deserve the opportunity to talk to Billy. You raised him, for crying out loud."

"Anyway, sorry to drag my own affairs into this," Freya said, trying to move the subject on for fear the burning flood behind her eyes would break their dam.

"Don't apologise."

"I'm just sensitive about my habits," she added. "Greg always used to complain about me being disorganised."

"I'm not Greg," Ben said.

"I know. I'm sorry, it's just that sometimes I let it get to me. I'm just frustrated. I'll get over it."

"Why don't you take off?" Ben suggested. "Grab an early night. Tomorrow will be the big one."

"Like today was meant to be?" Freya said. "No, I'd rather stay here. But you should. Go on. I can handle it here. I want to look into Emma's history a bit more."

"So let's do it together?" Ben said. He stood up, reached for the light switches, and flicked them all on, even those that lit Standing's end of the room. "I'll order pizza."

"You don't have to," Freya said. "I'm not much company right now."

"What am I going to do? Go home and watch TV? I don't think so. Come on, let's get to the bottom of this. Let's find out who Emma Blanch really was."

"It's not going to be a thrilling night," Freya said.

"Eh, listen, just don't fall asleep on me while we do real police work."

She offered him an appreciative smile. "Or, as Gillespie would call it," she said, mimicking their colleague's voice, "absolutely soul destroying police work."

CHAPTER THIRTY

"I found the Blanch case file," Freya announced, as Ben finished a call and slid his phone onto his desk. "Who was that?"

"Anna. There's no change in Jason Cross. The doctors aren't hopeful. There's a uniform on the door, so I sent Anna home. We're going to need everyone on form tomorrow."

"I suppose I should do the same with Gillespie," Freya said, then reluctantly, she dialled his number from her desk phone, using his contact details from an email.

"DS Gillespie," he said, sounding far more professional than Freya had heard in her earlier interactions with the man.

"Gillespie, it's DI Bloom. What's the news?"

"News? There is no news."

"You didn't find anything at all?"

"Clean as a baby's bum," he said. "We went through every single bag of rubbish by the door. It was mostly building stuff, you know? Plasterboard, coving, wood, and the like. What a job. I look like Bob the bloody builder, and I even managed to get his bloody takeaway all over me."

"Sounds like you had a good time, Gillespie," Ben called across the room. "At least he fed you."

"It's no laughing matter, Ben. I thought it was blood at first. I thought we'd got him. Turns out it was bloody chicken tikka masala."

"Did you check upstairs as I asked?" Freya said.

"Empty," he said. "Every single room. No carpets, no beds, no wardrobes, cupboards, or cabinets, or whatever else you might have. There's no chairs either, except for the ones in the conservatory. I was looking forward to tearing the place apart, as you said, boss, but he's already done it."

"So where's he sleeping?"

"From what I can tell, he's slumming it in a sleeping bag. Honestly, boss, I had more furniture when I was a student, and that was in a one-bedroom flat in the arse-end of Glasgow."

"That corroborates with what I saw on his laptop," Freya said. "In the past three months, he's sold more than two hundred items on eBay and Facebook Marketplace, not to mention the items of value that were auctioned. That'll be Cruz's job tomorrow. He can go through them line by line to make sure Garland's bank statements match up."

"Aye, have him check PayPal as well, boss. I doubt a man like Garland would be stupid enough to put his bank details online."

"PayPal, of course," Ben said, and he reached across to Chapman's desk. He opened the file and began skimming through the papers, which, of course, were in a perfectly easy-to-follow order.

"Good work, Gillespie," Freya called out, as she joined Ben. "I appreciate you working late. Do you need transport?"

"Ah, nay bother, boss. I'll catch a lift off Tweedle-Dee and Tweedle-Dum and meet you back at the station."

"No need. If you're done there, go straight home. I need everyone on the ball tomorrow."

"Why's that? Is it going to be the big one?"

"We're trying, Gillespie. We knew this would be a hard one."

"Aye, I know. But if you think I'm going home while you two

reap all the glory, you can think again, boss. I'll see you in half an hour."

"You don't need to, Gillespie—"

"Have you eaten?" he asked, ignoring her comment.

She looked up and Ben, who shrugged. "We'd be done quicker," he whispered.

"I'll grab some takeout. We should probably get these two some as well. They've been absolute legends. What d'ya fancy?"

Again, Ben looked up at Freya, and in unison, they both replied, "Pizza."

"Roger that," Gillespie said, his smile apparent in his tone. He called out to the uniforms who had helped him. "Hey, you two, let's wrap up. The boss says she's buying you both pizza. Bet you don't get that from Sergeant Priest, eh?"

Freya opened her mouth to argue, but saw little point in doing so.

"Get the napkins out, Benny boy," Gillespie said, and he ended the call.

"He's okay," Ben said. "You'll learn to love him."

"Maybe," Freya replied, and she was about to voice an argument when the incident room door squealed open. Looking up at the disruption, Freya found Cruz standing in the doorway. "What are you doing here, Cruz?"

"We just got back from the Blanch house, ma'am," he replied. "I saw the light."

"Did you think we were getting burgled?" Ben asked.

"No, I saw your cars in the car park. Figured you were still working."

"That's fine detective work," Freya said. "Is that an offer to help?"

He shrugged. "That's what we do, isn't it? That's what DI Standing does anyway."

"Does he buy you pizza?" Ben asked.

"Pizza? No. Why? We always have to buy our own dinner. Says he's not our mum or something."

"You're in for a treat then," Ben said. Then he appeared confused. "So where's DC Nillson?"

"I'm in here," a voice called out, and it was then they heard the rattle of chinaware. She backed through the door carrying a tray of steaming cups, and then set them down on the nearest desk. "Thought we'd need these," Anna said.

"Nearly a full team then," Ben said, and he clapped his hands together loudly, and rubbed them as if trying to keep warm.

"Do you want to call Gold and Chapman in?" Freya asked. "If we're going to hit this now, they could be useful."

"Jackie texted me earlier. Charlie is sick again," Ben said. "She's got her own issues to deal with."

"Fine. Anna, message Chapman, will you?" Freya said.

"Right then," Ben began, raising his voice to be heard by all. "DI Bloom and I were just saying that we need to alter our approach. Up until now, we've been focused on the murder weapon and the three suspects. We need a new perspective."

"That's right," Freya said, taking over from Ben with a gracious nod. "Three hours ago, we had three suspects, one with the means, one with motive, and one with the opportunity. Now we have one suspect, who had the opportunity, a weak motive, but as far as we can tell, not the means."

"So what do we do then?" Cruz asked. "If Cyrus Cross is the only one without a solid alibi, we should bring him in?"

"If only it was that simple, Cruz," Freya said. "We have nothing on him. Not really. We have to look elsewhere. If both Cyrus and Garland disliked Emma so much, then the chances are there will be others out there who feel the same way. We have to find them. Her trial was published, is that right?"

"Yes," said Anna. "Locally, anyway. I'm not sure if it got national coverage."

"That's fine. Find any articles you can. I want you to collate all the photos. Then get onto the local news station and see if they have any footage of Emma Blanch going into court, being arrested, that sort of thing. You're looking for an individual who shows up multiple times. I worked on a case a few years back in London, and we hit a wall like this. We tried a similar tactic and it produced leads. Good leads, at that."

"Leave it with me," Anna said, as she shook her computer mouse to wake her laptop.

"Cruz, go down to the evidence locker and fetch Garland's laptop."

"Grab Pope's too," Ben added, then he looked at Freya. "Seems kind of odd that one man sells everything he has on eBay, while the other makes his living there, doesn't it?"

She nodded her agreement. "When you have them, I want you to go through Garland's eBay account and check every sale against his PayPal account line by line. Do the same for Pope, paying particular attention to the bayonet he sold recently." Freya then turned to Ben. "Do we still have him in custody?"

"Sent him home," Ben said. "I didn't see much point in keeping him here. His laptop is due to be screened by the tech guys."

"His laptop is all we need," Freya said. "This is our last chance with Pope and Garland. Cruz, get to it."

"What about us?" Ben asked.

"Emma Blanch," she said. "I want to know exactly what she was doing before she met Jason. There's something missing. Something vital. If we're going to work out who killed her, we need to know everything."

CHAPTER THIRTY-ONE

"Get it while it's hot," Gillespie announced, as he kicked the incident room door open and entered carrying four boxes in one hand, as a waiter might carry a tray full of plates to a table. "And you'll never guess who I bumped into."

From behind his massive bulk, Jackie emerged, and then Chapman.

"It's nine o'clock," Freya said. "What are you two doing here?"

Jackie looked confused. She glanced at Chapman, then at Ben, and then finally back at Freya.

"Ben messaged Denise," she said. "Then she texted me."

"Did he tell you there would be pizza?" Gillespie asked, as he tore open the first box. "We have Hawaiian."

"He said we were pulling an all-nighter," Jackie said.

"I thought you were looking after your son?"

"I slipped out. My mum's there. She won't mind."

Freya looked across at Ben, eyebrows raised.

"Final push," he said in defence. "We need everyone we can get our hands on."

"Everyone?" said Freya, and she glanced up at DI Standing's empty desk.

"Well, not everyone," he replied. "Only those that matter."

"Final push?" Freya said, and Ben nodded.

"Final push."

"Meat feast," Gillespie announced, like a child opening Christmas presents. He tore off a slice, ripped a section of the lid off the box to use as a plate, and ventured to his seat. "What will you have me doing, boss?"

Freya looked around at her team, proud and in awe of each of them in their own way.

"You can start by passing me some of the Hawaiian," she said.

He groaned, then quietened, before standing and reaching for the box.

"I don't know how you do it, boss," he said, holding the box out for her to help herself. "Pineapple on pizza. It's like having a banana on a fry up. It just doesn't work."

"It's a ham pizza. Pineapple pairs with ham," she replied, covering her mouth while she chewed. "It's the same as having cranberry with turkey, or mint with lamb."

"Hey now, I won't hear a bad word said about mint sauce with lamb. I'd have mint sauce on everything if I could. Beef, chicken..." He paused, trying to think of more meats to add to the list.

"Lamb?" said Ben, with a smile behind Gillespie's back.

"Aye, lamb too," Gillespie said, taking a large mouthful of his meat feast. "But pineapple on pizza is just wrong. What do the Hawaiians know about pizza anyway?"

"Actually, it's Canadian," Cruz said from his corner of the room, where he sat with his feet up on his desk, and one hand filled with a giant slice of pepperoni.

"Eh?" Gillespie said. "Behave."

"It's true," Cruz said. "Some Italian family in Canada tried putting tinned pineapple on a pizza. You know? Like chicken tikka masala. It's not a real Indian dish, but it's still good."

"Or sweet and sour chicken," Jackie added. "You won't find that in Beijing."

"Or Chongqing," Cruz said.

"Or what?" Gillespie spluttered, with a mouthful of stringy mozzarella.

"Chongqing."

"What's Chongqing when it's at home?" Gillespie said, as if Cruz had lost his mind. "Some kind of Asian delicacy?"

"It's a city in China, Jim," said Cruz, as if everybody would know that.

Freya smiled at how easily the young and naive DC had outsmarted the older and more experienced DS.

"My point is, why is it called a Hawaiian pizza then?" Gillespie said, his voice at almost alto levels in pitch. "Why isn't it called a Canadian?"

"It was the brand of pineapple chunks they used, I think."

"How on earth do you know that?" Freya said. "And more importantly, why do you know that?"

"I don't know," said Cruz. "I just heard it once. I guess it stuck."

"Aye, right," Gillespie said, his deep voice bullish in contrast to Cruz's quieter tones. "So it could all be rubbish."

"Nope, I just checked," Chapman said, scrolling with her computer mouse. "Some Canadian family pizza restaurant created it in nineteen fifty-nine. Nice one, Cruz."

"Aye, well. It's still a rip-off. Not an original pizza topping. Not like a meat feast. Or even better, a meat feast with a crust filled with piping hot mozzarella."

"I'm pretty sure Italians wouldn't regard that as authentic Italian cuisine either," Ben said. "I'm pretty sure the stuffed crust thing is a western invention, too."

"Ah, it's like dining with savages," Gillespie said, and he took another slice before settling down. "Next time I offer to pick up the pizzas, remind me not to bother."

"Maybe next time, you can get Indian," Ben suggested. "I love a good chicken tikka masala."

The comment raised a few laughs, and heads lowered once more as the team continued their research. Freya scrolled through the original case files from the Emma Blanch manslaughter case. Links had been provided to the deaths of her parents, and Freya began reading about her father.

"So Emma Blanch's dad died using machinery," Freya announced. "It doesn't say anything about drug abuse, but a toxicology report found his body to contain exceptionally high quantities of caffeine, and he was a diabetic."

"Could have been a Red Bull freak," Gillespie suggested.

"At fifty-three? With diabetes? That's suicide."

"It takes all sorts," Chapman added. "My uncle gets through the stuff like water. I mean, granted he loads it with vodka, but still."

"How old is he?"

"In his sixties," she replied. "Drinks it religiously. The whole family knows he's digging himself an early grave. But I guess it's like smoking. People know it's bad for them, but they still do it. It's a choice, right?"

"Getting back to the victim's father," Freya said, "Ben, I'm emailing you the report. Have Doctor Bell look into it, will you?"

"No problem," he replied. "What about the mother?"

"I'm looking at her now. Her death looks innocent enough, too. Died in her sleep. She suffered a stroke when her husband's body was discovered. Never fully recovered."

"Hence the need for Emma to nurse her."

"It looks that way. I'll send this to you, too. No harm in getting Doctor Bell's opinion."

"I've got something here," Cruz said. "I'm looking at Edward Pope's eBay account. The bayonet in question was purchased by a Donald Higgs. Lives down in Brixham."

"Where's that?" Gillespie asked.

"South coast," Freya said. "Devon."

"About as far away from bonnie Scotland as you can go," Ben added.

"I've never been further south than London, and that was bad enough," Gillespie said.

"Too much sunlight for you?" Ben asked.

"Aye," he said, accepting the friendly dig. "That and the crowds."

"Brixham is a little coastal town. London is a two-thousand-year-old, thriving city. There's literally no comparison," Jackie said.

"Well, take me to the Isle of Skye any day. I'd rather face the wrath of the North Sea than the English crowds."

Freya was about to argue that both destinations were on the North Atlantic, but decided not to antagonise the debate further. She looked up at Cruz. "Well?"

"I've never been to either of them, ma'am," he said.

"Not the bloody places. The bayonet. You were telling us about Donald Higgs."

"Right, yeah. Donald Higgs. Well, actually, not Donald Higgs. There's no record of him. But the house the parcel was addressed to is owned by none other than..." He drummed a short drumroll with his index fingers. "Cyrus Cross."

"Cross?" Gillespie said, voicing the surprise that every other member of the team was able to internalise.

"And Donald Higgs doesn't exist?" Freya asked.

"Well, there are people called Donald Higgs. But none that live in Brixham."

"When was the bayonet purchased?"

Cruz made a display of counting the days, squeezing one eye shut and extending a finger for each day.

"Nine days ago," he said, then looked at the screen again. "That's weird. It wasn't sent until three days ago, and Emma was killed two days ago."

"Not exactly exceptional customer service," Gillespie added. "He'll be getting a poor review for that."

"How much did it sell for?" Ben asked, peering over his laptop, clearly with an idea in mind.

"One hundred and fifty quid. Give or take," Cruz said.

Looking across to Freya, Ben wore the expression of a man who had the answers but couldn't put them all in the right order.

"I think we need Devon Police to open that parcel," he said, then returned his attention to Cruz. "Can you track it? Some delivery systems allow you to track the delivery."

"Yeah, it's at the local sorting office," Cruz said, then read the message on the screen. "Your parcel will be delivered today. Not going to be home? Just tell us where to leave it."

"Shame we can't redirect it to Lincolnshire."

"Well, if you're going to send one of us lot down there, you can count me out," Gillespie said. "I have zero interest in venturing further south than this place. Going anywhere near London gives me a nosebleed. Why are we bothering anyway? If it was sent before Emma Blanch was killed, it can't be the weapon. Am I missing something?"

"We're all missing something, Gillespie. Something isn't right. What Cruz said earlier about the timing doesn't sit right. But nobody is going down there. We don't have time," Freya said. She paced a few steps forward, then retraced her steps. "Gillespie. Contact Devon CID. I want that parcel intercepted before it's loaded onto a van, and if they can't stop the van in time, I want a uniform on the door of the house. Cruz, do we have a delivery time?"

"Afraid not," he replied. "But I can set an alert for updates. I'll get an automated text message whenever the parcel goes through to the next stage."

"Do it," Freya said.

"Has anyone looked into Edward Pope's parents?" Chapman asked.

The team exchanged glances.

"Are they of significance?" Freya said.

"Could be," she replied. "Died in a gas leak at the family home. They were both retired. Must have had Edward quite late in life."

"He was an only child, wasn't he?" Ben asked.

"Yes," Chapman said, as she read the report. "His mother was quite ill. Looks like she had some kind of skin issue, like eczema. Oh god..."

"What is it?" Freya asked, and the room fell silent, save for Gillespie munching on his fourth slice of pizza.

"She had to have dressings cleaned on her legs and feet every day. She had open wounds that secreted a kind of pus."

Gillespie's chewing stopped. A string of cheese hung from his mouth to the pizza slice, and he stared at Chapman in disgust.

"The husband was unable to take care of her properly, so a private carer was assigned to her," Chapman said.

"Emma Blanch?" Freya asked, and Chapman nodded. Freya stared across at Ben and summarised her theory in two concise sentences. "What if Emma Blanch was responsible for the deaths of her own parents *and* Edward Pope's? That would give Edward Pope a motive."

"Want me to arrange uniform support?" Ben asked, his hand already hovering over the desk phone.

Freya nodded slowly.

"Let's bring him back in. This time, he stays until it's over. One way or another."

The team jumped up from their seats, almost in unison, save for Gillespie, whose delay Freya presumed was due to the volume of pizza he'd eaten. Ben closed the lid of his laptop and shoved it to the back of his desk. Chapman straightened her files and loaded her bag with everything she would need, and Gillespie stretched, then tapped his belly. Jackie was already at the door, ready and waiting, and her face dropped when she caught Freya's stare.

"What is it, ma'am?" she said, and a few of the team must have sensed the tension and looked up.

"Not you, Gold," Freya said.

"What? Why not?"

"Not tonight. Go home to Charlie. He needs you."

"But the team–"

"Will be fine without you for one night. You've given enough for one day. Your poor old mum deserves a break too, don't you think?"

Jackie looked at each of the team individually, then returned her gaze to Freya.

"I haven't done anything–"

"No," Freya said. "You've done nothing wrong. You're a valuable member of the team. But the fact remains that you have a child, and while I have the support of half of DI Neanderthal's team as well, I might as well make the most of it and make sure at least some of us can function tomorrow without one of Gillespie's weird pumpkin coffees."

"Hey," he said, from behind her, but there was no offence taken, and if there was, right there and then, it was Jackie who Freya was looking out for.

"You'll keep me informed, won't you?" she asked nobody in particular. "I don't want to be left out."

"Chapman, make sure Jackie is kept fully abreast of all updates by text message. That's an order," Freya said in a friendly tone. She fixed Jackie's stare and held it. "Go home, Jackie. Go and be with your boy. I can't be with mine."

She held the door for Jackie Gold, who looked like a little lost child on her own. The door squealed closed again, and Freya searched Ben's expression for support.

"You did the right thing, Freya," Ben said.

"Aye. With a little one and all. The boy should take priority."

"I'm glad you see it like that, Gillespie," Freya said, as she reopened the door and stepped out into the corridor. She waited for it to squeal closed behind her. Just as she was about to step into the stairwell, she looked back and admired them all following in a line. "Oh, and by the way, if anybody ever repeats what I said about DI Standing, you'll be back on his team."

CHAPTER THIRTY-TWO

A LIVERIED POLICE CAR FOLLOWED CLOSE BEHIND BEN'S FORD. There was no need for sirens or lights, and given Pope's weak nature, Ben saw little need for any more than the two uniformed officers as backup. It was getting on for eleven p.m. and the roads were quiet. But unlike at the Blanch house, there was a distinct lack of fog.

He indicated and turned into Pope's street.

"Are you ready for this?" he asked Anna and Gillespie.

"I'm ready," she replied. "I'm surprised, but I'm ready."

"Surprised at what?"

"Oh, come on. He's the most unlikely candidate to be a murderer. He's a bit of a wet lettuce."

"Aye," Gillespie said from the rear seat. "But he's damaged goods. Folk will do anything when they've been through it. Wet lettuce or not. Do you remember the fella that Steve and I nicked a few months back for harassment? He was only a wee fella, like a walking Twiglet."

"You mean the guy that was stalking his ex-girlfriend?"

"Aye, that's him, yeah. Scrawny little shite with a nose like a pickaxe. Didn't think I'd have any trouble with him, but he clocked me right in the plums. Took three of us to pin him down, including DI Standing. And we all know how many pies he eats. It was like watching a hippo put cuffs on a wriggly worm."

"That's why we brought you along, Gillespie," Ben said, smiling at the bizarre analogies. "Pope ran before, and no doubt he'll run again, given the chance."

"I heard about that little episode. I didn't realise you were a rugby player, Anna. I might have to get you down to the club one of these weekends. You could show the lads a thing or two, from what I hear."

"I'll take a rain check on that one, Gillespie," Anna said politely, and she turned to offer him a smile of condolence. "Wouldn't want to show you up now, would I?"

"I want you round the back with one of the uniforms, Gillespie," Ben said. "We'll go through the front with the other."

"I heard he ran because he'd been up to no good on his laptop," Gillespie said with a childish laugh. "Been looking at things he shouldn't have, the mucky pup."

"Well, now we know that was a pack of lies, don't we? He panicked and ran, and needed an excuse for it. But we now know he's not as naive as he seems. No more sympathy votes with this one. We treat him just like any other."

"You mean slap him around a little?" Gillespie asked. "Show him who's boss."

"That might be how DI Standing does it, but I can assure you, if DI Bloom hears you've assaulted a suspect, you'll be up on a charge."

"Aye, right," Gillespie said, dejected. "I was just kidding. Anyway, we've got Anna on our side. We won't *need* to rough him up. He'll probably drop to his knees and surrender himself just at the sight of her."

Ben pulled the car to the side of the road, then waved for the driver of the liveried car to pull alongside. He lowered his window.

"Griffiths," Ben said, "good to see you."

"Now then," Griffiths said, by way of a greeting. He held onto the steering wheel but leaned across the PCSO beside him in the passenger seat to talk to Ben.

"Do me a favour. It's the house up there on the left with the green door. Drive past and turn round. The suspect has run before. If he does it again, we may need more than DC Nillson to catch him."

"No problem," Griffiths replied.

"What's your name, son?" Ben asked the PCSO.

"Taylor, sir," he replied.

"Don't call me sir. I'm DS Savage, this is DS Gillespie in the back, and DC Nillson," Ben said, by way of an introduction. "If you're in doubt, follow their lead. You'll be with DS Gillespie round the back of the house. Do what he tells you and you won't go far wrong."

"Will do," Taylor replied.

"Good," said Ben, and he looked back at Griffiths. "I want you parked facing this way in case he runs. You go ahead and turn around. I'll be right there. Don't wait for any instructions. We are go go go. Understood?"

Griffiths nodded, put the car in gear, and drove off. The few times Ben had worked with him in the past, he had been a solid uniform to have by his side, and an excellent driver. He watched as the marked car passed the house at normal speed, then slowed, turned, and began making their way back.

"Here we go," Ben said, engaging first gear. He pulled into the road, timing his approach to match Griffiths'. Both cars nosed into the side of the road at the same time, and five doors opened in unison. Taking the lead, Gillespie gave Taylor a tap on the shoulder, and led him into the side alley. Meanwhile, Griffiths made his way to the front door and banged on the wood three times.

The neighbour's curtain twitched and Ben glanced at Anna, who had also seen the movement.

"Edward Pope, are you in there?" Griffiths called out.

He slammed his hand against the wood three more times.

"Pope. Last chance."

Griffiths' radio crackled, and Taylor confirmed that he and Gillespie were in place. Griffiths looked at Ben, who nodded, giving him the all clear.

"Whatever's happening?" said the old man from next door. He was peering through the gap between the door and the door frame, the security chain in place.

"Close the door, sir," Anna shouted at him, and she jumped over the fence to make sure they didn't come out, just as the heel of Griffiths' boot connected with the green front door.

They were inside in seconds and ran into the hovel of a living room just as Gillespie and Taylor came in from the kitchen.

"Gillespie, Taylor, stay down here," Ben said. "Griffiths, you're with me."

He led the way upstairs, making no attempt to be quiet.

"Edward Pope?" he called out. "If you're here, make yourself known."

No reply came, and when they reached the landing, Ben nodded for Griffiths to check Pope's bedroom, while he lined himself up to kick the war room door open.

Wood splintered and the brass handle fell to the carpeted floor.

But there was no movement from inside. Cautiously, Ben moved forward. He took a large enough step that, should Pope have been hiding behind the door, he would have time to block any attack. But Pope was not hiding behind the door, and Griffiths called that he wasn't hiding in the bedroom either.

Edward Pope had been tied by his wrists to one of the eye bolts that was fixed to the ceiling. Even though his head hung forward limply, Ben could see the gash across his neck.

"Griffiths," Ben said quietly, and the uniformed officer stepped out of the bedroom.

"Ben?"

"He's here," Ben said, and he turned to face his colleague in the doorway, feeling the blood drain from his face. "Somebody beat us to it."

CHAPTER THIRTY-THREE

THE SINGLE LIVERIED CAR THAT BEN HAD ASSUMED TO BE sufficient for his needs had been joined by three other marked BMWs, an ambulance, two marked CSI vans, and Freya's little rental. Uniform had blocked the road off at either end and, on Ben's instruction, Cruz was managing the door to door effort with very little argument.

Freya ended the call she had taken and pocketed her phone before joining Ben, Gillespie, Anna, and Chapman at Ben's car. Of the two men, Ben was the larger in height but they were both big men, and as they leaned on the Ford's wing, the suspension lowered dramatically.

"That was Devon Police," Freya said, in answer to each of their unspoken questions. "They managed to intercept the package before it was passed to the driver."

Ben said nothing. He knew how Freya preferred to distribute information and waited patiently but attentively. Gillespie, on the other hand, demonstrated rather less patience.

"Well?" he said. "Do they have it?"

"It was addressed to a Donald Higgs, addressed to the right

house, and DCI Granger managed to get a warrant issued in time."

"And?" Gillespie said, unable to contain himself.

Freya stared at each of them in turn. The significance of the contents of that box would have a drastic effect on the investigation. She needed to know that each of them knew that.

"It was empty."

"Ah, the conniving little..." Gillespie began, and he pushed himself off the Ford, heading toward the house. "If he weren't dead already, I'd–"

"Arrest him, and take him in?" Freya said, cutting him short before the neighbours heard his outburst. She peered around at them all. "Whoever is behind this is still out there."

"But why kill Edward Pope?" Chapman said.

"He's covering his tracks," Ben said, the result of his quiet contemplation. "Gillespie, how long ago did you leave Garland's house?"

Shrugging, Gillespie checked his watch, which unsurprisingly was the type of digital watch a teenager might wear. "Three hours? Enough for the old bastard to do this, that's for sure."

"The neighbours seem to know everything that happens on this street," Ben said. "Anna, go and see what they can tell you. It'll be an hour at least before Cruz gets to them."

"Typical," Gillespie said, turning to watch Cruz and a uniform further along the street. "He's only started with the wrong neighbours. Look at him, the dozy–"

"Give him a break. He doesn't know," Ben said. "Gillespie, stay close to CSI. I want you inside as soon as you can. Chapman, you're quiet. What's up?"

"I'm just thinking," she said, and Freya took notice. When Chapman put her mind to it, she could be brilliant.

"Go on," she said, urging the young DC to voice her thoughts. "See if you're thinking what I'm thinking."

"Well, the money came through for the bayonet ten days ago,

but Pope didn't post the empty box until three days ago. Why was it empty? And why wait?"

"Because the knife was collected by hand by the killer, and the killer sent the empty package," Freya said.

"Which means Emma Blanch's murder was planned meticulously," Chapman added. "But it makes sense that Pope didn't kill Emma Blanch, and he didn't have the bayonet. Someone else does."

"Which means Pope was just a puppet. A bloody decoy, and a spent decoy at that," Gillespie said, his eyes revealing the processing of information.

"Garland, Cross, and Pope all had a motive to kill Emma," Freya said. "So, in light of recent events, the chances are that it was either Garland or Cross that killed Emma *and* Pope, and whoever it was knew that Emma used to care for Pope's parents."

"What's the significance of the bayonet?" Gillespie asked. "He could have used a kitchen knife."

"There *is* no significance. Forget about the bayonet," Ben said, and Freya nodded. "The bayonet was a device to, first of all, lead us to Pope, and then make sure we cleared him. He sold the item before Emma was killed. As far as we were concerned, Edward Pope was in the clear."

"But if the killer wanted him dead..." Gillespie said.

"Then Pope knew who he was," Ben finished. He looked at Freya. "It's your call, boss."

"Sorry, Ben. I need to pull rank here. Gillespie, forget about CSI. Have Cruz stay and take care of it. You're with me. We're going to Garland's house."

"Aye, right. About time that smarmy old bastard got what was coming to him," Gillespie said, by way of confirmation.

"I'll take Chapman," Ben said. "We'll hit Cyrus Cross. I'll call Will on the way to arrange warrants. If we're quick, uniform can deliver them."

"I'll call him now," Chapman said, retrieving her phone from her pocket. "I'll give him a full update."

"Wait for uniform to arrive before you go in," Freya said, while Chapman made her call. "Nobody goes in alone. I don't want any heroes."

"Sounds like you're speaking from experience, boss," Gillespie said, and his smile faded with Freya's scowl.

"One day, I'll tell you about it," she replied. "If you live long enough, that is."

"Ben, have you checked your emails?" Chapman called out. She walked back to them holding her phone. "Have you seen the one from the lab?"

"No," Ben said, as he pulled his phone from his jacket.

"They've identified the footprints as being a direct match to Jason Cross. They used a sample print they found in some cement inside the bed and breakfast."

"Boots," Gillespie announced. "I knew it. I knew there was something."

"What?" Freya asked, and the team all waited for Gillespie to process his thoughts.

"Jason Cross," he said. "When I found him, he was burned beyond recognition. I mean he–"

"Okay, okay," Freya said. "What's your point?"

"Aye, well. He had clothes on, all stuck to him and that, but he wasn't wearing any boots. I figured they'd melted or something. I don't know."

"For god's sake, Gillespie," Ben said. "Were you going to tell us that?"

"It doesn't matter," Freya said. "There's nothing we could have done with the information until now. If Jason Cross in fact did not have any boots on when Gillespie found him–"

"Which he didn't, eh. To be clear," Gillespie added.

"Then whoever did this may have taken his boots."

"A dead man's boots. Not something I'd like to be walking around in," Gillespie muttered under his breath.

"Something tells me this wasn't a fashion statement," Freya said gravely. "It was a decoy. Just like the empty box. They wanted us to consider Jason as a suspect."

"They also processed the glove that Cruz found," Chapman said. "It's full of Cyrus Cross' DNA."

"Cyrus Cross? What about the solution?" Freya said, and she faced Pope's house one last time. "Tell me it's a match."

"Bisley gun oil," Chapman said. "It's a perfect match."

The weight of four lives hung on Freya's shoulders, but the incessant ache she had been suffering seemed to fade with the news.

"Forget Alex Garland, Gillespie," Freya said, as she turned to face her team. "We're going to get Cyrus Cross. In fact, we're all going to get him."

CHAPTER THIRTY-FOUR

THE CONVOY OF CARS BEHIND FREYA'S RENTAL CONSISTED OF Ben in his Ford with Chapman, two liveried BMW estates, and a transport van. Once again, they kept the blue lights off and approached Wasps Nest in silence.

"If there's one thing I can't stand, it's bloody liars," Gillespie said from the back seat. "And to think, the old bastard even torched his son."

"We don't know that yet," Freya said. "Anna, what did the neighbours have to say?"

"They didn't see a thing," she replied. "Which is a bit odd, seeing as they've poked their noses in both times we've been there."

"Do you believe them?"

"I do. They're a sweet old couple. If anyone got into Pope's house, it was through the back door."

"Aye, but I can't see old man Cross sneaking around in a bala-clava, can you?" Gillespie said.

"Perhaps he didn't need to sneak," Freya said. "Perhaps he simply knocked on the door and Pope let him in."

"Eh?" Gillespie replied.

They were approaching the house, so Freya slowed to let Ben draw up alongside. The fields around them were in total darkness, and in contrast to the residential street where Pope had lived, a blanket of fog had rolled in off the fens.

"You take Chapman and two uniforms round the back," she called out. "I'll go in through the front. Nice and quick. No fuss. Let's get him down to the station as quick as we can. When you hear the front door go, you move in, okay?"

"No problem," he called back. "I'll follow you."

Using the hill to get the car moving, Freya found second gear and kept the revs low. She turned into Cyrus Cross' property, leaving room for the convoy behind them. Ben had pulled up beside her and was out of the car before Freya had even unfastened her seat belt. He waved for uniform to follow, and then led his trio around to the back door.

Gillespie, with his broad shoulders and long, heavy jacket, seemed to amble to the front door, yet with his long strides, he covered just as much distance as Freya in her smart yet impractical skirt suit and high boots. He was joined by two uniforms.

"You knock it down," Gillespie whispered. "Then stand back, sonny."

The uniform turned to his colleague, who handed him the enforcer – a red, steel ram with handles at either end. The officer grunted slightly, then looked up at Gillespie, who in turn glanced back at Freya, who then gave him the nod.

He swung the enforcer back and aimed just below the door handle. The wood splintered with ease and was sent flying back into the wall. A picture frame fell and crashed to the floor, and Gillespie was in there, clambering over the broken door before the enforcer had even completed its return swing.

"Police," he called out, slamming his hand onto the light switches as he passed them. He reached the end of the hallway, where the door to the lounge was, and glanced back at Freya, who held up one finger for him to wait. She peered through the front window, squinting to see clearly, and she thought she saw movement inside.

She gave him the nod.

There was no need for the enforcer on the internal door. Gillespie's boot did the work with half the effort but twice the bravado.

"Police, nobody move," he called out.

And nobody did move, except for Ben, Chapman, and the uniform who had all entered from the kitchen.

"Where is he?" Gillespie said.

"Ben, you check the garage. Gillespie, Anna, take the bedrooms and bathroom."

Freya followed Ben out to the back of the house, where he found the rear access to the garage. With much less need for bravado, Ben applied his weight to the door in what seemed like no more than a shove, and the wood cracked. No light spilt onto the concrete hardstanding, only gloom. Ben searched inside, then turned to the uniform behind Freya.

"Torch," he said, and held out his hand, taking the small pocket Maglite from the officer.

He turned the bezel to illuminate the scene inside, holding one hand up to keep Freya out of harm's way. From where she was standing, his face was silhouetted against the low clouds. And in that moment, all the strength and resilience she adored in him failed, and his features slumped. He closed his eyes in defeat.

"Ben?" Freya said quietly, but with enough authority that he could no longer keep her from harm's way.

He let his head fall backwards, and exhaled audibly through his nostrils.

She took a single step forward and peered inside, taking the torch from Ben's hand that was now hanging by his side.

Cyrus Cross was kneeling on the concrete floor inside the garage, his head hanging forward and only the structure of his skeleton keeping his body from tumbling. He was semi-dressed, as if the perpetrator had knocked on his door late at night, and taken him by surprise.

"We're too late," Ben whispered.

But then she saw it. Something dark on Cyrus' face. She stepped inside further, flashing the torch around into the dark spaces to make sure the killer wasn't waiting to jump out.

"Ben?" she said, as she crouched by Cyrus' side. "You need to see this."

He joined her, though he was clearly annoyed they had been led along another garden path. "What is it?" he said, when he saw what Freya was referring to. A piece of leather had been stuffed into Cyrus' mouth. "Is that..."

"The other glove," Freya said, finishing the sentence for him.

She stood and caught the attention of the uniformed officer.

"You, what's your name?"

"PCSO Taylor, ma'am," he replied, and looked to Ben for support.

"Have this place locked down. Get everyone out until CSI get here."

She turned back to Ben but said nothing, leaving the officer a little dumbfounded and not knowing where to start.

"Get Griffiths," Ben advised the PCSO. "He'll help you."

"Where shall I say you're going?" the PCSO replied.

Ben stopped, took one look at Freya, and they both nodded.

"We're going to find the bastard who did this," he said, and the weary features that had dropped only moments before now drew taut. "And we're going to put a stop to him."

CHAPTER THIRTY-FIVE

"Gillespie, Chapman, on me," Freya called, as she walked into the centre of the broad driveway. She started pointing at the uniformed officers who were being ushered from the building by Taylor and Griffiths. "You, you, you, and you, grab a car, any car. You're with me. Who's driving the meat wagon?"

"That's me," a voice called from behind the melee of uniforms that loitered in the mist. A tall uniform in a bright high-vis jacket.

"You too," she said. "Let's go. Follow me." She strode over to her car, searching for her keys and thinking the plan through as she walked. "Chapman, call DCI Granger, bring him up to speed. And get CSI on site. I want the place brushed, scanned, photographed, and whatever else they need to do. And have that lump of meat in the garage taken away."

She opened her car door and climbed inside, firing up the engine to get the heater going.

"I've got Chapman," Ben called. "We'll follow you."

Without replying, Freya slammed her door just as Gillespie was climbing into the passenger seat. "Let's go," he said, pulling on his belt, and Freya reversed out onto the road, quietly pleased he hadn't cracked a joke or tried in any way, shape, or form to make the situation any worse than it already was.

The fog was now thick. Visibility could be measured in feet, and with it came the cold. Gillespie blew into his cupped hands, then rubbed them together.

"It's a brutal night, boss," he said, which Freya deemed to be his attempt at starting a normal conversation. But she was in no mood for chit-chat. Possibilities ran through her mind, interweaving, spiralling out of control, dancing like bright, glowing ribbons against the dark sky. "What do you think we'll find?"

She checked in the rear-view mirror and saw the dim glow of headlights behind her somewhere, but the distance was hard to tell. Garland's house was just a mile away, and at the back of those spiralling and dancing thoughts, her own advice was the constant. Wait for the backup. Wait for Ben to arrive.

She had Gillespie with her, which added some comfort. Aside from Ben, he was the most capable of handling himself. Of the two men, it was as if Ben had won the toss in nearly every area. He was taller than Gillespie, broader, smarter, faster, friendlier, more professional, and dare she even think it, more handsome. Yet, in a pang of realism, she considered Ben to win against any man when measured for those attributes and traits.

And then there was Martin, or Mark, or whatever his name was.

"Boss?" Gillespie said, and she glanced across at him.

"Mm?"

"Are you okay? You haven't said a word to me."

"What did you say?" she asked.

"I asked what you thought about the glove."

"Which glove?"

"Well, both of them. The one Cruz found, and the one in Cross' mouth. He's bloody taunting us, boss, the sly bastard."

"Who?"

"Eh?"

"Who's taunting us, Gillespie? Sorry, I'm a little distracted."

"Distracted? It's one a.m., boss. You've been at this all day. Shall I drive?"

"No," she said, or snapped, or mumbled, or something. "No, we're nearly there. Listen, I can't help but think we've been led up the garden path here. I'm not sure exactly what we'll find."

"Aye, boss. Round the houses and back again. We should have just nicked the bastard and let him fester in a cell. To hell with rights. Some bastards don't deserve rights."

He was right. It had been a long day, and the distractions were coming thick and fast at a time when her focus and attention were needed the most. Greg waited in the shadows of her mind with Billy standing before him, his arms draped over the boy's shoulders. The shadows moved like clouds, and every so often, his sneering face would be revealed, while Billy cried. A moment later and she would see Greg in another light entirely. In the throes of ecstasy with his back arched and her, the bitch, straddling him, climaxing together, and turning to face Freya as they caught their breath in a lover's embrace.

"Boss?"

"Mm?"

"You missed it. It was back there, I think."

"Are you sure?" she said, suddenly both embarrassed and confused.

"Aye, look," he said, leaning forward to peer into the side mirror. "They're going in without us. Are you sure you're up for this, boss? I mean, I'm sure we can handle it–"

"I'm up for it, Gillespie," she said, as she came to a stop, crunched the gearbox into reverse, and made the turn. "Like you said, it's been a long night, and all I get is bloody questions. So don't you dare ever accuse me of not being able to do my job."

She fought with the clutch and the gears in her haste.

"Tell me," he said calmly, as she found first gear, and he

applied the handbrake, keeping his hand there so Freya couldn't drive off.

"Gillespie, what the bloody hell–"

"Tell me what happened. I know something happened to you. The whole station knows something happened to you. But nobody knows what it was. Talk to me."

"Gillespie, now is not–"

"Talk to me, boss. What was it? A case? Illness? I won't say anything."

"Gillespie–"

But he held the handbrake fast.

"If I let you go into that house like this, I'd be negligent. Aye, you might be my boss right now, but I'm also a human being, just like you. We all feel something. We all have our stories. Me especially, come to think of it."

She glanced ahead at the dark road. A dim glow came from Garland's driveway.

"They're not going anywhere. We've got a minute. Get your head together. Talk to me."

"What is this, some kind of truth bonding thing?"

"No, it's about not bottling things up. It's about clearing your mind. You want to hear my story?" he said. "Bullet points, right?"

She laughed. "Right."

"Parents didn't want me. I was sent to a home. I was bullied and beaten by the other kids. So I stole, I cheated, I fought, won some, lost some, and I did some things I'm not too proud of to people who deserved better. I was destined to become another statistic, boss. That's when I found the force. That's why I came to be here. I found the force, but Glasgow was too painful for me. I have a new family now, aye. I'm happy now, believe it or not. I got through it. But I still think of those days, boss. I think of them whenever I get knocked down, because it's only me that gets me back up on my feet."

"You've been through it, haven't you?"

"People do crazy things when they're traumatised, right? I said that from experience. It wasn't some do-goody-good claptrap."

She nodded.

"Your turn," he said. "We've got about thirty seconds before Ben calls, so do try to keep to bullet points."

She laughed again, this time a little harder and with more sincerity.

"There was a serial killer in London. I was glory hunting. I was stupid and went after him alone. He caught me and held me captive for three days. I was found, luckily, and we saved a girl's life. But it left my own life in tatters. I was in tatters, if we're being honest. My husband cheated on me shortly afterwards. I had to make the choice of staying but never truly being content with him, or leaving him and his son, and starting again."

"You started again."

"Lincolnshire seemed as good a place as any to recuperate."

"And the boy?"

"Billy? Now I'm not allowed to see him."

Gillespie let go of the handbrake and peered out of the window.

"What happened?" he asked. "The three days. Can you talk about it?"

"No," she said softly.

"If you want to, just say. I know some pretty good techniques from when I had counselling."

"That's all behind me now. Memories I don't want or need."

"It's okay, boss."

"It's not about the ordeal. Not for me, anyway. It used to be. Honestly, it used to be. But now it's about finding a normal. Now it's about the time I *do* have. The future I *can* have. I hoped Billy would be a part of it. What happened to me wasn't his fault. What his father did wasn't his fault either. So why should he suffer? Why shouldn't he get to enjoy me? I'm the closest thing he has to a mum. And I walked away when he needed me the most."

"You're afraid he thinks you don't want him anymore?"

She nodded, and Gillespie silenced for a moment, then exhaled audibly.

"I thought that too," he said, and she looked across at him. "My parents, I mean. I thought they abandoned me. I found them a few years back. Looked them up on the internet, took some leave, and went back up there. I watched them for a few days, sleeping in my car. I felt like one of those private detectives you see on the TV, you know? Dropping nutshells out the window. Part of me wanted to kick the door in and tell them what I thought. I was so full of hate, you know? Like I was possessed by it. I even followed my pa to the pub and stood a few feet from him at the bar."

"No?"

"Aye, I did. Just so I could hear his voice, so I could know him."

"That's wonderful. Did you talk to him?"

He shook his head.

"He was there a while when another lad walked in. He stood beside my pa and bought him a beer."

Freya had an idea of what he was going to say next, and steeled herself against the reality of Billy's future.

"He called him Dad," Gillespie said, his voice soft and somehow vulnerable. "It was my brother. They had another kid."

"You should have said something."

"Ah. I didn't see the point. I know where they are now. I've got that choice. The point is, boss, that I went there to try make myself happy. But you know what? I realised I am happy, and they are, too. I used to think they were bastards. I had this image of them, you know? In my head. Scumbags. But they weren't. They were nice. Normal people. It gave me a choice. I know that, whenever I want, I can go to them. I have that choice, that power. That's enough for me right now. That's all that matters."

"If that's supposed to make me feel better, Gillespie, about my relationship with Billy, you're way off the mark."

"Really?" he said. "It didn't help?"

She smiled at him, stiff-lipped.

"It did help. Thank you," she said. "I see a different side to you. You're alright."

"Ah, don't pay too much attention to how loud and obnoxious I am, boss. I'm just a bloke," he said with a laugh, then softened. "I won't say anything. About what happened to you, I mean."

"That's because only one other person knows what happened to me, Gillespie," she replied, slipping the car into first gear with ease now that her nerves and anger had abated. "His name is James Marley and he's currently on remand awaiting trial for the murders of five young women."

CHAPTER THIRTY-SIX

"Where did you get to?" Ben asked, when he saw Freya climbing from her car. The frown she had worn for most of the day had gone, and when she spoke, her voice had lost the bitter edge it had carried.

It was Ben's first visit to Garland's house, and he was still none the wiser as to what the place looked like. The house and grounds were shades of blacks and greys, and the mist left a layer of dew on his skin.

"It's been a long night," she said. "Who have we got where?"

"Uniforms are covering the rear and side entrances," he said, pointing to either side of the huge house. "Griffiths has the key, so I kept him out front."

"The key?" Freya said, then gave a little grin when she saw the silhouette of Griffiths with the enforcer hanging from one hand. "It's a skeleton key," Ben explained. "Opens all kinds of doors."

"He'll know we're coming," Freya said. "Be ready for anything."

Ben was ready. Despite being the one to discover both Pope and Cross in the last few hours, he was ready.

"Are you okay?" Ben asked. "Gillespie didn't drive you up the wall, did he? I know it was only a five-minute drive, but that's long enough for him to get under your skin."

"He's okay," Freya said. "I had a little chat with him. There's more to him than meets the eye, you know."

"Aside from being an arrogant prick?" Ben said, and Freya actually laughed.

"There's a reason he is the way he is. I'm learning to like him."

"Wow, in one car journey, he managed to convince you he's okay?"

"Let's just say that beneath that wild and complex exterior is the beating heart of a red-blooded male just finding his way, just like the rest of us," she said. "Shall we get this over with? I plan on leaving Garland to rot in a cell while I'm sleeping for a hundred years."

"I'm sure Martin would enjoy that," Ben said, and felt her sharp elbows in his ribs. It was playful, but she was back, and that pleased him.

"Griffiths, do your stuff," Freya said as they approached the waiting team. She checked her watch. "Chapman, alert the teams. Entry in exactly thirty seconds from now. Gillespie, stay with us. I want you up the stairs as soon as Griffiths breaks through. Ben, you take the downstairs."

They huddled on the broad top step, and Freya counted down in a hushed whisper.

"Four, three, two," she said, then gave Griffiths the nod.

The enforcer landed square against the door plate, and the wide door slammed back against the wall, shattering the two narrow glass inserts.

"Police," Gillespie, shouted, as he entered the house. He took the stairs two at a time, calling out as he ran, "Garland?"

"Griffiths, up the stairs," Freya said, as he discarded the enforcer to the ground. Ben ran past him, getting his bearings in the house. He kicked through the first door he came to and found a lounge, or a dining room; it was hard to tell being void of furniture. Freya entered behind him.

"Clear," he called out, and approached another internal door, as the team came into the house from the rear and side doors. Ben burst through, scanning his surroundings fast to make sure Garland wouldn't jump out in some kind of crazed final act, but again, the room was empty. Faded squares on the wall marked the spots where pictures had once hung, and the once-polished wooden floor only shone in those places where furniture had been.

All around the house, voices announced rooms were clear, and as Ben entered the last of the downstairs rooms, his gut tightened with the thought of what he might find.

"You okay?" Freya asked, when she saw him holding the door handle.

He nodded.

"It's been a long night," he said, mirroring her earlier excuse.

"Want me to do it?"

He laughed once, but it wasn't really a laugh, then entered. The room was an old office. Ben imagined it had once been furnished with chesterfields, bookcases, and perhaps a silver tray with a glass decanter.

But more importantly, it was empty, and a small part of Ben was thankful for not having to witness the grim sight of another body.

"Boss?" Gillespie called out from upstairs. "You might want to see this."

Together, Freya and Ben ran to the stairs and looked up, finding Gillespie standing at the top holding something.

"The place is empty. His bag is gone. His van isn't here. He's done a runner," Gillespie said. "But he left this. Must have dropped it in his rush to get out."

Ben climbed the wide stairs beside Freya. Three uniforms

looked on, and Gillespie descended a few steps and held up a photo in a gloved hand.

"It's Emma," she said, glancing at Ben briefly before studying the photo. She had seen it before somewhere, although she couldn't remember where. The portrait photo had been taken by a professional photographer, that much was clear. The plain, grey background, the lighting, even the pose screamed professional. It wasn't a snap taken on somebody's phone or against a wall.

"What is it?" Ben asked.

"Nothing," she replied, unable to remember where she had seen the photo. She pulled herself away from the image and huffed in defeat. "We need to find Alex Garland."

"Chapman," Ben said, kicking into gear. "Check with traffic to see if we can get him on ANPR. His vehicle details are in the notes. Gillespie—"

"Wait," Freya said, and she sat on the top step to think. She massaged her temple with the tips of her index fingers, and gave a deep sigh. "Get the alert out to traffic. Get in touch with his bank. I want to know when and where he used his bank card last. Lastly, get a uniform to watch this place. Two, if possible. I don't want anyone left alone. When you've done that, go home."

"Freya, we can find him—"

"I said go home, Ben. Everyone. Go home. It's one a.m. and he's one step ahead of us. I'll talk to Granger in the morning. It was my fault we hit Pope first. It was me that let Garland walk. I'll take the rap for it."

Ben stared at her, but she refused to make eye contact, and said nothing until she reached the bottom of the stairs.

"Two men died today. That's on me. I can't ask anything else of you. Not until you're all rested," she said. She turned back to look up at them. "Tomorrow, we make a new plan. Tomorrow, we find him."

CHAPTER THIRTY-SEVEN

It was the morning, of that Freya was sure. But it felt like she had only just closed her eyes. The winter sun was notoriously lazy, so when she saw the light shining through the gap in her curtains, alarm bells rang somewhere in her subconscious. She stood, and let the duvet fall to the floor as she held onto the window ledge for balance. Her phone stated that she had five missed calls and a large number of messages.

She despised cold toilet seats, and groaned when she sat down. But the shock of the cold on her backside awoke memories from the previous night. Pope. Cross. The flashing, blue lights. Garland's empty house. And, oddly, her chat with Gillespie. Her dressing gown hung from the bathroom door. Every morning, she cursed having to walk to the bathroom to find it, and then an hour later, she would hang it there again to shower, and so restarted the cycle.

She had promised herself she wouldn't rise to Greg's comments. That she would remain professional and mature. Yet when she checked her phone, and the blurred text came into focus, she was seething.

I've asked her to marry me. Thought you should know.

Suddenly, all the bitterness and spiteful comments over the past few days made sense.

She dialled his number before she'd given it thought, then regretted the move almost instantly. The dial tone began, by which time it was too late to stop. He'd see her missed call and sense her hesitancy. She took a breath and pulled back the curtain to see if she could spot Ben's car outside his house. But the fog was still clinging to the damp ground.

"Freya," Greg said. It was the first time she had heard his voice since she had walked out. He had been begging then, his voice high with emotion, and he had offered himself all kinds of punishment as recompense for his infidelity. "How are you?"

Now his voice was deep with shame and guilt. But, she thought, at least he had the gumption to answer her call.

"Is that what you want, Greg?" she asked, ignoring his question, which she was sure had only been said out of habit or politeness anyway.

"It's what we both want."

"So she said yes, then," Freya said, and a little part of her heart died.

Greg said nothing.

"She did say yes, didn't she?"

"Not yet," he replied. "She said she wants some time to think about it."

"Naturally," Freya said, unable to stop herself thinking how the woman had broken their marriage and owed Greg at least some kind of assurance.

"We're spending Christmas at her mum's place. I'm hopeful I'll get an answer while we're away."

"That'll be a nice present for you," Freya said, then thought about what he had said. "Wait. You're taking Billy to her family's house for Christmas?"

"Well, I can't leave him here on his own, can I?"

"Does he know?"

"Know what?"

"Greg, does he know about you and…" She had to refrain from the insults. She wouldn't lower herself to his level of arguing. "Her?" she said finally.

"Well, I guess so. We haven't really said anything."

"Greg, he's not stupid."

"He thinks we're just friends."

"Does she stay over?" Freya asked, aware of the resentment in her tone and unable to shake the image of the bitch lying where she used to sleep. "Of course she stays over. What do you think that's going to do to him?"

"He's fine, Freya. Relax."

"He's impressionable is what he is."

"He's *my* son is what he is," Greg said, and the inference to Freya's inability to claim maternal, or any kind of parental, governance was clear in both choice of words and tone.

She waited a while, to digest the statement with several parched swallows.

"I raised him," she said, and hated the weakness in her voice.

"I know."

"I raised him and fed him, and held him when he cried, and…" She stopped, unable to list all the things she had done, said, and felt over the years that had helped her form what she had once thought was an unbreakable bond with the boy.

"And you walked out," Greg said finally.

"That's not fair. Look at what you did."

"Let's face it, Freya, you were checked out long before you physically left. Where were you? Eh? In the six months before you left, you were nothing but a shell."

"How dare you? I was recovering from being abducted."

"That's what you say."

"What? Are you serious?"

"It's funny how you can go back to work as easy as that, yet you couldn't hold a two-minute conversation with me."

"It wasn't easy. I had to do it."

"And you're still there. What is it, three months now?"

"Four."

"Right. How come we haven't heard from you? How come you don't answer my messages?"

"I've been…" Freya said softly, but her voice trailed away as she realised her own selfishness.

"How come the first time we heard from you in four months is when you want something?"

"I just wanted to see him."

"Yeah, you want."

"Greg, don't make this about us. I want to see Billy. For him and for me."

"He's over you."

It was as if somebody had thrust a blade deep into her heart. A long knife. Like a bayonet, a World War Two Landing Service bayonet, number seven, mark two, with a nick two-thirds of the way down the blade.

"Don't," she said. "Don't say that."

"I tried to make it easy for you, Freya."

"Don't do this, Greg."

"I messaged you, called you, and even considered coming up to find you."

"Greg, no."

"But you know what I thought?" he said. "Why should I? Why should I put myself out for you? Why shouldn't I see her? Why shouldn't I be happy?"

"Greg, I need to see him. I need to see Billy."

"You know what I realised? After all those unanswered messages and calls?"

"Please."

"I realised that we don't need you. I don't need you. Billy doesn't need you."

"No," she said, her voice close to a scream.

A silence ensued, and she could almost hear the pleasure on his breath rasping against the phone.

"You're not welcome, Freya. It's taken four months to get my boy back. To stop him crying himself to sleep. To convince him that none of this is his fault, that he did nothing wrong."

"You didn't blame *me*?"

"I told him the truth," Greg said. "I told him how your job is more important than anything, including us."

"How could you do that to him?"

"He needs to know the truth about you, Freya. I wished I had known all those years ago."

"He's just a boy. Telling him that could mess him up."

"Not as much as leaving us would," Greg replied.

He waited for Freya to say something, to stoop to the next level down. She had already ventured further than she had panned. She had already shown how weak she was, and worst of all, had shown emotion.

She said nothing.

"Have a nice Christmas, Freya. Enjoy your life up there. I won't be sending you an invite to the wedding."

He ended the call and Freya was left holding the phone, staring out into the fields.

She was still staring two minutes later when her phone rang again. She answered it, ready for another barrage of insults and heartbreak.

"I can't do it anymore," she said.

"Do what?"

"This. You win," she said weakly.

"Win what?"

"Ben?"

"Who did you think it was?"

She inhaled, long and slow, and blinked away her tears, as she held the phone away to clear her throat of emotion.

"Ah," she said, testing her voice. "Nobody. I was just... It doesn't matter."

"Are you coming in today?" he asked. "It's going to be the big one."

"I'm sorry... I, erm–"

"You okay?" he asked.

"I was up late."

"Billy?" Ben said, needing to add nothing else to give context.

"Yeah."

"Want to talk?"

"Not really. I'm all talked out, if I'm honest. Is everyone else in?"

"They're in, but not exactly bright-eyed. Except Jackie, that is. She's the only one who had a decent night's sleep, even though Charlie had her up all night..." He stopped. "Sorry. I guess you don't want to hear about Charlie right now."

"It's okay," she said. "Life goes on. I'm glad he's okay. Listen, give me half an hour to an hour. I need to get ready. If Granger says anything–"

"I'll handle it."

"Thanks, Ben," she said.

"I've got Cruz typing up a report on his door knocking exercise. Chapman and Anna are researching Garland's family to see if he has any allies close by. Gillespie is currently on a coffee run."

"I'm sure he'll love that."

"It'll keep him out of mischief for a while."

"Good," Freya said, as she ventured down the stairs. "I'm going to go to the Blanch house to see if we missed anything. I'll be in later."

"Sure you're okay?"

"I'll see you later, Ben," she said.

She ended the call as she entered the kitchen and flicked on the kettle. A shadow passed by her window, followed closely by a knock on her door.

She sighed for the fourth time in under ten minutes.

The dark shape could be seen through the frosted glass. He was tall, broad, and waited patiently, just as Ben would have. She glanced at her phone. Ben had definitely been in the incident room; she had even heard the door slamming in the background.

Clutching her dressing gown by the collar, she opened the door.

"There she is," he said. "Sleeping beauty."

"Martin?"

CHAPTER THIRTY-EIGHT

HE SMILED THAT DEVILISH GRIN. IF HE HAD BEEN A CARTOON, Freya could have sworn that a bright, gleaming sparkle would have flashed from his teeth, such was the heroic manner of his pose. If the cold toilet seat hadn't woken Freya up, the mere sight of him, along with the freezing wind that stormed across the fields, would have.

But he stood there like a statue, as if nothing could touch him, or break him. A picture of confidence.

"You didn't reply," he said sheepishly. "I, erm…"

"You wondered why? You wondered if somehow you had messed things up, and you thought maybe a visit in person at seven o'clock in the morning would somehow spark some romance?"

"Well, to be honest, it's actually eight-thirty, and I was less concerned about the romance part for the time being."

"And you were doing so well," she said, with a pitiful expression. She leaned against the door frame and closed her eyes, while the decisions battled one another in her mind.

"I would have left it until later, but well… See, I was just on my way to work. I figured I'd just see if you were around."

"And you saw my car and thought you'd try your luck, because you want your answer right now? It's Christmas and you've been invited out to a few parties, and well, let's face it, you need to know if you're single or not so that when you sidle up to the office slut, you know if you should feel guilty or not. I suppose I should consider myself grateful. Most men wouldn't have cared. At least you had the decency to consider my feelings, at the cost of forcing an answer from me. Am I right, Martin?"

"It's Mark," he said, a look of sheer disappointment spread across his face. He held out an envelope with her name printed in neat capital letters. "And no, you're entirely wrong. I have some family nearby. In Woodhall Spa. They're doing a Christmas lunch, and well, being on your own and all…" His voice dropped a few decibels to a disappointed murmur. "But I guess it doesn't matter now. You've clearly got your own issues to get through, your own life to lead. Stupid, really. Fortune favours the brave. That's what I told myself. I was close to turning around at least three times. You take care now, Freya Bloom."

He turned his back on her and walked toward the cars parked on the lane. Freya watched him. He didn't turn. He didn't say anything spiteful. He just walked to his car, opened the door, and…

"Wait," she said, and he stopped with one leg inside the car. He no longer wore his carefree look, and his shoulders hung low as if they carried a weight. Nor did he gaze at Freya with anticipation or joy. "I've just been through a divorce. We were arguing. Just then, we…"

She stepped out in the freezing cold, and the wind lapped at her pyjama bottoms as she walked. She stopped beside his car, and spoke to him across the roof, just as she had with Ben so many times.

"I was rude," she said. "You don't deserve it. I should have responded to your messages. It's something I need to work on, it seems."

He nodded, but remained standing where he was.

"I need to sort a few things out. My head. It's..." She paused again, and sighed. "It's not fair on you. Plus, I'm in the middle of a significant investigation."

There it was. The excuse she had used with Greg so many times before. The chisel she nestled in the cracks of every relationship she had ever had.

"I'm not a bad bloke," he said. "Maybe look me up when..."

His voice trailed away. It was all Freya could do to watch him climb into his car and start the engine. He lowered the window and gestured at the envelope in her hands.

"The offer still stands. If you want some company on Christmas Day."

"Then I'll phone the Samaritans," she answered, sure that he was about to declare how he'd love to escort her to the family dinner.

He nodded, disappointment written across his face. He pulled away slowly and was lost to the fog in less than a minute.

She sighed and watched him leave. It could never work. Not with her head where it was at. She heard some distant memory of Ben's voice.

"Swipe left and carry on," it said. But there would be no more swiping in any direction for Freya.

CHAPTER THIRTY-NINE

GILLESPIE ARRIVED IN THE INCIDENT ROOM IN A FAR LESS amateur-dramatics style than he had previously, and his claim to hold the elixir of coffees was held at bay. The team worked in silence for the most part.

"How's Charlie?" Ben asked, assuming the role of team lead in Freya's absence.

"He's okay. He's getting used to it now," Jackie replied. "There's some kind of bug going around. You know what kids are like. They spend more time sick than healthy. I can't remember the last photo I saw of him when he didn't have snot running down his face. Poor kid."

"My dad used to make us sweat it out," Ben said. "He'd force us to go to bed fully dressed, and then tuck the blankets in so tight we couldn't move. Then he'd sit in the corner of the room to make sure we didn't try and get up."

"Sounds like the bloody Victorian days, Ben," Gillespie said. "I can see you now, standing in front of your pa with your wee bowl and spoon. Please, Pa, I want some more." Gillespie did his best impression of Oliver, but few laughed.

"No, my dad's just set in his ways," Ben said. "He didn't know any better."

"Yeah, but blankets?" Jackie said. "Didn't you have a duvet?"

"No, we had itchy blankets and old sheets," Ben said. "He still uses them, I think."

"Aye, we had that, too. Sheet, blanket, blanket, sheet," Gillespie explained, gesturing the sandwich of layers as he spoke. "Bloody awful, if you ask me. We had to make our own beds, too."

"Sounds like it was *you* that grew up in the Victorian days, Gillespie," Jackie said.

"Aye, well. It did me no harm. Taught me a few things."

"Oh yeah?" Jackie said, as she checked her phone for messages, which Ben presumed would be from her mother who was caring for Charlie. "And what's that then? What did your parents teach you? Listen up, everyone. Gillespie is going to share some wisdom."

The spotlight was on Gillespie. Normally, he would have thrived in the limelight. But for some reason, he faltered.

"Aye, well..." he said, seeming downhearted.

"You said you had a lesson for us," Jackie said, winding him up just as he would have wound her up, given the opportunity.

Gillespie stared at each of them in turn – Jackie, Cruz, Anna, Chapman, and then Ben.

"Where's Bloom?" said a voice from Ben's right. It was Steve Standing, who had ventured down from his end of the office; his interruption was less innocent than it seemed, and designed to protect Gillespie.

"She's heading to the crime scene," Ben said.

"On her own?" Standing asked.

That was when Ben saw a different side to Standing.

"Maybe somebody ought to meet her there?" he said, and he gave Ben a knowing look. Only a handful of the team knew what Freya had been through in the James Marley investigation. Standing was one of them, and he was right.

Nodding his agreement, Ben stood and pulled on his jacket. "You're right, Steve. Cheers. Anna, Chapman, Cruz, carry on with Garland. Build a network of everyone he knows, friends and family. And if his bank card—"

"We'll call you," Anna said, professional as ever.

"Jackie, seeing as you had the most sleep last night, I want you to drop in on Jason Cross. See if there's been any change in his condition. When you're done, meet with Emma Blanch's brother. He wants to see his sister," Ben said. "Though I cannot for the life of me think why. Just remember, as far as he's concerned, she's the victim, okay?"

"Got it, Ben," Jackie replied, and reached for her coat. "I'll walk out with you."

"Any problems, call me," Ben said to the team, as he left the incident room and let the door slam behind him.

"Ah, Ben," Granger said, opening his own office door. "I've been waiting for DI Bloom to give me an update on last night."

"She's just at the Blanch house—"

"I don't mind being woken up in the middle of the night to authorise warrants, Ben, but I do expect to be kept in the know. I don't expect to find out that we dealt with two murders from Detective Chief Superintendent Harper. It should have been me telling him."

"I'm sorry, guv. It was a late one."

"It's not for you to apologise, Ben," he replied, and must have seen the grave expression on Ben's face. "I gather Alex Garland is missing, too."

"He is, guv. We've got ANPR on alert and the bank is on board. He'll show up. He can only get as far as a tank of diesel will allow."

"He planned the decoy box to be sent to Devon."

"Yes, that's right."

"And he planned for Cyrus Cross' glove to be found."

"We think so, yes."

"Do you honestly believe he hasn't planned his escape with the same meticulous level of detail?"

He stared at Ben, but there really wasn't an answer Ben could provide. He was right.

"Whatever Bloom is doing, tell her to stop. I want to see her immediately. I'm supposed to give a press conference this morning, and so far, I have nothing new to give them aside from two dead bodies and a missing suspect. Pass that on for me, Ben, if you would."

"Will do, guv."

Granger's office door closed, and Jackie, who must have heard the interaction between them, emerged from the incident room just as it ended.

"I'll be glad when this one is over," she said, as she zipped up her mac. "Everyone seems to be down in the dumps."

Ben thought about what she'd said, turned, and walked with her toward the stairs.

"Everyone except you, Jackie," he said, and gave her shoulder a friendly squeeze.

He held the door open for her to enter the stairwell, and followed her in. The stairwell was the unofficial location for off-the-record chats, and was a place deemed to be rank-free, where individuals could speak their minds without fear of reprimand.

"What's wrong with everyone?" Jackie said, and she stopped at the top of the stairs. "DI Bloom explodes with no warning, DCI Granger is always grumpy, and even Gillespie seems to have lost his sense of humour."

"We're dealing with a man who has murdered at least three people, Jackie, and one of those was responsible for the deaths of five others. That's a lot of death for people to deal with. It's a hell of a lot of negativity."

"There's more to it than that."

"There's nothing that you or I should be concerning ourselves with."

"I just thought maybe if we sparked some life back into Gillespie, he could raise a few smiles in the others. He's good like that."

"He is good like that. But he'll push through it," Ben said. "You know what your problem is, don't you?"

"Sticking my nose in where it doesn't belong?"

"Well, yeah, that. And you're too bloody nice," Ben said, and he smiled at his oldest friend. "Go on. Call me if there's any news of Jason Cross."

"I'm not looking forward to it, if I'm honest," she said.

"No. I don't blame you. I know it's wrong to say," Ben began, "but a part of me hopes he doesn't wake up at all. For his own sake."

CHAPTER FORTY

THE WANING FOG DID LITTLE TO MAKE THE PROPERTY SEEM homely. The converted stables on the right side of the driveway were skeletal, and the house, in its state of disrepair, had a sad feel to it. It had been loved by both Emma and Jason, from what Cyrus Cross had said anyway, but it now awaited its fate in the gloom.

Freya parked and sat for a minute, marvelling at the eerie stillness that follows death. When she climbed from the car and made her way to the back of the house, her footsteps seemed to be disturbing the peace. Blue and white police tape flapped in the wind, and the little flags that marked the pathway of Emma and her killer fluttered. The chickens on the far side of the property clucked loudly at her presence, and Freya guessed they hadn't been fed for some time. There was nobody to deal with them now. She made a mental note, amid the chaos of her mind, to tell Ben about them. He would know what to do, being a farm boy.

The back door was open, and Freya was always surprised at how CSI teams, who were renowned to obsess over preserving crime scenes, always left such a mess when they were finished with a space. Combined with the team that had been through the property looking for the murder weapon, and the already dishevelled walls, the place was, in Freya's mind at least, inhabitable. The kitchen cupboards had been emptied into boxes, the doors had been left open, and the sink, which hadn't been used since the night Emma Blanch had been killed, had begun to smell. A few dirty dishes were inside, and somebody, presumably either Emma or Jason, had thought to rinse them with water with the intention of cleaning them later. But they hadn't got around to it. Given Emma's plans to leave, perhaps it had been Jason who had left them there. Before his world was shattered.

The living room offered little of interest to Freya. It was a decent size, but sparsely furnished with just an old, hand-me-down couch and an even older armchair that had surpassed the hand-me-down phase and long ago entered the take-outside-and-burn-me phase. In the bedroom, the search team had stripped everything from Emma's case, which had previously been placed on the bed. Its contents were in a number of sealed, clear bags, and the case had been positioned against the wall with an ID tag sticking up like it was a feature in sale.

Freya moved on, drawn to the office, which was at the end of the hallway around a ninety-degree bend. The mess that Emma's killer had made had ironically been tidied by the search team. The papers that had been sprawled across the floor were now stacked on the desk using much the same filing system that Freya had used – one big pile that she'd deal with later. She took the seat, and stared through the little window which overlooked the side of the house and down to Cyrus Cross' house. The windows had yet to be double glazed, and the wooden frames were rotten with flaking paint. But even so, Freya could imagine how wonderful it must have been to turn that shell of a property into a home. She could see their vision. The bed and breakfast would bring in a nice little income. The small field would provide their vegetables and, of course, the chickens would provide eggs.

After sifting through the paperwork for ten minutes, Freya

had put together the story of how the project had got to the stage it was currently at through a sequence of invoices, printed emails, and receipts, all correlated with the bank statement Chapman had supplied. The exterior work on the bed and breakfast had been completed, and the latest invoices were for interior materials – plasterboard, timber, bathroom suites, and PVC piping. They had been just weeks away from completion.

She sat back on the chair and followed the line of photos across the wall. A few were of either Emma or Jason, perhaps when they had first met. But most were of the happy couple in various places. Freya recognised an image of them in the Lake District beside a waterfall that she, Greg, and Billy had visited once. Aira Force, it had been called. She remembered how scared Billy had been when they had walked across the bridge at the top of the falls, and how he had held onto her with that uncompromising trust that children have.

She wondered if he would hold onto her now, or if he would cling to his father instead.

A few other photos had been spliced into the collage, one of which Freya presumed was of Emma's parents. They seemed happy enough, and they appeared to be healthy, although photos can be deceiving. There was another photo that Freya had seen during her first visit, but had thought nothing of it. But now that she saw it again, she recognised the boy's features. It was a portrait photo of Tom Blanch. The grey background, the lighting, and even the pose...

"Professional photographer," she said aloud, and something clicked in her mind.

A breath of wind caught the papers, and the top-most sheets fluttered, threatening to fall. Freya glanced up at the corridor, noting her lack of escape.

The back door slammed, and that eerie silence fell over the house. Had the wind opened the door or...?

She looked about the room for something to defend herself

with. But it was void of anything useful, except for a heavy-looking stapler, which at best, would only help if she threw it at the intruder, if there was one.

Footsteps shuffled out of the kitchen. Freya recognised the change in sounds from lino to the carpeted living room, and then to the wooden floor in the hallway. Whoever it was approached the bedroom. If they went inside without looking down to the office, she might stand a chance of slipping past and out of the back door. But if they looked left, they would see her without a doubt.

She stood from the chair and left the room, fearful of being trapped. Slowly, step by step, she approached the turn in the hallway. With one hand, she stifled her breathing, taking long, slow breaths to stay as quiet as she could. Whoever it was had stopped, and was perhaps waiting for her to turn the corner.

She reached out for the wall to steady herself, as she leaned forward vying to catch a glimpse of a coat, a boot, or anything.

A phone rang out, loud in the silence, and she pressed herself flat against the wall at the sudden noise.

"Jackie?" Ben said, and Freya could have dropped to her knees. Breathless, she stepped into view and found him staring at a photo on the wall, holding his phone to his ear. He nodded at her by way of a greeting, completely unaware of what Freya had been through during the past two minutes. Losing interest in the image, he caught Freya's eye and spoke to Jackie.

"Hold on, I'll put you on loudspeaker," he announced.

"Ben?" Jackie said. "I'm at the hospital. The doctor said Jason has made progress during the night. He's letting me in to see him."

"Only for two minutes, detective," a voice called from nearby in a warning tone.

"Did you hear that?" Jackie asked.

"Yes, we heard. Is he stable?" Freya asked, and she moved closer to Ben to be heard over the phone. He wasn't the type of man to wear aftershave, but still, he always smelled good, and was a blessed relief from the smell of damp and dust.

"No. Well, he is for the time being. Hold on, let me find somewhere private," Jackie said, and the sound of her footsteps on the linoleum floor came over the phone. "Sorry about that. They're giving me the eye for being on the phone. I hate to say it, but this might be our only chance. I thought it might be good to have Ben on the phone while I talk to him. I was thinking I could put you in my pocket so you can hear."

"Is that allowed?"

"Probably not, but from what I can gather, they're preparing for him to crash. They've been asking for details of his next of kin."

"*She's* in another part of the hospital," Ben said.

"I know. I did tell them that," Jackie said. "Shall I go inside?"

"Yes," Freya said with hesitation.

"One last thing," Jackie said. "Should I tell him about his father?"

Both Ben and Freya exchanged glances and came to the same conclusion.

"Only if there's time," Freya said, though she hated herself for it. The fact of the matter was that the news would upset the man, and he would be far less likely to be able to help them find Emma's killer.

"Okay, hold on," Jackie said, as if she had been expecting the answer.

A scratching sound followed, and they could just about hear a muffled conversation, presumably the nurses advising that she should be brief, and that should Jason Cross crash, then she should leave immediately.

"Okay," Jackie said, and the ambient noise altered.

"She's in," Ben whispered, and Freya nodded her agreement, moving closer to Ben.

"Jason?" Jackie said, her gentle approach more suited to the task than Gillespie's gruff tones. "Jason, my name is Jackie Gold. I'm with the police."

A rasping sound followed, and then Cross coughed.

"How are you feeling?" she asked.

"Numb," Cross said, after a pause. He sounded like a ninety-year-old man, and Freya could imagine the injuries the flames had caused.

"I just have a few questions to ask you. I hope that's okay. We want to find who did this. We think you can help us."

"I don't..." He coughed again, and bed sheets rustled. Freya imagined how uncomfortable he must be. "I don't know who did it. I didn't see his face."

"So it was a man?" Jackie said.

"Yeah," he rasped. "Strong."

"What happened, Jason? Tell me about your last conversation with Emma. I know it's hard, and if you don't feel up to it–"

"It's okay. I can." His breathing was louder, like he was fighting for every breath.

"Emma's bag was packed. Can you tell me a bit about that?"

"She was leaving me."

"Why? Did she say, Jason? Did you have an argument?"

"No. Not an argument," he said between laboured breaths. "She was scared."

"Scared? Scared of who?"

"Everyone. She said they hated her. Wherever she went, people hated her. I saw what he did to her. I saw it. She was right."

"What did you see, Jason? Tell me, if you can."

"He drugged me. I couldn't move..." His voice rose in pitch, and his breathing grew heavier.

Ben eyed Freya, and mouthed, "He's not going to last."

Biting her lower lip, Freya nodded her agreement again.

"It's okay to cry, Jason. You've been through a lot. So you were on the ground?"

"I couldn't move. I couldn't scream out for my dad. But I could see. I could see it all like some sick, slow-motion film."

"Do you know where he took you? Did you recognise it?"

If he answered, it was either a nod or a shake of the head.

"Can you tell us anything about the place, Jason? What did you see?"

"A shed or a barn, I think. Overgrown. Full of old tools."

"That's good, Jason. That's really good. You're doing really well. That's helpful," Jackie said, encouraging him to give more detail. "Who could have done this, Jason?" Jackie said, and the question seemed to appease Ben, whose facial muscles tightened in anticipation.

"Garland, maybe?" he said. "He hates us. Her, anyway. Wherever she went, she was recognised as the girl who got away with murder. It was him spreading the lies."

"But she was innocent, right?" Jackie said. Freya frowned at the question, but agreed with the approach, surprised at Jackie's subtlety.

"Of course. But..." He coughed again, louder this time, and he fought for breath.

"Take your time, Jason."

"She said she was plagued, or cursed, or something. She said she was a loser. She lost..." The sound of a man dry-retching was unmistakable. He spat, presumably into a bowl or a vessel of some description, then regained his ragged breathing.

"Why would she say that?" Jackie asked.

But Jason didn't answer. His breathing was the only sound in the room, save for the incessant beeping machines that kept what remained of him alive.

"Jason?" Jackie said, and there was a slight panic in her voice.

The sound of doors crashing open followed, and voices, lots of voices, one of which was clear, articulate, and strong. "Out. Out now," the woman said.

Freya found Ben staring at her. They were standing in the

hallway of the man's house as the team fought to keep him alive on the other end of the line. But even just from the call, Freya guessed he would never be coming home.

"Ben?" Jackie said. Her voice was filled with emotion and thick with restrained tears.

"It's okay, Jackie," Ben said. "It's okay. You did well."

"Really well," Freya added. "We're proud of you. Let's make his last words count."

"Yeah," she said, still distant, and she ended the call.

CHAPTER FORTY-ONE

BOTH FREYA AND BEN EXHALED LOUDLY, AND MOVED INTO their own space, each of them taking a few moments to deal with what they had just heard.

"A barn," Ben said. "Is there a barn on Garland's property?"

"No, I checked," Freya said, suddenly connecting dots in her mind. The constant battle between Greg's words was cast aside, and fragments of the previous few days came to light, but never quite came into focus.

"You okay?" Ben asked.

She nodded, still pondering the ideas.

"Granger wants to see you. Shall I wait in the car?"

She stared up at him, and something clicked.

"Gillespie said he waited in his car for days once," she said.

"Right?" Ben replied, clearly not seeing the link.

"To see his parents. He was sent to a home for children when he was a child."

"I think we should be going," Ben said. "Let's grab a coffee on the way back–"

"Tom Blanch said the same thing."

"Who?"

"Emma's brother. He said he waited in the car to see her."

"I don't see where you're going, Freya–"

"Let me show you something," she said, and coaxed him toward the little office. He slid in behind her, and she pointed at the photo of a young Tom Blanch. Ben reached across her, leaning on her shoulder to get a better view. She could have moved to make it easier for him, but his touch was warming. Comforting. She thought of Mark in that moment, but with far less desire or want than before.

"Is that Tom Blanch when he was younger?" he asked.

"It is. But what do you notice about the photo?"

"It's professional. The type a loving parent might want to give to family."

"And?" she said, teasing him, hoping he would stay in that position for longer.

"I give up."

"The colours. The grey background. The pose."

"The photo of Emma in–"

"Alex Garland's house."

"It's from the same day."

"How would Garland have an old photo of Emma?" Freya said, and she met his curious gaze, watching with fascination as his mind worked overtime.

"Maybe he stole it?" Ben said. "You said he was obsessed, and even Jason just said–"

"Or maybe Tom Blanch left it there when he took Alex Garland?"

"Eh?"

"What were Jason's last words?"

He paused for thought and moved away, leaving a cold spot on her back where he had been.

"Something about being plagued?" he said. "About her losing. I don't know. I can't think."

"Emma didn't kill all of those people. She killed her father, at least that's what Tom Blanch believes."

"How did you come to that?"

"Imagine this. Emma's father suffers a heart attack and dies. But somehow, her brother suspects it was her."

"Why would she kill her own father?" Ben asked. "She was just a kid."

"She didn't. The mother did. Tom Blanch said that the parents argued."

"So? Everyone argues."

"He also said that it was a boys versus girls thing. The dad would always team up with Tom."

"Freya?" Ben said, shaking his head. "You're not making sense."

"The report said that a large life insurance claim was paid out. The toxicology report suggested large amounts of caffeine. What if the mother had been lacing his drinks?"

"The mother's a killer now?"

Freya held her hands up in defence. "What if the mother laced his drinks and Emma knew about it. Helped, even?"

"What, boys versus girls? The endgame?" Ben said jokingly.

"It makes sense. Tom Blanch said he left for the sake of his family, but that's rubbish. He left because he couldn't stand to be around his mother, or Emma. And the idea that she got away with it gets to him. They had won."

"So, he plans his revenge," Ben said. "He lost his only friend."

"Yes, he planned his revenge. But not by killing Emma. Not straight away, anyway. But by terrorising her, haunting her with death. The mother is next, a drug-induced murder just like his father's death. Seemingly innocent."

"Then Emma was on her own," Ben said, following along, nodding.

"Then, as far as we know, Edward Pope's parents die in a gas leak while they're in bed. While Emma is the mother's carer."

"There could be more."

"Lots more."

"Then it's Harold Garland," Ben said. "But it goes wrong. She was arrested and tried."

"She got away with it. Tom wasn't expecting that. He needed a plan to bring all this to an end. He needed a fool-proof plan to make sure he wasn't the only one to point the finger at."

"I didn't even suspect him."

"Nor me. Why would we? Even Cyrus Cross said they hadn't spoken for years."

"The meticulous plan," Ben said, and she could see cogs falling into place in his mind. "That's why he left the photo there. To throw us off."

She smiled at him. "Did you see the newspaper articles of the story?"

"A few, yeah."

"Alex Garland was there on every court date. Cyrus was there too, of course."

"And Pope?"

"Pope didn't need to be there. All Tom had to do was convince him that Emma was responsible for his parents' deaths. He could have told Pope exactly how his parents died. He could even have described the scene."

"Because it was actually him."

"Then, all Tom had to do was bring them all together in a blend of circumstantial evidence. We spend three days chasing our tails–"

"And Tom just slips away again," said Ben.

"Tom Blanch has Alex Garland," Freya said, and Ben's face turned deathly pale. "What is it?"

"Jackie," he said. "She's meeting Tom Blanch at the mortuary."

CHAPTER FORTY-TWO

"Come on, come on," Ben said, holding the phone to his ear as he ran to his car. "Pick up, for god's sake, Jackie."

"The number you have dialled is unable to take your call," the message said, annoyingly stating the obvious.

"Damn it."

He wrenched open the door, climbed into the driver's seat, and hit the ignition button to start the car. Freya joined him moments later, and Ben was reversing out of the drive before she even had time to reach for her belt, let alone click it into place.

"Sorry," he said, when he saw her being thrown around in her seat. He found first gear while the car still rolled backwards, and again, while Freya was still pulling her belt across. The wheels spun on the loose gravel, and only when they had gained traction and Ben was climbing through third gear did he drop his phone in her lap. "Call Pip. See if Jackie has been there yet."

"Do you mean Doctor Bell?"

"Pip," Ben said. "That's her name in my phone."

The call played through the Bluetooth system in Ben's car, but seemed to take an age to be connected, and when it did, at least eight rings had passed before the call went silent.

Ben groaned, anticipating the annoying message telling him that the caller was unable to take his call, when…

"Now then, if it isn't Lincolnshire's answer to Inspector Poirot," Pip said, her voice calm and collected enough that Ben could imagine her peering into some sort of body cavity as she spoke. "I'll have to start charging soon."

"Pip, where's Jackie?"

"Eh?" she said, taken aback by Ben's blunt approach.

"Jackie Gold, Pip. She was coming to see you. Where is she?"

"I don't know, do I? Who do you think I am, Mystic Meg?"

"She's missing."

"We don't know that she's missing," Freya added. "Doctor Bell, it's DI Bloom. We have reason to believe the man DC Jackie Gold is with may be dangerous. Can you please confirm with a yes or a no if she's been to see you, and if she was with anybody if she has?"

"Well, I'd have to say yes, and yes, then," Doctor Bell replied. "What do you mean by dangerous? The girl's brother, wasn't he? Blanch?"

"That's right. How long ago did they leave?"

"I don't know. Enough time for me to suit up and open a chest. No more than that."

It was typical of Doctor Bell to answer a question with an answer that nobody else would understand.

"Doctor Bell," Ben said, with as friendly a warning in his voice as he could muster.

"Fifteen minutes, I suppose," she said. "Left by the back door. Funny fellow, he was. Said he felt a bit queasy. Well, there's a shortcut out back. I showed them the way. Jackie said she'd help him to his van."

"His van?" Freya said.

"That's what I said, didn't I? His van."

"Did you happen to see it, Pip?" Ben asked. "The van. Do you have a description?"

"As it happens, I did. I followed them out for a smoke. It was sign written. Some kind of builder's van. Ladders on the roof, you know?"

"Was it a joinery firm?" Freya asked.

"That's it. Garnish or something. Do you know it?"

"I'm afraid we do."

"I can normally tell just from the look of a man if he's a grafter. I took one look at that boy, and I thought to myself, he's a pen pusher, that one, or at least something light duty. Do you know what I mean? Hands as soft as a baby's buttocks, he had. Didn't have the weathered face of an outdoors man either. Baby faced."

"That's him. He's a porter," Freya said.

"That sounds about right."

"Pip, are there cameras on the back entrance?"

"There's bloody cameras everywhere round here now. Can't even fart without being caught on camera, I can't."

"Doctor Bell, I have one last question," Freya said. "Something I think we've overlooked."

"Okay," Doctor Bell said tentatively.

"Your initial assessment about the bayonet was right. You said the killer was tall. Something about the angle of his hand over her mouth."

"Yes, it was the angle of his fingers. Almost horizontal, it was. If a shorter man reached around from behind her, his fingers would be at more of a vertical angle. It's a simple evaluation, really. Not a very scientific one, I'm afraid."

"Do you still have Emma Blanch's clothes?" Freya asked. "She was wearing jeans."

"Course I do. They're right here," Pip replied, and a rustle of plastic followed as she retrieved them from the bag.

"Check the knees," said Freya.

"Dirty," Pip replied, and her voice held just a hint of apology. "Filthy, in fact."

"If Emma Blanch was forced to her knees, a shorter man's fingers might have been more horizontal, as you described. Is that right?"

"Well, yes," Doctor Bell said.

A silence followed, during which time both Ben and Freya became more certain they were on the right track and Doctor Bell experienced doubt.

"Still an excellent analysis," Freya said, massaging her confidence. "You've been absolutely brilliant."

"Are you sure?" Doctor Bell replied. "I told you it was a large man. Feel like a right wally, I do."

"The fact that you found the chemical on Emma's face at all is a wonder," Freya said.

"Agreed. Thank you, Pip," Ben said. "I owe you one."

Freya ended the call and dialled the incident room.

"DS Gillespie," said the gruff voice that answered the call.

"Gillespie, DI Bloom," Freya began.

"Are you bringing the coffees in this morning, boss? Or should I take a wee stroll down the high street–"

"Is Chapman there?" Freya said.

"Aye, but I don't think she'll be able to carry them by–"

"Put her on the phone," Freya said. "In fact, put me on loudspeaker."

"Hold on. It's a new phone."

"Now, Gillespie, please."

"Ah, there we go. You're on," Gillespie said, the penny finally dropping that Freya was in no mood for banter.

"Chapman?"

"Ma'am," Chapman replied.

"Get onto the hospital security team. I want the CCTV footage from the rear entrance of the mortuary."

"How far back?" Chapman asked, with her usual no-nonsense approach to a task.

"One hour. Gillespie?"

"Aye, boss," he said, his voice deeper and without humour.

"Are you at your laptop?"

"I am, aye."

"Search the satellite imagery for Tom Blanch's address. It should be in the case files. We're looking for a shed or a barn on his property. It might be overgrown."

"Sit tight," he said, and Ben heard him flicking through the notes. As much as he could play the idiot well, when push came to shove, the man was a solid detective, and Ben was grateful to have him on their side.

"While he's doing that, Cruz, what are you doing?"

"Looking up Garland's family. He has cousins in Norfolk and–"

"Forget them. Alex Garland is not the killer, not directly anyway. I want you to go down to Sergeant Priest. Tell him I need every available uniform on standby. As many as he can give me."

"Detective Inspector Bloom," a voice rang out, far different from those of the team, and carrying much more authority.

"Guv?" she said, and she closed her eyes, cursing beneath her breath. Ben glanced across at her, and she ignored him, knowing full well he was looking her way.

"My report. Where is it?"

"It's been a difficult few days, I–"

"Before you set about causing any more mayhem all over Lincolnshire, I want to see you."

"Guv, we've got a strong lead."

"In my office," he continued. "Thirty minutes."

As much as Ben knew she was holding out from upsetting the team, he knew as well as she did that the only way DCI Granger was going to give on this one was for her to make an announcement.

And if she wasn't going to, then he would.

"Guv, it's me," Ben said, and Freya glared at him for addressing him on her behalf. There was little time for formalities. Ben had known the man for his entire working career, and they had become good friends over the years. There was a time when formalities were mere obstacles.

"DS Savage?" he said, referring to Ben's rank in an effort to maintain his position.

"Will, we found the killer. It's Tom Blanch."

"This isn't helping, Ben."

"He's got Jackie."

The room was silent. So much so that Ben had to check the phone's screen to make sure the call was still active.

"DC Gold?" said Granger, and a murmur built up in the background. "Okay, okay," he said, calming the team down. Ben pictured him with one hand raised. So much control in one of those shovel-like hands.

"We believe he's taking her somewhere, and we believe Garland is there, too. He may still be alive."

Granger pondered the scenario. But it took far too long for him to see reason.

"Why Jackie?" he asked.

"I don't know. Maybe he saw an opportunity? Maybe he knows we're closing in?"

"Because he needs to win," Freya said. "He needs to win, and he needs somebody to see it. He wants to kill Garland, but if nobody knows about it, it's not much of a win, is it? It's boys versus girls, guv. This is his endgame."

"What do you need?"

"Men, guv," Ben said, spying Freya turn her head away to look out of the window. "As many as Priest can spare. Cruz, are you still there?"

"Yes," he called out.

"You heard. Go and see Priest."

"Yes, boss," he replied.

"I've got it," Gillespie called out, and his voice grew louder as he stepped closer to the phone. "There's no barn there though, Ben. It's just an empty field."

"There must be something. Look harder."

"I've just had a ping on the ANPR," Chapman called out. "It's Garland's van."

"Where?" Freya called.

"Heading east on the B1190. Towards Horncastle."

"Where's he going?" Ben asked nobody in particular. "Think. What's he doing? Chapman, scan the folder for the search term Horncastle. See what comes up. We may have missed something."

"Wait," Freya said, so quietly that Ben didn't hear her at first. "I've got it," she mumbled, and the room silenced, waiting for her to air her suggestion.

She peered across at Ben, and spoke as if it were only the two of them, "It's his parents' house. The father died from an accident in the barn. He's reliving his father's death. He's going to show Jackie how he can win."

CHAPTER FORTY-THREE

"There's nothing here," Gillespie said. "I've checked the parents' address in the files and there's no barn."

"Chapman, help him look," Ben said. "It could be in a nearby property. The father died eleven years ago. Anything could have happened since. The new owners could have sold land off."

"Or knocked the barn down," Gillespie said. "I can see a few outbuildings, but you couldn't call them barns. A shed maybe, but small."

"I'm looking now," Chapman said. "DS Gillespie is right. It's just an open field with some trees down the back. Looks like an orchard or something."

"That's it," Freya said. "It'll be in the trees somewhere. Can you zoom in?"

A few seconds of silence passed, and Ben imagined Granger leaning over Gillespie's desk, while Chapman and Cruz worked frantically on their own laptops.

"There it is," Granger said.

"It's a dark patch in the trees," Gillespie countered. "It could be anything."

"Wrong. It's the only dark patch in trees."

"Ping us the address," Ben said.

"It's on its way to you already."

"Ben, I've had an email back from hospital security," Chapman said, her voice flat and serious. "They're sending the footage over, but that'll take time. They've sent a screenshot for the time being. Oh Christ, Ben. It's her."

"Tell me what you see."

"I'm sending it on to you now," Chapman said. "Brace yourself, Ben."

Freya opened the email the moment the notification showed on Ben's screen.

She exhaled and turned away from Ben to peer through the window again, thinking that Ben hadn't seen her dab at her eye.

"Show me," he said, but she didn't respond. "Freya, show me the photo."

Slowly, Freya turned to face him, her eyes shining crimson against her pale skin.

"Show me," he said, keeping an eye on the road.

She held the phone out into his line of sight, so he could see both the road and the photo. The image was of low quality to the extent that it would not serve as evidence alone, as neither Jackie's nor Blanch's defining features could be ascertained. And although the photo resembled a short, broad man holding a white rag to Jackie's mouth, and her leg kicking wildly, the lack of detail would deem it as unsubstantial in a court of law.

But Ben knew. He knew without a shred of doubt that the girl in the image was his friend, and although he hadn't met Tom Blanch, he knew it was him dragging her into the back of his van.

"It doesn't mean anything," Freya said, to which Gillespie concurred.

"Aye, Ben. She's a tough girl. She can handle herself, alright?"

Ben stared dead ahead, focusing on the road and trying to get the distorted image out of his head.

"How far out are we?" Freya asked.

"Twenty minutes," Ben replied. "A bit less if we're not held up."

"I don't need to tell you how precarious the situation is," Freya said, addressing the entire team. "DC Gold is in serious danger and Alex Garland may also still be alive. DS Savage and I will be the first on the scene. We'll do our best to control the situation. Chapman, arrange for armed response to attend, and if we can get it, have the air ambulance on stand-by. Gold is one of us. If she's hurt, we owe it to her to get her out fast."

"You're not going in there without backup," Granger said. "I know you want to get her out, but we have to maintain safety."

"We'll go in as far as we can," Ben said, and nodded slyly to Freya. "We'll make our assessment when we're in position."

"Chapman, Cruz, lead the uniforms in. Is there rear access to the property?"

"Aye, boss," Gillespie said. "Looks like the property backs onto a farm. There's a wee track close by."

"Have a unit cover that," Freya said, then swallowed hard. "Get to the scene and wait for my instruction. Is that understood?"

"Ma'am," Chapman replied.

"Aye, boss."

Freya ended the call, and they rode in near silence for the next few minutes while Ben navigated the winding lane from memory. Had the fog not been so heavy, he may have driven faster, but he was already pushing the limits of safety, and twice he had to brake hard to make a turn. For the inexperienced, the roads were perilous. Deep dykes ran alongside the tarmac as drainage for the fields. Without them, a single hard downpour could flood the fertile soil, destroying crops and livelihoods with a single bitter sweep of Mother Nature's hand. Many a car had found its way to the bottom of the dykes, usually in the hands of a young driver who hadn't the experience or foresight to consider the bends and the road surface.

"Five minutes out," Ben said, recognising the road into Horn-castle. "Want to go in through the back?"

"What's fastest?"

"The front. I know the road."

"Then we'll do that. We don't even know if he's there yet."

The little dashboard screen lit up again, signalling a call was about to come in. One of the incident room numbers flashed up, and he hit the green button to answer the call immediately.

"What do we have?"

"Ben, it's me," Gillespie began. "Chapman's done some digging. The property is up for sale, so it might well be empty."

"The perfect opportunity for him to use the barn, then."

"Aye, that's what we thought. Armed response are on their way, as are uniform, and the air ambulance is on standby. What's your ETA?"

"A few minutes, tops," Ben replied. "Has anyone spoken to Jackie's mum yet?"

"No. We didn't think it wise until..." Gillespie faltered for a moment. "Well, you know?"

"You're right."

"She'll be fine, Ben. I know the two of you go way back–"

"She will be fine. I'm going to make damn sure of it," Ben replied. "What time is Granger's press conference?"

"In about an hour. Anna's helping him put the facts together now," Gillespie said. "Listen. I think I should come. I can be there in thirty minutes."

"I need you there, Gillespie," Freya said, and the ensuing silence conveyed his disappointment. "You've done a lot already. What I need now is a safe pair of hands to coordinate the effort. If Blanch isn't here, we'll need to divert the resources elsewhere. You'll lead that effort."

"Aye, boss," he said, somewhat consoled by the responsibility.

"Good to have you on the team, Gillespie," Freya added, by way of a closing statement.

"We're here," Ben advised, as he pulled into the property. "We'll call in with updates."

He hit the button to end the call before anybody could argue, and ignored Freya's approving expression.

The detached house was set back by fifty metres or so, providing ample parking space. Although the building was fairly large, it clearly hadn't been maintained for many years. Wild ivy had cleaned much of the brickwork and windows, and a few of the roof tiles had fallen away.

Ben spied Garland's van, which hadn't been parked so much as dumped in the top corner of the driveway close to the alleyway that ran down the side of the house. Dark lines marked the places where the vehicle had skidded to a stop and the front tyres had dug into the gravel.

Ben had his seatbelt off and was opening the door before the car had stopped. He sprinted to the rear of the van. The doors were open and inside was empty, save for all the things a man might need for what Blanch had in mind – a roll of gaffer tape, a length of old rope, a white rag, which Ben presumed would reek of chemicals. He gave it a sniff.

"Rohypnol," he said, turning to find Freya standing beside him, and together, they peered down the alleyway. At the far end of a three-acre field, tall trees dominated the skyline.

She opened her mouth to answer the unspoken question on his mind when something spooked a flock of birds that had been roosting in the trees, and milliseconds later, a deathly scream filled the air.

CHAPTER FORTY-FOUR

"That was a man's scream," Freya said, wide-eyed.

"I don't care what it was," Ben said. "I'm not waiting to find out if you're right."

He ran a few steps, but Freya stopped him. "Wait," she said, hearing the panic in her own voice. In the short period of time she had known him, she had shown her weaknesses, had shown her strengths, and had even experienced those moments of teenage lust, when she would have gladly given it all up for an hour alone with him. But now, this was a whole other side of her she was showing, and she was powerless to hide it.

"What is it?" he hissed.

She took a deep breath and stepped closer to him, peering into the alleyway at the trees beyond. The fog was as thick there as it had been on the road, and despite the cold, her cheeks burned with fear.

"I've been here before," she said. "Not here, but..."

"Oh, Freya. I'm sorry, I didn't think–"

"We have to wait," she said. "I know you think we should go in alone, but–"

"Then you wait," he said. "Armed response will be here any minute. Send them in after me."

"No," she said, allowing her terror to be aired. "The last time I did this, I barely survived."

"And if I don't do it now, Jackie might not survive," he countered, and he backed away from her, preparing to run to his friend. "I've got to go in after her."

She nodded. Even if she did outrank him, even if she could manipulate him, and have him bend to her needs, she knew there was no stopping him. Such was his loyalty and tenacity, Freya found herself in awe of him. She saw what a good friend she had in him.

"It's not James Marley down there. It's Tom Blanch. And it's no ordinary victim who's with him. It's Jackie."

"Then I'm coming too," she said, and she stepped forward to stand beside him. "But we stay together."

He nodded, and together they ran alongside the building. Ben led the way, leaping over a fallen wheelie bin. Freya, in her boots, had to slow down and step over it.

"Go," she called, and he ran into the field ahead of her.

Then the worst happened.

From behind the house, Tom Blanch stepped out. He whipped a thick arm out, catching Ben by the back of his collar, and yanked him backwards as he ran. Ben's legs flew into the air and he landed in a heap on his back. But before he could react, Blanch had a length of rope around his head, and he dragged Ben to his knees by his neck.

"Don't move," he told Freya.

Ben struggled and fought the man, reaching back to grab a handful of anything he could find. Blanch was fast and strong, avoiding Ben's clutches at every attempt. But tenacious as he was, Ben wouldn't give up. His face reddened from the lack of air, and he pushed up with his legs. He knocked Blanch off-balance, and for a moment, Freya saw hope, but a swift kick from the squat man sent Ben back to the ground on his knees.

Slowly, he drew something from behind his back, and Freya froze in horror as the blade of a World War Two bayonet grazed Ben's skin.

"Stop, Tom," Freya called, stepping forward. "You don't need to do this."

"Get back," he snapped, breathless from the exertion of restraining Ben. Spittle flew from his lip as he panted, and his wild eyes widened so that Freya saw the curvature of his sockets within.

"It's over, Tom," Freya said, finding calm from somewhere deep within her. "In a few minutes, this whole place will be teaming with police. Dogs, helicopters, men. It's over, Tom. You lose."

"It's over when I say it's over."

"Just let him go. He hasn't done anything to you."

"You don't know anything," he said, and he pulled Ben back by his neck, keeping the blade firmly in place.

"I know she killed your father," Freya said, and Blanch paused. He cocked his head to one side, curious, like a dog. She nodded. She had his attention, but time was running out. "I know how that must have felt, Tom. He was your world, wasn't he?"

"He was a good man."

"And your mother took him from you."

He stared at her in disbelief, as if there was no possible way anybody could comprehend his loss.

"And Emma. They won, didn't they? The girls won, and the boys lost. So you haunted her," she said, and he laughed crazily, until his breathing became hoarse. She stepped forward. Just one step. "You haunted Emma with death, didn't you? To tell her the game wasn't over. You were still playing. You could still win. All this time. How many were there, Tom? First, your mother. But that was easy. You were never a mummy's boy anyway, were you?"

"You don't know," he said, but there was doubt in his tone. "You can't…"

"Then there was the Popes. But that wasn't until years later, was it? What happened in that time?"

"I was busy," he shouted, as a boy might shout at his sister. "They're my memories. Mine."

"And then Harold Garland. Your pièce de résistance. The one that was supposed to see her suffer for the rest of her years."

Ben's legs kicked out, scrambling for purchase. His face was a deep red, but Freya needed just a few more moments. She stared at him, made eye contact, and willed him to still if only for a few seconds more.

"But your plan didn't work, did it? You couldn't send her mad. You couldn't even send her to prison," she said, her voice rising to a bitter shout. "You lost, Tom Blanch. You failed him. Your father. Where's the revenge now?" she screamed.

"Stop," Blanch said, his chest rising with each sharp intake of breath. The bayonet pressed harder into Ben's skin. "Just stop."

But now was not the time to relent. Now was the time to strike.

"What did you ask her, Tom?" she said, quietening her voice so that he had to focus on each and every word. "What was it you said to her? You had her on her knees, didn't you? Just like you have Ben now. You were in control. You gave her a choice. What was it?"

"I-I…" he stammered, and for a moment, the Tom Blanch that Freya had met just three days before showed his face. The weak Tom Blanch. Freya glanced at Ben, whose strength was waning; his fingers clutched at the rope, but his attempts to grip it were feeble.

"What was it, Tom?" Freya shouted, loud enough that she might rouse Ben from his semi-consciousness.

"A choice," Tom said proudly, and for the first time, he raised his knife hand, pointing the blade at Freya. "I gave her a choice. Tell me I've won," he said, then smiled cruelly. "Or die."

Freya was stunned at the response and his callousness, and Blanch saw he had made an impact on her. He smiled the smile of a winner. Of a man whose lifetime goal had just been achieved.

But it was short-lived. With a final heave, Ben put every ounce of energy he had into his arm, swinging back wildly, and connecting with Blanch's gut. Blanch let go of the rope and doubled over, but not before shoving Ben to the ground where he clambered to safety, toward Freya, sucking in air as fast as his body would allow.

Freya tore the rope from his neck and tossed it to one side, and Ben rolled onto his back. He raised a hand, touching the tiny slice of skin the blade had cut. They both stared after Blanch, just as he disappeared into the forest.

CHAPTER FORTY-FIVE

THEY ENTERED THE COPSE OF LIME TREES AND SLOWED TO A stop. The path on which they ran had been recently used, judging by the fresh boot prints and the two unbroken lines, which Freya assumed to be the marks of Jackie's heels as she was dragged. The barn was set deep into the trees, camouflaged by the natural foliage. A decade or two of neglect had allowed nature to reclaim the land, and wild ivy had formed a mask across its surface, much as a spider might cocoon its prey, until its insides were ready to be consumed.

Ben led, and Freya, still reeling from her own ordeal, followed, glancing behind them every few seconds and scanning the surroundings for movement.

A breath of wind caught the corrugated steel door, opening it a few inches before dying off and letting it clatter against the thin barn walls. They stopped outside with their backs to the barn. Ben turned away from her, edging toward the door with a hand up for her to stay and keep watch. Then he moved forward. He waited patiently for another fortuitous gust of wind to take advantage of, and when it happened, teasing him with a view inside the barn, he placed his foot to stop the door from closing again. He gave Freya a nervous glance, then carefully, he peered through the space.

Unnerved by the sudden return of the roosting birds, Freya scanned the trees around them, keeping one eye on Ben, who was half inside the barn already. She tugged at his jacket, and he turned to face her, seeming irritated by the distraction. He opened the door a little further, just enough for him to peek around the corner. Then, without warning, he slipped inside and out of sight.

"Ben?" she whispered. But he didn't reply. She cursed and followed suit, catching the door before it slammed. As quickly as she dared, she peered inside then pulled back. The open door cast a beam of light across a concrete floor, but the suffocating gloom from within concealed anything else.

On three, she told herself.

One.

This is stupid.

Two.

The memory of that night returned. It was dark. She was alone in the forest, staring at James Marley's cabin. The world was still, save for the ever-restless birds. In her mind, Marley's hand reached out for her. She glanced behind her.

Nobody there.

Three.

She took a breath, and in one swift movement, before she could convince herself otherwise, she stepped inside.

A strong hand caught her mouth and she was pulled backwards into him. And there he held her. So close that his warm breath licked at her nape.

But unlike James Marley, her captor's breath was fresh, and his touch was firm yet gentle, respectful almost.

"Shh," he whispered, and he relaxed his hand, letting it fall to her hip. "Don't look behind you."

She didn't turn, choosing instead to do exactly as he instructed. She stared ahead of her. The room was a picture of gloom. Each wall had been filled with shelves, on which only a sample corner or surface of each item was visible, but nothing more. She recognised a few items as garden tools, a roll of tarpaulin, and even terracotta plant pots. But the darkness revealed little else. The floor was clear, for the most part, save for the spaces near the walls, in which barrels of oil, tins of paint, and some agricultural machinery had been stored, and left to ruin in the decaying building. A bundle of sheets had been tossed into one corner, and from the rafters, a chain hung, its hook clearly silhouetted against a mildew-covered window on the far side of the barn. And on the ground beneath the window, a dark stain had embedded itself into the concrete. A memory. A catalyst for events that nobody could have foreseen.

It was a place of death.

"Who is it?" she whispered, hoping for the lesser of the two evils.

"Garland," he said, and she exhaled with relief.

"Is he..."

"Very much so."

Slowly, she pulled herself from his grasp, but stayed within his arms, turning to face him. There was very little she hadn't seen or witnessed. Bodies in the dozens. Mutilations, stabbings, and worse.

With eyebrows raised in question, she glanced down at his hands, which still held her tight.

"I didn't want you to call out," Ben explained in a breath of a whisper.

"It's okay," she said, and she peered over his shoulder to see the horror he had saved her from encountering and thus crying out in surprise.

Alex Garland's body was hanging from the only clear part of the walls. Behind the door where the dark gloom suffocated all but the shiniest of things. Beyond that narrow strip of light from the open doorway. As if he had passed into darkness and was out of reach.

Garland's lifeless eyes stared back at Freya. His form was the dark shape of a limp man against a black backdrop. But it was him. Freya knew it. The palest light glistened from a wound across his neck, but there was no need to look harder. He wasn't the first.

"I think we lost him," Ben said, nervously peering out of the door, and speaking out loud for the first time. His voice was still raspy from the rope around his neck, and subconsciously, he rubbed at the red mark across his throat. "He must have taken off across the fields."

"Where's Jackie?"

"I don't know," he said. "She's not here."

"Is there somewhere else? The house maybe?"

But Ben peered past her, over her shoulder. His expression fell from that hardened frown to something Freya could only describe as hope. His hands fell from her and left her cold. He brushed past and dropped to his knees at the bundle of sheets on the ground. Frantically, he began tearing them away, discarding them to one side, until...

"Jackie?" he said, and he collected her dark form in his arms, raising her head.

Freya ran to Ben, dropped down beside him, and instantly began checking Jackie's vitals.

"She's breathing," she said, hopeful. "Keep her head up. I'll call Gillespie."

Grabbing her phone from her pocket, she dialled the incident room, wedging the handset in place between her ear and her shoulder.

Three beeps, each one a higher pitch than the last, announced that she had no service. She checked the screen, and the tiny single bar of signal strength disappeared.

"Shit," she hissed.

"Jackie, come on," Ben said, no longer caring for stealth. "Wake up, damn it."

He brushed his hand through her hair, and felt again for her pulse, seeming to find relief in its gentle rhythm.

"Stay here," he said. "If Blanch comes back, call for me."

But Freya reached out and grabbed his arm as he stood. This time, she wouldn't let him get his own way.

"We said we'd stay together. They're coming, Ben. We wait," she said, and with another look at Jackie's face, he relented.

It was as he crouched beside Jackie again and held her hand in his own that she stirred. A soft murmur. Her fingers tightened on his, then relaxed. And she gave a deep exhale, like somebody waking from a terrible dream only to find themselves in a gloomy, old barn belonging to a serial killer with two people staring down at her in the darkness.

But the shock was short-lived, and recognition set in.

"Ben?" she said, her voice dry and rough.

"It's okay. You're safe now. We've got you," he said.

Freya dropped to her knees and exhaled, long and loud. Her head hung limp, and she closed her eyes as the adrenaline that soared through her waned. There was so much she wanted to say. So much she felt she could offer. But instead of her offering those reassuring words to Jackie, she heard them being spoken to her. Three days locked in a dark room, arms and legs bound, and slowly dying of thirst. And all they had to say to her was, "It's okay, you're safe now."

And she realised. There was nothing else they could have said. Nothing in the world would have mattered more than to hear those words.

"Help me sit her up," Ben said, and together, they raised her torso, dragging her up against the wall.

"Are you hurt?" Ben asked. "What do you need?"

But just as Ben had stared past Freya when he had spied the

bundle of sheets, Jackie now stared through them, between them, squinted with irritation as if they were blocking her view on purpose. And just as nothing Freya said seemed to penetrate his distracted mind, she too seemed oblivious to their presence.

"Jackie?" Ben said. "You're safe now."

But her eyes widened. Her mouth hung open, and even in that gloom, her skin turned pale with fright.

Freya glanced across to Ben, and slowly they craned their necks toward the entrance. Beyond that slice of light, in the deepest shadow, Alex Garland's hand moved. It seemed to float to the right a little, and a third leg emerged. Then another arm appeared, and inch by inch, Tom Blanch stepped out of the bleak shadow and into the light from the doorway. His face was half-lit; the rest was buried in darkness. But that winning grin of his was unmistakable. He was blocking the only exit and enjoying every second of his winning move.

"I don't lose," he said, as he raised the bayonet into the light. He lovingly touched the blade, caressing the steel shank with admiration. Then he turned his attention to them and took a single step forward, revealing himself to the world outside the barn. A single gunshot rang out, echoing around the old, metal building. The shot was deafening, but so struck with terror was Freya that she never once let her gaze fall from Blanch's.

He hit the floor in a heap, writhing in agony, and let out a scream so wild it could have come from the forest outside. From his bloodied hand, the bayonet clattered across the dust, stopping just inches from Freya's boot, just as the barn door was wrenched open and four men stepped into the room, sweeping the dark corners with their weapons before pinning Blanch to the ground. The fourth man came and stood over Freya and Jackie. He dropped to one knee, holstering the handgun he carried.

"Everyone okay?" he asked, to which they all nodded silently.

He relayed the message through his radio.

"Suspect is down. Suspect is down. Require urgent medical assistance. Three survivors. I repeat, three survivors." He glanced around at his team who all confirmed the barn was clear, and, seeing that Ben and Freya were mostly unhurt, he spoke directly to Jackie. "You're safe now," he said. "You're going to be okay."

CHAPTER FORTY-SIX

At Freya's request, Alex Garland's body had been removed once the gunshot wound in Blanch's leg had been dressed. It was her way of drawing a truce with the deceased. He had done little to deter her from believing he may be a suspect, leading her along the garden path exactly as Tom Blanch had known he would, and his arrogance had fuelled that belief, exactly as Tom Blanch knew it would. But still, he deserved to be removed with dignity and ahead of his killer.

Ben watched the two ambulance men roll Tom Blanch onto the stretcher. He lay helpless, staring up at the ceiling, biting down on his lower lip to ease the pain. His leg had been dressed, although it was no more than a flesh wound. He flinched when Ben stood over him, then defiance showed in his eyes, but it was futile, and gave way to the madness.

"Thomas Blanch, I'm arresting you for the murders of Emma Blanch, Alex Garland, Edward Pope, Jason Cross, and Cyrus Cross. You do not have to say anything, but it may harm your defence if you do not mention when questioned something which you later rely on in court. Anything you do say may be given in evidence."

He stared up at Ben, his mouth open as if he might offer some insult or verbal attack. But nothing came.

"Nothing to say, Tom?"

He shook his head. "Only that I'll see you around, DS Ben Savage," he said, as the two paramedics bent to pick him up.

"Can you give us a minute?" he asked the paramedics, and they nodded and left the barn, leaving Blanch helpless on the ground beneath Ben. He crouched, and looked down at him with disgust. "You're going to prison for a very long time. You may never walk as a free man again. So, you see, you won't be seeing anyone around, except the men you share a wing with. And my guess," Ben said, allowing his lips to form a thoughtful grin, "is they aren't really the sociable type."

"One day, I'll make you eat those words. One day, when you're fast asleep in your little farmhouse." He nodded. "That's right, Ben. I know where."

"You'll never be released," Ben said. "And don't even attempt to plead insanity."

"Oh, I won't be pleading insanity. Insanity is for the weak of mind. No. No, I think I'll just go for plain old not guilty, your honour."

"You killed your sister," Ben said, and his face twisted with sickened incredulity. "And Edward Pope, and Jason. The list goes on."

"Prove it," Blanch said, and he smiled once more. "Where's the proof? Ah, you don't have any, and you won't find any."

"We'll find it. We have CSI at Pope's house and Cyrus Cross' house, and they'll be in here too, when we're done. Plus, we have a statement from Jason Cross. That was interesting. His dying words."

"I wish I could have been there," Blanch said. "You know? When the time came. Gives a whole new meaning to dying with your boots off, doesn't it?"

It was at that moment that Ben saw it. The truth. He finally understood what Freya had been saying about the master plan.

"You used Jason's boots?" Ben said, fitting the pieces of the puzzle together. "You wore them when you killed Emma, and in Edward Pope's house."

Blanch's smug grin said it all. But he said nothing.

"And you used gloves belonging to Cyrus Cross," Ben said. "You used Cyrus Cross' gloves on Emma and you made sure they were found. You purposefully coated them in gun oil so we'd find them." Tom Blanch grinned up at him. "What about your mother? And Pope's parents? How many others were there? You sick bastard—"

"Now, now," Tom Blanch said. "Don't be a sore loser."

"The only evidence you ever left behind shines a light on somebody else, doesn't it? That's what you do," Ben said, shaking his head in disbelief; here he was staring down at a man who had it all planned out.

"I win," Blanch whispered. "I'll be seeing you around."

Given the circumstances, and the effort Blanch had put in, for the first time, Ben really did have his doubts.

Blanch called out to the paramedics, offering Ben a wink goodbye, "I'm ready."

Ben watched as they carried him out, and he followed Blanch's smug expression until he was out of sight, then watched their shadows fade in the light on the concrete floor.

"What will they do with him?" Jackie asked.

"Hospital first," Freya said. "Though I dare say he doesn't deserve it. However, if he gets anything less than excellent treatment for his gunshot wound, it'll go in his favour during the trial. It's a bitter fact."

"If I had my way, I'd let him bleed out on the floor," Ben said.

"He'll get his dues," Freya said, and she turned her attention to the bayonet. "He'll be found guilty for Garland for sure, so that's one count of murder."

"Eh?" Jackie said. "Will he really get away with all those murders?"

"This was his master plan, and if we hadn't caught him here, he would have got away with this too," Ben said, and he stared at Jackie. "And who knows what else."

"But he killed Pope, and Cyrus Cross, and–"

"And Emma?" Freya said. "Not to mention her mother, Edward Pope's parents, and Harold Garland. Probably Jason Cross as well. But you try proving it. He might be crazy, but he's not stupid. He's had *us* running round in circles for three days."

"What about Emma's innocence? People need to know that. They need to know it was her brother," Jackie said.

"How can you sit there so calm?" Ben said. "Doesn't it infuriate you that he might get away with–"

"With murder?" Freya asked, and she turned her hand to reveal her phone. The screen was lit. A call was live. She hit the button to enable the loudspeaker. "Did you get all that?" Freya called out.

"Aye, boss. Loud and clear. Even recorded it too," Gillespie replied, his voice tinny but unmistakable over the phone's loudspeaker.

"He's proud of what he is, of what he's done," Freya said. "He's proud that he outsmarted us all. I knew you'd say something, Ben. I knew you'd try and understand him, and I very nearly stopped you."

"Why?" Ben asked.

"Because it gave him pleasure. Did you see the look on his face? I knew he'd boast to us, in private, out of earshot. With no way for us to prove it. His one chance of glory that will keep him going for years. His final win."

She reached up from where she leant against the wall, and Ben pulled her to her feet. Together, they hauled Jackie up, and Ben held her for a while, until he was sure she was able to walk.

"Right, let's get out of here so CSI can do their stuff," Freya said. "Gillespie, get yourself down the high street."

"Aye, boss. I'll get the coffees in, eh?" Gillespie said. "One flat white coming up."

"No. Get me one of those things you had. The pumpkin thing," Freya said. "In fact, get everybody one. It is Christmas, after all."

CHAPTER FORTY-SEVEN

"I'D LIKE TO RAISE A TOAST," GILLESPIE ANNOUNCED FROM THE bar of the Fox and Hound. He reached over and handed Ben a pint of pale ale, then checked the entire team had a drink in their hands. "To DI Bloom, and her dream team."

They sounded more like a rugby squad than a team of police officers as they raised their glasses and chorused, "The dream team."

Even Chapman, who was usually so reserved, clinked her glass with Cruz's so hard that she spilt much of her wine, then laughed it off, carefree. Their din formed just part of the overall hum of festive drinks in the pub. Nearly every table was filled with glasses, and every seat was taken. The jukebox played some eighties crap that Ben didn't consider to be Christmas music, or tasteful in the slightest. But it was Christmas, nonetheless. Tinsel had been wrapped around the uprights on the bar and across the rows of spirits. Flashing, coloured lights hung in the windows and each of the bar staff had adorned themselves with some kind of festive accessory. One girl had glittery stars for earrings and a shiny ribbon in her hair. Another wore reindeer antlers in the form of an Alice band. The only bloke behind the bar seemed to be lacking in Christmas spirit. That was until he stepped back to pour a measure of vodka and Ben noticed the pair of baubles hanging crudely from his fly. The man winked at Jackie, who turned away with a wry grin on her face.

"Are you sure you want to be here?" Ben asked her. He wanted to put his hand on her shoulder, or give her a squeeze, but even as close as they were, the gesture would have been inappropriate. "I can run you to the hospital if you want. I'll wait—"

"The duty MO checked me over, Ben. I wouldn't be here if I didn't want to be," she snapped, her cheeks flushing a little.

"I'm sorry. I just want to make sure you're okay."

"I know, Ben. I'm okay. Honest. He didn't really hurt me. Ruined my bloody boots though," she said, trying to find a light-hearted angle to deflect the attention from herself. That was typical of her.

He nodded, accepting that he would have to trust her judgement.

"Thanks though, yeah?" she said. "Thanks for coming after me. Gillespie told me you were going nuts."

"I wouldn't call it going nuts—"

"Oh yeah? Speeding down the lanes, shouting down the phone, ordering people about. I heard DI Bloom had to take over the call."

"Well, I just wanted to get you back," Ben said. "I'd have done the same thing for anyone."

She smiled. "You know how to make a girl feel special, don't you?" she said, then reached her arms through the crowd and held her drink aloft. They silenced waiting for her to speak. For a moment, Ben thought she had lost her nerve at the last minute, or that the emotion had caught in her throat. But she spoke finally, "To my good friends. May you all have a very merry Christmas."

They raised their glasses once more in response to the toast, then drank. Gillespie slammed his empty glass down on the bar.

"Right then, who's having another?" he asked, then, without asking, performed a circular motion to the barmaid, indicating he'd like a full round.

"Not for me, Jim," Jackie said, and she signed to the barmaid to be excluded as she put her empty glass down. "I should really get back to Charlie. It's been a long day, and I think I just want to be with him."

Had it been anybody else, Ben was sure Gillespie would have countered the escape by forcing a drink into their hand. But even the rough and ready James Gillespie had heart enough to understand Jackie's plea.

"Aye, Jackie. You're a trooper," he said. "We'll see you on Boxing Day, eh? Go and give that boy of yours a big hug."

She nodded, said her farewell to the team, and then turned to Ben.

"Thanks again," she said, and leaned in, stood on her tip toes, and gave him a peck on the cheek. "You're a good friend, Ben Savage."

The door was still closing after she had left when a large hand caught it and pushed it back open, letting a draft of bitter cold air blow through the saloon bar. Wrapped in a long, grey, double-breasted jacket, DI Steve Standing entered, glanced around, then approached the team. He came to stand beside Ben, spying the only break in the wall of people at the bar.

"How you doing, Steve?" Ben said, nodding a greeting. "You all set for Christmas?"

"Ah, you know how it is," he replied, as he reached forward and tapped the pump in front of him, indicating to the barmaid that he wanted a light ale. "The wife does all the shopping. I just turn up and pretend I know what we've bought the kids. What about you? Are you still at your old man's place?"

He pointed at the bar and Ben's glass, silently asking if he wanted another. But Ben held his hand up and shook his head.

"Just the one for me. I have the furthest to drive. And yep, I'm still on the farm. And yes, I'm still enjoying the single life," Ben said.

"Nothing brewing in the pipes then?"

"Not this year," Ben replied, raising his voice to be heard over the laughing and chanting from the team behind them. "It'll happen when it happens. This lot keep me pretty busy."

They both turned to find Gillespie and Cruz racing to down a pint, egged on by Anna and Chapman.

"They'll keep you busy alright," Steve said. "They're a good bunch really. I'll miss them when I'm gone."

"Are you going somewhere?" Ben asked, unsure if he had heard him correctly.

"Lincoln HQ," he said, his voice grumbling below the din. "Not everyone knows, so..."

"Promotion?" Ben asked. "Why didn't you say?"

But before Ben could get too excited for him, Standing held out a hand.

"It's not a promotion. It's a sideways move. Bigger team. More opportunities."

"Less Freya Blooms?"

"Something like that," he said, as he took the drink from the barmaid and handed her a five-pound note. "It used to work well when DI Foster was alive. We'd split the workload, you know? There never really used to be any competition. I don't know. It's not the same anymore, is it?"

Ben shrugged. "Things change."

"That they do," Steve said. "Anyway, like I said. Keep it on the down low for the time being."

"Why are you telling me?" Ben asked, suddenly suspicious that the man was merely fabricating some kind of endeavour to get at Freya, which wouldn't be out of character. "You've barely said ten words to me since Dave died."

"Because, Ben, you're the most likely to get moved up," said Steve, glancing over his shoulder. "Gillespie wants to make DI, but we both know who is next in line. You deserve it, mate. You should go for it.”

“Right,” Ben said, unconvinced. “Thanks.”

“You would, of course, be up against Freya, but I’m sure you’ll work her out better than I’ve managed to. Now, if you don’t mind, if you’ve finished with my team, I’d like to go and buy them a drink. Might be my last chance.”

“Of course,” Ben said, and tapped the side of his glass against Standing’s. “Have a good Christmas.”

“You too, Ben,” he replied. “You too.”

Ben watched the man join the throng. Somehow, he seemed different out of work. Perhaps it had been his news that had softened him? Or maybe he was just able to relax without Freya being around. Checking his phone, Ben saw the time. He was going to interrupt Gillespie’s account of the time Anna took Edward Pope down, even though he wasn’t actually there to witness it, but he thought better of it. He slid his empty glass onto the bar, nodded his thanks to the barmaid, then slipped through the hustle and bustle of a local business having its Christmas drinks, and out through the door.

The cold air hit him in an instant. He thrust his hands into his pockets, and walked the two hundred yards back to the station. Searching for his keys, he unlocked the car without removing his hands. He climbed inside, started the engine, and then adjusted all the heating controls to heat his feet as fast as possible. Rubbing his hands together, he blew into them, and was about to release the handbrake when he noticed something on the passenger seat. It was a brown paper bag, which he opened and let the contents fall into his lap. It was a garment of some description wrapped in tissue paper. Undoing the paper, he discovered a set of men’s leather gloves and a small piece of card with some handwriting on it. He flicked on the interior light, and read it.

Big heart, cold hands. Happy Christmas. F.B., was all it said.

He smiled at the gift, and tried them on. A perfect fit. Of course they were.

Pulling his phone from his pocket again, he found Freya's number. His finger poised over the button to call her. He thought of where she was, and what she might be going through, and if she would appreciate a call, or if she wanted to be alone. She had every right to be there tonight, celebrating with the team, but had slipped away early.

The truth was – and he hated to even think it – there was nobody else he would rather be sharing Christmas with than her. Even if they sat in silence, away from the bustling crowds, away from the chaos of family. Just in her company.

"Happy Christmas, Freya," he said.

CHAPTER FORTY-EIGHT

Nearly one hundred and seventy miles away, in a backstreet of a South London suburb, a small rental car was parked. The spot had been strategically chosen. Nestled between two other parked cars, with a clear line of sight to the house she once called home. There was a car on the drive. Greg's car, she presumed. It looked like a Greg car – boring, and as vanilla as a car could be. It most likely had a brown interior and had been purchased for its efficiency rather than any form of style.

There were lights on inside, but it was the only house on the street not to have some kind of Christmas feature on the front lawn. He had at least gone to some effort to decorate the inside. The downstairs windows had flashing, white lights, and she could see through the curtains that he had bought a tree for Billy.

She thought of all the Christmases they had shared there, watching Billy grow up through the years, and how he had always wanted to stay up late on Christmas Eve yet fallen asleep before nine p.m. every single time.

She wondered if Billy might look out of the window, perhaps looking for signs of Santa's arrival. She wondered if he might see the stupid toy dog that was sitting on the doorstep waiting for him, and venture downstairs to get it.

But her questions were answered within five minutes, when, one by one, the lights inside the house were extinguished.

Freya opened her car door.

The Christmas lights were turned off last, casting the house into total darkness, and the front door opened.

She climbed out.

"Billy?" Greg called, as he stepped outside carrying a small suitcase and his overnight duffel bag. It was the one she had bought him. The leather one he had wanted.

Keeping to the shadows, Freya edged closer to the house until she was standing behind the caravan that belonged to the house next door.

"Billy, come on, we'll be late," he called out again, and Freya thought she heard his little voice calling from upstairs. His bedroom light turned on, just as Greg discovered the toy dog sitting where the milkman used to leave the milk. He searched it for a tag or a message, then glanced up and down the road in confusion.

"What's that?" Billy said, and he appeared in the doorway in his pyjamas and slippers, lit only by the porch light above them.

"Nothing," Greg said, as he held the toy dog above the boy and coaxed Billy toward the car. "Go on. In you get. And strap yourself in. I'll be checking."

He opened the back door of the car and waited for Billy to climb in.

"I'll just be a minute, okay? I'll put this inside and lock the house up."

"Okay, Daddy," Billy replied.

Seeing her chance, Freya darted across to the car, keeping to the side furthest from the house. She opened the door, peered inside, and held her finger to her lips.

"Shh," she said, smiling at him.

"Freya," Billy exclaimed, and his face lit up with excitement. His feet started kicking and she reached in to give him a hug.

"I can't stay," she said. "Are you okay? Are you happy?"

He nodded enthusiastically, the way kids do, and he beamed at her from his car seat. She double checked his seat belt, and then slipped him the little box from her pocket.

"I got you this," she said.

"What is it?" he asked, as Freya quickly unwrapped the present for him and opened the box. She pulled the pendant out by its chain, and let it hang before him, marvelling at how his eyes lit up in wonder.

"It's a Saint Christopher," she replied.

"A Saint what?"

"A Saint Christopher. It's to keep you safe wherever you go. He watches over you for me, okay?"

"He's your friend?"

"Yes," she said sadly. "Just remember, when you have this with you. I'll be there too, keeping you safe. Keep it in the box, and keep it very secret. This is just between you and me, is that okay?"

He nodded, beaming with delight.

"I have to go now," she said, and she leaned in to kiss him on the cheek. "Just remember, if ever you want me, you just look at that. My number is engraved on the back. You be good now, and don't tell Daddy I was here."

"Daddy already knows you're here," a voice said, deeper and duller than Billy's and filled with resentment.

"Good evening, Greg," she said, as she backed out of the car.

"I suppose the stuffed dog was your idea of a present for him, was it?"

"I thought he should have something for Christmas."

"He'll have plenty from me, and from–"

"Don't say her name," Freya said. "Please."

Greg's face twisted in disgust. "I told you not to come."

"You also told me you'd be faithful. Remember? Right about the time you said you'd be with me in sickness and in health."

"Do you want to do this now?" Greg asked. "Here? On Christmas Eve?"

She shook her head.

"No. No, I don't. Look, I didn't come here to fight."

"Then why *did* you come?" he hissed, keeping his voice low and out of Billy's earshot.

Freya held his stare, unable to quite believe that she had once loved this man. She had once longed to be in his arms, and to wake up beside him.

"To say goodbye," she said, and his expression softened. "To Billy. I came to say goodbye to Billy. I didn't get a chance–"

"When you walked out?" he finished, eyebrows raised. But then he nodded, relenting a little. "Be quick. We're running late."

Seizing her chance at one more hug with Billy, Freya leaned into the car, put her arms around the boy she looked on as a son, and held him until the tears in her eyes abated.

"Are you crying?" he said, with that child-like naivety.

"No," she said, and held him tighter. "No. You?"

"Not anymore," he said, and she pulled away to look into his eyes. "I thought you weren't coming back."

She leaned in to whisper in his ear, "Call me whenever you want. Anytime. Anywhere. Our secret. Okay?"

He nodded, and glanced out at the street where Greg was busy on his phone, probably texting the slut.

"I love you, Billy," she said, loud enough for Greg to hear, and she touched his nose, the way he liked. His face wrinkled up as he laughed, but the joy was soon quenched by Greg who was standing close by.

"That's enough," he said. "Time's up."

"I love you too, Freya. I miss you," Billy called, as she backed from the car again.

Greg loaded the case and the bag into the back of the car, as Freya closed the door with a final wave to Billy. She exhaled loudly and stood with her hands in her pockets.

"Thank you," she said, conveying as much sincerity as she could.

He nodded. "No doubt I'll be picking up the pieces again for the next month. So do try to be grateful, won't you?"

"I'll try," she said, with a smile that he rolled his eyes at. "So you're really going through with it, are you? Popping the question?"

"The question is popped, Freya. Things will be different after Christmas. We'll be family. I can't have you turning up out of the blue."

"I'll call ahead then," she said.

"You'll do no such thing. We'll work something out," he said, as he opened the driver's door and climbed inside. He lowered the window as soon as the engine was running. "It hasn't been easy, Freya."

"No. No, it hasn't," she said, and she watched the car pull away, with Billy's face pressed against the glass.

She watched the car turn at the end of the cul-de-sac, and then took a slow walk to her own car. Freya fired up the heater and set it on her feet, then let her head fall back onto the headrest.

From inside her pocket, she withdrew an envelope. Inside, she found a mildly amusing Christmas card featuring a black and white image of a lady resting her head in her hands with a bottle of wine beside her. A crude attempt at suggesting Freya drank too much, perhaps? Inside the card, she found that familiar neat handwriting.

Whatever you decide, I hope it works out for you.
Happy Christmas, Freya.
Mark (a.k.a Martin).

He had even printed the address of his relative in Woodhall

Spa at the foot of the card with a final message.

> *Dinner's at 2 p.m.*

CHAPTER FORTY-NINE

CHRISTMAS DINNER WAS A SOMBRE AFFAIR, JUST THE WAY FREYA liked it. There was none of the shouting and family arguments that she had experienced in the past, and there were no children running around making a racket. All of which meant Freya could enjoy her third glass of wine in peace.

Although, there were multiple occasions when she spared more than just a passing thought for Billy.

There was turkey, and all the trimmings, and the man opposite her demonstrated his gratitude for her coming with a silent yet admirable presence and the occasional smile to make sure she was having a good time. His broad shoulders were relaxed, his smile natural, and even the way in which he ate was calming. That was an odd thought, but it was true.

She raised her glass to the man on the other side of the table, and he met her halfway with a chink.

"To new beginnings," she said.

"And old friends," he replied.

They drank and ate, and when they were done, the plates were left in place.

"What do you normally do on Christmas Day?" he asked.

She thought about her response, then summarised it with, "I'm in the market for a new usual. What about you?"

"This," he said, and cast a sweeping hand across the table of food. "Nothing else. It's the one day of the year I get to relax. This is enough for me. Boring, aren't I?"

"I could get used to it."

"Having said that," he continued, "I do like to spice it up a bit later."

"Don't tell me, you sit and watch TV?"

"No," he said, looking offended. "I often have a nap."

"You don't strike me as the napping kind."

"Oh, I'm a napper alright. I'd happily leave everybody else to it, and nap beside the fire with my feet up on the footstool."

"And you ridiculed me for falling asleep?"

"Ah, come on," he said. "You left yourself wide open for that one."

She laughed and finished her last, perfectly cooked roast potato, wiping her mouth with her napkin, and scrunching it into a ball on her plate.

"Thanks for coming," he said. "It means a lot."

"It means a lot to have been invited. And thanks for the present. I'll find somewhere suitable to hang it." She glanced across the empty room at the framed Bovril advertisement with a large crack in the glass. "Would you be offended if I hung it somewhere I don't have to look at it every day?"

"I'd expect nothing less from a stuck-up cow like you. Besides, you left it in my car."

She nodded her gratitude, grinning inwardly at the joke.

"I think, though, that a Bovril ad, as nice as it is, isn't really much compared to the gloves you bought me."

"It's the thought, Ben, and—"

"I've got some news," he said, cutting her off. "Good news."

"You're being promoted?" she said, then thought about it. "No, I would have heard."

"Standing."

"Promotion?"

"He's leaving," Ben said with a grin. "Transferred to Lincoln HQ."

"What about the team?" she asked, delighted, but there were so many questions.

"DC Moray and DC Vaughan have gone with him."

"Which means Nillson, Cruz, and..." The punchline hit her hard, and she could only smile. "Oh god, Gillespie..."

"All report into you," he replied, raising his glass again and taking a sip.

"All my Christmases rolled into one," she replied, returning the gesture by raising her own glass.

"What are you going to do about Martin?" he asked.

She laughed again and took a sip of her wine.

"That would never have worked," she said with a smile, and he matched it with one of his own.

"Are you happy, Freya?"

"I'm happy, Ben," she replied, and raised her glass once more and smiled at her friend. "To crime."

"To crime," he replied, and they chinked glasses.

"The fireplace sounds good," she said. "Do you happen to have two armchairs?"

"We'd have to share the footstool," he replied, and stared at her over the rim of his glass.

"I'd like that," she said. "I'd like that very much."

The End

Emily Treverne's laugh carried through the trees, carefree with youth and unquestionable innocence.

"Ready or not, we're coming to find you," she called.

Marie pressed her back up against a tall elm and crouched down so that she could just turn her head to peer over the line of nettles beside her. It was a good spot. The best spot. They would never find her. She had run for more than a minute and taken the path of most resistance to throw them off the scent. She had even doubled back on herself to confuse Digby.

Now, she watched with a glee she could barely contain as Digby came into view, accompanied by his snorts and gruffs as he followed Marie's scent the wrong way. Wearing her bright yellow rain mac, Emily tip-toed behind Digby with her hands over her mouth trying to mask her squeaks and giggles.

But Digby stopped in his tracks. He sniffed at the ground, searching for the scent. The smart pup hadn't fallen for Marie's trap. He doubled back, followed closely by Emily, and he pounded along the forest track until her scent stopped and disappeared into the stinging nettles.

"Wait for me, Digby," Emily called out, and she joined him a few moments later, peering into the space, while Digby found a path through the thick undergrowth.

"Ah, you found me," Marie called out, as Digby pounced on her, and Emily squealed with delight. "What a clever little dog he is."

"I helped him," Emily said defensively. "We both found you."

"Okay, then," Marie said, as she stepped over the nettles and onto the track. "You guys win. You're the best at hide and sniff."

"Better than you?" Emily asked, searching for some kind of accolade.

"Far better than me," Marie conceded. "How about we go home and get some soup? My feet are so cold they're frozen."

"Like ice?"

"Like ice," Marie said, as she gave the working cocker a treat. "I could even ice skate home, they're so cold."

Emily laughed. "No, you couldn't."

"I could. All I would have to do is whip my shoes and socks off and I'd slip and slide all over the place. I should really get them to the fire at home, so they can thaw out. What do you say?"

"One more game," Emily said, and she looked longingly up at Marie, who peered up through the trees to the sky above.

"I don't know. It's getting quite late–"

"Oh, please, can we? We'll be super quick. Digby and I will find you really quickly." She looked up at Marie, pleading with those big eyes. "Come on. You've been so sad recently. I haven't heard you laugh like this for ages."

"Really quickly?" Marie asked.

"Really quickly. The quickest ever."

"Well, okay then," Marie said. "But if you don't find me in two minutes, I'm coming out. It's getting dark and we need to get you home to Dad. Okay?"

She nodded, thrilled to have one more game.

"Okay, you'd better hold onto Digby's collar. I'll call you when I've hidden, okay?"

"Okay, Marie," the young girl said, and she held the dog's collar tightly.

Marie slipped into the trees, zig-zagging through the brush, off the beaten path. She ducked beneath a fallen tree and then crouched in the hollow of its roots. But she was too exposed. She moved on, deeper and further, searching for the ideal spot.

And there it was, beyond the stream. A drain or something. She splashed into the stream, running through the water to throw the dog off her scent, and then climbed up the bank on the far side. She hadn't seen the drain before. She hadn't ventured this deep into the woods before, and from the undergrowth, it looked like nobody else had. The drain was circular, and she could see that at one stage, a metal grill had covered the top. But it had long since been removed and discarded. The small brickwork structure was about two meters across, and on the inside, metal rungs had been installed, presumably for men to go down and clean or unblock it, or something. She wasn't really sure. But the rungs would hold her weight.

She slipped one leg over, searching blindly for the rung, and then the other. She clung to the topmost rung and took a deep breath. "I'm ready," she called, then climbed down two rungs, so that she could just peer over the top of the bricks.

While she waited, Marie glanced down at the old drain twenty feet below. It clearly wasn't used anymore. Even Marie could see that, and she thought that perhaps it had serviced the old, abandoned water tower that stood derelict in the old hospital grounds. But after so many years of neglect, the bottom of the drain was filled with rubbish. Plastic drinks bottles mainly, plus a few old beer cans, and she shuddered to think what else. Rats maybe?

There was no sign of Emily, even after two minutes had passed. Her feet began to ache on the iron rungs, and Marie was about to slowly poke her head up above the bricks to see if she could spy them. Then a nearby branch cracked.

She smiled to herself as footsteps grew closer. But then they stopped, and a sinking feeling grabbed Marie's gut like a strong hand was crushing her stomach. Something wasn't right.

Slowly, she craned her neck to peer up.

And then she saw him. Two feet away. Dressed in black.

Her grip on the iron rung failed.

Above her, a circle of light framed by darkness grew smaller as she fell.

And then pain. Pain like nothing else. Her vision blurred, and the figure of a man leaning over the drain peering down at her from above faded to black.

Then nothing.

ALSO BY JACK CARTWRIGHT

The DCI Cook Murder Mysteries

A Winter of Blood

A Secret to Die For

The Wild Fens Murder Mysteries

Secrets In Blood

One For Sorrow

In Cold Blood

Suffer In Silence

Dying To Tell

Never To Return

Lie Beside Me

Dance With Death

In Dead Water

One Deadly Night

Her Dying Mind

Into Death's Arms

Join my VIP reader group to be among the first to hear about new release dates, discounts, and get a free Wild Fens novella.

Visit www.jackcartwrightbooks.com for details.

VIP READER CLUB

Your FREE ebooks are waiting for you now.

Get your FREE copy of the prequel story to the Wild Fens Murder Mystery series, and learn how DI Freya Bloom came to give up everything she had, to start a new life in Lincolnshire.

Visit www.jackcartwrightbooks.com to join the VIP Reader Club.

I'll see you there.

Jack Cartwright

COPYRIGHT

www.ingramcontent.com/pod-product-compliance
Lightning Source LLC
Chambersburg PA
CBHW051249210726
48287CB00002B/412